Dear reader,

When I began writing this book, I simply wanted to tell the story of a girl pretending she got into her dream college to avoid getting in trouble with her family and embarrassing herself among competitive classmates. I quickly realized that exploring this idea wouldn't be simple at all: it would require me to dig deep into what would make someone go to such lengths to hide a truth that could shatter their life and self-worth.

If you find this premise unbelievable, ask yourself this: Who among us hasn't fudged the truth to make ourselves shine brighter or at least avoid losing luster? Think of all the times you told your parents you were already on your way home when you were barely leaving your friend's place across town. Or when you chose not to mention that less-than-favorable exam score.

I took this idea many steps and stumbles further, and what I thought would be a fun, simple story expanded: it encompasses cultural concepts of internal debt, the inadvertent harm we may be doing to young people by forcing a singular idea of success, and the persistent, damaging myth that some Americans need to be *model* to be accepted.

The main character, Perla, is fictional, but the competitive environments and narrow, rigid expectations that constrict her may be all too real and relatable for some. Perla is a mirror of how we falter and crack under the extreme pressure—internal and external—to be perfect. This may sound heavy, but I promise there's some light and joy in here too.

It's my hope that any readers who find Perla's statements more personal than they'd like find ways to soften the pressure put on them by others or even themselves: you're doing the best you can, and there will always be a way forward, even if it's not always the one you planned for. And if you're reading this for the sheer mystery of whether Perla will get caught, I hope you enjoy this story for the stressful romp that it is and perhaps rethink any trespassing plans you may have for the evening.

Thank you so much for reading.

Sincerely,
Tracy Badua

this is not a PERSONAL STATEMENT

TRACY BADUA

Quill Tree Books
An Imprint of HarperCollinsPublishers

Quill Tree Books is an imprint of HarperCollins Publishers.

This Is Not a Personal Statement
Copyright © 2023 by Tracy Badua
All rights reserved. Printed in the United States of America.
No part of this book may be used or reproduced in any manner whatsoever
without written permission except in the case of brief quotations embodied
in critical articles and reviews. For information address HarperCollins
Children's Books, a division of HarperCollins Publishers, 195 Broadway,
New York, NY 10007.
www.epicreads.com

Library of Congress Cataloging-in-Publication Data
[TK]
Library of Congress Control Number:
ISBN 978-0-06-321775-1

Typography by Erin Fitzsimmons
23 24 25 26 27 PC/LSCH 10 9 8 7 6 5 4 3 2 1
❖
First Edition

For my parents and grandmothers
(This isn't about you at all)

ONE

A low current of joy and despair from the latest college admittances and rejections hums through Monte Verde High.

Once the last bell rings, the entire senior class whips out their phones for news. Conversations crackle around me on the parking lot curb. I pretend to focus on spotting Dad's Lexus among the dozen other luxury cars in the distance, but it's hard not to react to the bursts of happiness and heartbreak around me.

Two other seniors, Edie Anderson from my PE class and Camilla Kang-Jansen, the daughter of one of Dad's law firm partners, pause near me on their way to their cars.

"Did you hear? Wendy got into Stanford, but Gabriel didn't. You think they'll break up over this?"

Hard-earned futures are being made and broken this very second, and people chatter about them like they're reality show bombshells.

I adjust my backpack straps as an excuse to angle toward the murmured conversation. Edie and Camilla don't seem to notice or, if they do, care. Being the lone sixteen-year-old senior at Monte Verde and a tad well-known for my overachievement—my mom sent a press release to the local paper when I started high school at twelve—means that I'm blocked out of the social scene and its related whisper networks. But I do like to stay informed.

At most schools, gossip would center around who's dating whom, who has the most expensive this, the flashiest that. At Monte Verde High? I attend one of the most academically competitive high schools in California. People spend their life savings on tiny, dilapidated houses in this school district so their kids can come here because our grads go on to be governors, CEOs, and all manner of brag-worthy intellectuals and notables.

Everyone talks about the record-shattering achievements of the Monte Verde student body.

No one talks about the intense competition, the unhealthy lack of sleep, the grueling lineup of forced extracurriculars, the expensive standardized test prep classes, or the underground market of cheat sheets and pills.

But I don't care about any of those right now: they're as much a fixture in my school life as my creaky locker and my wobbly chair in AP Comp Sci. I don't even really care about Wendy or Gabriel.

I care about which schools' acceptances are out.

Three others join the girls chatting a few feet away from me. I'm in at least one class with each person in that group, but they barely acknowledge my proximity. Through Dad, I've known Camilla for ages. Aside from the way our parents seem to play us against each other to make us work harder, we tend to get along outside of school. She's often the one friendly face at firm picnics and award dinners, but she keeps her distance on campus and I don't force it.

At least I don't have to hide my eavesdropping if I'm functionally invisible here.

I peer at them through the curtain of long, straight black hair on either side of my face and act like I'm scrolling through the latest PicLine posts on my phone. The group compares notes. Two people in my physics class got their MIT acceptances today. Tennis star Arnell eyes Columbia: eir first choice, but not eir parents'. Oscar faked a rejection to Duke just so he wouldn't have to explain to his parents that his dream school is here in California. Edie dabs at her teary blue eyes as she gripes to her friends that she's wait-listed at two Ivy Leagues.

I try not to roll my eyes as Camilla comforts her. Edie is the debate team captain who introduced some of the seniors to her sister's Adderall-prescription-happy doctor friend in exchange for a hefty, under-the-table referral fee. I've been cut enough by Monte Verde's ruthless streak to recognize that Edie's tears are a cover for her rage. She must be livid that underground Adderall went to those same kids who likely edged her out of those Ivies' incoming classes.

"What about Little Miss Perfect? Where do you think she's going?" Arnell's voice drifts over to me, a hint of amusement in eir voice, like the mere mention of me is a joke. My body tenses. My thumb continues to mindlessly scroll so I can keep up the ruse that I don't hear them.

A harsh shush from Camilla. "Arnell, quit it. She's right there."

A snort from Arnell. "So?"

So they do know that I'm standing right here, listening. They just ignore it, like they ignored me for the past four years. I barely feel the pinch of sadness about it now. Perfect Perlie Perez—a nickname that I obviously didn't come up with myself and haven't managed to fight off—is better than this. Better than them and their pettiness.

I only have to endure a couple more months of high school before I can escape with my diploma. Then it's on to Delmont University, the shining light at the end of the tunnel. It's number one on the list of universities curated by my parents and me. That list is the first page of Perlie's Academic Plan, a dog-eared red plastic binder crammed full of report cards, standardized test scores, articles about college prep, and everything needed to click my PhD path into place. The plan serves as a road map for the life my parents and I have planned.

It helps that we all want the same thing: for me to graduate from this prestigious university, attend a top med school, and go on to be successful and scandal-free. Be as perfect as the world sees me. The goal may reek of elitism to some, but there's generations' worth of trauma alive and well in the fact that we hold certain professions as the mark of success and belonging.

A brown woman? The table's full, sorry.

A brown woman wielding a PhD from an illustrious school? We'll find an extra chair, ma'am.

My parents and their parents left friends, family, and livelihoods to cross the ocean and settle in Monte Verde. Calling this place home didn't come easily. They found themselves separated from others here by their faces, their tongues, their skin. For them, making a home was trickier than just finding shelter and sustenance: it was proving that they belonged here.

And I'm supposed to be part of that proof.

Sometimes, with all this pressure on me, I think of myself as a tree growing on the side of a cliff. People say a seed should've never landed, taken root, and thrived there all by itself. But I found a way. I grew sideways to get my share of the sun, letting my roots claw into the unwelcoming rock.

Withering is not an option.

The familiar silver glint in the distance is a beacon through this storm of social awkwardness. Dad's car approaches. He's speaking, his black eyebrows as furrowed as they can get with all the filler Mom injects him with. His youthful appearance is part our Filipino heritage, part religious sunscreen usage, and part perk of Mom's boutique aesthetic clinic. He shakes his head at something, and his neatly gelled black hair doesn't even move. He must still be on a work call.

I step closer toward the curb, ready to leap into the car when Dad stops.

I've had enough of the other seniors whispering and staring at me. They must have the same idea, because Camilla suddenly shrieks, waving her phone in the air.

"I just got a text from my mom. The UC's admissions portals are up! And I've got mail from Delmont too. We're going to check it all together when I get home."

The mention of Delmont hits me straight in the chest.

"Delmont did actual paper letters?" Edie asks.

Camilla isn't fazed by the incredulous note in Edie's voice. "Still old-fashioned, I guess. They opted out of electronic notifications entirely. Paper's prettier for PicLine pics though."

I bite back a smile. My ticket out of this dreadful, hypercompetitive high school and into my bright future might be burning a hole in our mailbox as we speak. I wonder if Camilla has the same big envelope, stuffed with welcome materials and deposit deadlines, and how long it will take for our parents to compare.

I try to shake the nerves off, but it's hard to unload stress that's been riding on my shoulders for sixteen whole years. In accordance with Perlie's Academic Plan, I applied to nine schools, and half already sent me their boilerplate regret-to-inform-you rejections. My parents chalked it up to me being on the younger side of the applying class, but I doubt the admissions people had my birth certificate next to my personal statement. When my second-grade teacher hinted that I was advanced academically enough to skip a grade or two, my parents were initially thrilled at the suggestion. So was I, because this external proof that I am exceptional brought a whirlwind of praise and an impromptu ice cream stop. But then my parents and school administrators questioned whether I was mature enough to handle this leap forward. The thought of going back to being a regular, ice-creamless second grader left a bitter taste in my mouth. I pleaded with them that I was ready, and because I truly am exceptional, I won.

Now, every day that I bring home a stellar test grade or a

compliment on an assignment, I prove that being the youngest isn't holding me back academically at all. These college rejections aren't helping my case, but they hadn't stung much; those weren't the schools I was destined for anyway.

Delmont is where I'm headed. It features one of the most highly rated undergraduate premed programs among all American universities and therefore serves as one of the best feeders into the top medical schools in the nation. It's an almost-guaranteed ticket into a successful career, a lifetime of respectability, and my name being whispered with a hint of awe when strangers meet my parents.

Dad's car slows to a stop in front of me.

I slide in as he's saying his goodbyes to whoever's on the phone. He taps a button on his steering wheel, hanging up the call, before turning to me with his usual greeting.

"How was school?"

I open my mouth to reply, only to be interrupted by a racking sob from Edie on the sidewalk. Camilla rubs her back. Edie must've gotten another rejection. My stomach flutters as I imagine the Delmont acceptance letter in our mailbox.

"Good." My usual answer, if you forget about the strained group project in Spanish class and mispronunciation of my name by the physics substitute. I know not to bring up the not-so-perfect details with him and Mom. They'd accuse me of complaining, of being ungrateful after all they've done to get me to where I am.

All that aside, today actually was a good day.

And I have a feeling it's about to get even better.

TWO

Dad glances into his side mirror before sending the car gliding out of the school parking lot.

"Was that Camilla?" he asks, his eyes on the road. "I wasn't sure because of the haircut." A lie. She and I have both had our black hair waist-length since freshman year.

I fish my water bottle out of my backpack to delay an answer. I sense a trap. My parents rarely ask about Camilla unless it's to make some pointed comparison between us. Dad and one of Camilla's moms, Jan Kang, jockeyed for top spots at their law school together and impose that same sense of rivalry on their children.

Camilla and I live in the same pressure cooker: a suffocating mix of aggressive parents, intellectually elite classmates, and microscope-eyed college admissions staff. Comparison to her has been inescapable all my life. You'd think it'd be enough that I'm keeping up with her academically even though I'm two years younger, but that doesn't stop my parents from reminding me of her many, many accomplishments.

"Yeah, it was," I reply, letting him slide. Sometimes it's easier to let a little lie hang in the air than to reach for it and shake up trouble.

"You know, Ms. Kang told me the other day that Camilla's heading for NYU in the fall."

My shoulders tense despite Dad's tone staying as easy as if he'd been talking about the weather. I know where Dad's line of thinking is headed.

"That's great for Camilla. She works really hard. I'm sure she earned it." And I mean it. Not because she and I actually get along every once in a while and she's the only person who can beat me at *Mario Kart*. The sheer fact that we're academic rivals means she must work her tail off like I do.

I leave the *Mario Kart* compliment out of the conversation with Dad. I've loved video games since I could first swipe open an app on an unattended phone. I learned history through *The Oregon Trail*, soared daringly over dark alleys and rooftops as a superhero, reinvited myself in iteration after iteration of *The Sims*. When most of my week is spent in regimented academia and extracurriculars, games provide me a thrilling escape I can't get elsewhere.

But for all the joy it brings me, my parents don't see "the point" of it. To them, video games are not a serious academic pursuit, and they won't make me money or win the admiration of friends and family, so why waste time? As long as I bring home As, though, I get to keep this guilty pleasure hobby. Mom changed the password on my Origin and Steam accounts the last time I brought home a B-plus on a progress report.

I try to steer this conversation in a direction that doesn't lead to a Hollywood-style spotlight on Camilla. "NYU wasn't on our college list, remember?"

Dad purses his lips and lets out a short breath through his nose. He does this whenever he's trying to keep in words that he worries will hurt my feelings, but I hear the disappointment in his exhale. He tries to cover it with a quick smile. "But why wasn't it, again? It's a great school."

I shift in my seat, fighting back the tears that flow into my eyes whenever someone implies that I and all my efforts aren't enough. I can't cry now. Dad asked a simple, albeit loaded, question. My parents would judge the tears as a sign of my supposed emotional immaturity and not being ready for "the world," which is not the case. I can't control the direct line between my brain, heart, and tear ducts.

I untwist my water bottle cap—I'm even perfect at staying hydrated—and take a swig to buy myself a minute to stop the emotional spiral. "You're the one with premium access to that college database. We even highlighted the rates of graduates specifically going to medical schools. Delmont's at the top."

I had dedicated extra time and effort on the Delmont application. This notoriously hard-to-get-into (and therefore more prestigious) university doesn't use the Common App like almost all the other top schools. It demands your individual awe and attention the way an Oscar winner does on the red carpet. My parents had paid a recent Delmont grad to act as my application coach, and they took turns proofreading the personal statement that swore Delmont and I were a match made in premed heaven. It was smart, mature, Delmont-worthy.

"Ah, right. It would've been nice to have that NYU acceptance though."

"And waste that time and application fee? Come on, Dad."

My joking appeal to Dad's priorities—time and money—makes him smile, almost dissipating the tension. The ring of his phone blares through the speakers in the car and cuts our talk short, which I'm perfectly fine with. I know he and Mom are just trying to push me to excel, but the moments immediately after a long day at school and before a draining night of homework are not my favorite times to have big, analytical discussions about my future. He puts a single finger up to shush me, then fumbles for his headset and starts talking to someone else about a big filing due today.

Dad adjusts his work hours as best he can to accommodate my school and extracurricular schedule, but there's only so much generosity his hungrier law partners extend to him. He works from home or leaves the office early to be both my chauffeur and taskmaster. That time out of the office has cut into the career he thought he should have by now. We don't talk much about the lucrative time-intensive business opportunities he's had to pass along to another person at the firm just so he can maintain that flexibility to shuttle me from school to SAT class to volunteering at the church. I know better than to interrupt him right now.

I pull up PicLine and scroll, looking for connection but finding only content. I am more than ready to leave Monte Verde behind and start fresh.

Dad's still on his call when we pull into the garage. He heads inside to continue his negotiations, away from the noise of lawn mowers and children and cars whizzing by way above the twenty-five-mile-per-hour speed limit. I beeline for the mailbox.

I know I got in, but anxiety swirls in my stomach as I pad across our immaculate lawn anyway. I wipe my clammy hands off on my jeans and tug the metal mailbox door open with a creak. I pull out a handful of envelopes. Bill, bill, credit card offer, Delmont. My heart stumbles over its next beat.

The envelope is thin.

I blink to make sure I'd read the return address right. Yes, it's there in neat, printed text, and yes, that's the blue-and-green Delmont seal printed in the upper left. I bite my lip.

Why is the envelope so thin?

I don't have any frame of reference for paper acceptances. Maybe Delmont's envelope is supposed to look like this. Delmont might have decided to save some trees by referring accepted students to materials online.

That must be it.

How very eco-friendly of them.

My hands shaking, I reassemble the stack of mail and head inside. Dad nods his head, cell phone held up flush against his ear, when I plop the rest of the mail down on the already-mail-cluttered kitchen table. I poise to sprint up to my room when he lays

12

his hand on my arm. We're the same shade of not-enough-time-in-the-sun brown, thanks to us spending all day indoors. Even our limited free time together is movie theaters and restaurants rather than beaches and hiking trails.

His dark brown eyes fix on the Delmont envelope in my hand.

He squeezes my arm, flashes me a grin, then refocuses on his phone call.

My heartbeat erratic, I take the stairs two at a time up to my room. I nearly trip on the top step I'd crossed thousands of times before.

Backpack down, door shut, envelope in hand. I launch myself onto the bed, ruffling the light pink pillowcases, sheets, comforter, and two stuffed bears—Bip and Bop—perched on top. Other than the laptop on my desk, my room hasn't changed in years. It's the room of a bright-eyed eleven-year-old who picked out a daisy rug because it looked like something she'd seen on TV.

I tuck my legs underneath me and grip the envelope. I turn it over and slide my finger under the seam, earning myself a paper cut as I rip it open.

I ignore the smart of the fresh cut and unfold the paper. There it is, the Delmont seal in all its glory at the top, then *Dear Ms. Perez, we regret to inform you that . . .*

No.

No. No. No.

. . . we are unable to offer a place in our first-year class at this time.

The oxygen disappears from the room. I feel like I've been flung into space: breathless, unanchored.

The words on the page blur as the tears start to burn in my eyes. Unable to offer me a place? That can't be what it says.

Because I'm supposed to get accepted into Delmont. I get in. That's what's written in blotchy blue ink in Perlie's Academic Plan in the bookcase downstairs, what's tattooed on my soul. Delmont is the next big stepping-stone in my heavily mapped-out future. I get in.

This damn letter is telling me otherwise.

I read the lines over and over again, as if a hidden acceptance lies behind it, if only I am smart enough to decipher it. Trembling, I fold the paper back up along its neat creases, covering the words like they never existed. But the truth of those ground-shaking words sears into my brain.

I didn't get into my dream school. My parents' dream school. They'll be more than angry: they'll be ashamed. All that money spent on tutors, coaches, and prep classes, all that time wasted whisking me from activity to activity, all those comments to friends and family about how intelligent and impressive their daughter is? All for nothing.

Everyone at school will find out, and, worse than their ignoring me, they'll side-eye me with those pitying looks. They'll shake their heads and whisper about that Perlie Perez kid who kept to herself because she thought she was better than everyone; then they'll be the ones going off to their dream colleges. They'll be the ones proving how much worthier they are.

And what does this say about me? I, Perfect Perlie Perez, am not good enough for the future I'd been tailoring myself for all my life. Something in me wilts. I'd prepared for acceptance, a first year at a prestigious school, killer finals, new social crises.

I hadn't prepared for rejection.

A tear hits the paper and soaks in.

Dad has seen the envelope, so there's no hiding this. Once he's off his phone call, he's going to come up here and ask me about the letter. Judging by the heat on my face and the heaviness on my chest, I don't think I can tell him about the rejection without full-out sobbing. And the crying will reaffirm his erroneous belief that I'm still only a child, one who is not emotionally mature enough for any of this college business. One whose life still has to be carefully crafted and controlled by her tough but well-meaning parents because clearly she can't be trusted to handle even the slightest thing on her own.

I rub my palms against my eyes; then my gaze lands on the quote above my desk. The words, in rich navy blue, pop against the white background: one of the few non-pink bits of decor in my room. We had found the print and its gilded frame in an antique store back in eighth grade, and it's been hanging above my head ever since.

Only those who attempt the absurd can achieve the impossible.
—Albert Einstein

An actual genius: a parent-approved role model for a sixteen-year-old.

My eyes narrow in on a few words, the rest fading.

Attempt the absurd.

An idea ignites in my brain, one so wild—so absurd—that my heart thumps that extra beat it'd missed earlier, when I'd seen the thinness of the Delmont envelope.

I'm at my desk, one hand on the laptop keyboard, the other on the mouse, before my brain registers that I've moved.

I can fix this.

I will fix this.

I unfold the letter, purposely averting my eyes from the evil *we regret to inform you*. I place it into the feed of the four-in-one printer my parents moved into my room from their office so I could print and proofread my essays without disturbing them. The scan button flashes bright yellow, and the hum of the scanner soothes my jagged, jittery nerves.

I open up the image in Photoshop, and it's quick work to splice out the letterhead and pull sample acceptance language from the internet. I throw in a line about welcome materials being available online, to explain the shamefully tiny envelope. I match the font type, the size, even the graininess. I didn't get an A-plus in digital arts for nothing.

Footsteps thud against the wooden stairs. Dad's done with his call, and he's coming up.

I hit print and stretch for the ripped envelope on the worn carpet. My revised Delmont letter finishes printing, and, despite the shaking of my limbs and the rioting of the blood in my veins, I fold it into thirds. I crinkle and play with the paper a little to give it a worn, not-fresh-from-the-printer feel, and four knocks

rattle my bedroom door. Dad's knuckles might as well be batter-
ing rams.

"Can I come in?" he asks.

I do one last swipe across my eyes to dry any remaining tears
and force my voice steady. "Sure."

He swings the door open and leans up against the doorframe.
His suit jacket and tie are off, and he looks relaxed, even happy. Of
course he'd be happy. He believes his daughter got into Delmont.

"So?"

I hand him the envelope with the fake admission letter. The
real denial letter is toasting in the scanner bed.

Drawing from every bit of that A-minus I'd gotten in drama, I
paint a small smile on my face and hope a glimmer makes it to my
eyes. "See for yourself."

Dad draws out the forged letter and reads. The world goes
silent and still then, and my forced breathing sounds ragged in
my own ears.

Will he spot this as a fake immediately? Maybe I spelled something wrong. I should've proofread it. Acid rises up in my throat,
and I shift in my chair. It squeaks beneath me, but Dad keeps
reading despite the distraction.

I pinpoint the exact moment my lie takes root, because the tiny
pinch between his brows loosens. I thought I'd be relieved, but
the acid surges once more. This isn't some small white lie about
finishing a project early or that no one's gotten their AP practice
test results back yet. My whole identity, my whole future, hinges
on what's on that flimsy piece of paper. It's too late to come clean

now.

Dad raises his sparkling eyes to me and pumps his fist in the air like his team just got a win at work. Despite knowing the truth, I curve my mouth into a big goofy grin that matches his.

He hands me back my forgery then pulls me in for a quick, tight hug. "You did it! Good thing we didn't waste that time and money on NYU, then, right?" He reaches for his phone and dials Mom. "I just knew you'd get accepted into Delmont, Perlie. I didn't doubt it for a second."

I lean back into my chair, that grin stuck painfully on my face like I stapled it there. "Neither did I."

THREE

When I tuck Bip, Bop, and myself into my fluffy pink bed, my blood buzzing with sugary lemon frosting from Mom's store-bought congratulations cupcake and growing guilt over my fraud, I remind myself of the four other schools that owe me responses. They're all what our high school counselor would call "reach schools," ones whose typical admissions qualifications like grade point average and test scores are above mine. My counselor recommended everyone add a handful of "safety" schools that were more likely to offer admission, but my parents and I sniffed at the idea of lowering our family's standards. I only applied to the lofty schools listed in Perlie's Academic Plan. Still, that leaves four whole chances to get back on slightly derailed track. I can convince my parents that I'd changed my mind and decided to go to another school instead.

Not the least bit tired, I gaze out at the darkened windows of the cookie-cutter houses across the street. Among the other thousand worries in my head, the conversation between Camilla and her friends in the school parking lot earlier today still needles me. Edie had people to immediately turn to when she was hit with a rejection.

I don't.

I obviously can't talk to my parents about this, so I squeeze Bip and Bop closer. "You two love me no matter what school I go to, right?"

Their inanimate plastic eyes gaze back at me, and I frown into the darkness. I'm looking for reassurance from two teddy bears: this is how desperate I've become. I shut my eyes, if only to hide from Bip's and Bop's gazes.

Hours later, in the bright light of day, it's obvious that I can't tell my usual lunch crew—Leah, Yin, and Marcus—about it either. They haven't noticed my silence since I plopped myself onto this metal bench.

We usually prefer to keep discussion light, despite the fact that our combined brainpower could probably build and launch a satellite. Never anything too personal, mostly sci-fi and fantasy fanfic and video games. My Nintendos, gifts from my self-proclaimed "fun aunt" Auntie Trish, were my key into these lunchtime friendships.

Auntie Trish is the director of a major tech giant–funded nonprofit, a position that Mom said she stumbled into because she burned out from her much-higher-paying advertising job. Judging from Mom's tone alone—the same one she says "video games" with—I can never burn out. I have to continue burning brightly forever.

Yin gripes about some level of *Luigi's Mansion* that she can't beat. Leah nods in sympathy, her mouth stuffed with an oil-dripping quesadilla from the cafeteria. Marcus balances his calculus book and a binder on his legs, trying to finish homework due next period.

I poke at the dry turkey wrap Dad packed for me this morning while the others strategize. All three are on some medical track like I am, whether future dentists or pharmacist hopefuls. I wonder if I'll stay in touch with the lunch crew when I'm off at college, and I realize with a twinge of sadness that, no, I probably won't. We'll hug at graduation and say we will, but the only thing binding us together was the brief half-hour respite from the intense intellectual competition that crushed us the rest of the day.

A shadow casts over my turkey wrap, and I gaze up, expecting the pitter-patter of unexpected rain during an outdoor lunch period.

But it's worse than that.

It's Camilla.

Camilla tucks her thumbs into the pockets of her dark jeans. Her narrow jaw is tense, and her eyes are slightly puffy, like she was crying or was up late, or both. "My mom told me you're going to Delmont. Congratulations."

It doesn't sound like a true congratulations with how monotone it came out, but I thank her anyway. It's better than what I'd initially thought of saying, a slew of choice angry words at her for outing me for a lie I wasn't ready to drag my lunch crew into yet.

Before I can shoo Camilla away and minimize the damage,

Marcus holds up a hand for a high five. "Wait, Delmont? That's awesome, Perlie!"

I smack my palm to his, and the impact stings my skin. It's like every cell of my body rebels at my dishonesty.

"It's not a sure thing yet. I'm still waiting on four more schools," I hedge.

"But Delmont's your dream," Camilla says. "You've talked about it since you were a kid. Why would you think about going anywhere else?"

Why, indeed? I honestly haven't had the chance, or the fortitude, to think through every tiny detail since my rash letter printing less than twenty-four hours ago. My mouth goes dry as I reach for any possible response other than that I didn't, in fact, get in.

Part of me wants to tell the truth. Who at this school hasn't fibbed to keep parents, teachers, and coaches off their backs for just a moment?

But this isn't like faking a stomachache so I can get out of a physical fitness test. It was a little white lie to Dad yesterday, but if Camilla knows, then my parents' colleagues must know. And now everyone at Monte Verde is going to know too because Camilla just announced it in the middle of the open-air quad. My brief streak of honesty fades. I need to think of a better way to handle this than to make me and my family the subject of ridicule.

Besides, I'll get in somewhere else. Then I'll say I changed my mind.

"Delmont's great, but I'm keeping my options open, you know,"

I say before focusing intently on my lunch.

Camilla seems to take the hint that I don't want to talk. "Well, Delmont is a pretty good option as it is. Congratulations again." She nods at my lunch crew before walking over to her usual table with Edie and Arnell.

Yin flips a strand of long black hair behind her shoulder. "Yikes, what was that about?"

"I don't know," I say, even though I can guess. I didn't ask Camilla about what was in her own Delmont envelope, but I assume her triteness means she didn't get in either. I can't even commiserate with her the way we used to over *Mario Kart* now that my Delmont acceptance lie is out in the world.

Leah bumps her shoulder to mine. "Don't let her bring you down. Good for you. I got into Yale, Yin's sent her deposit into Johns Hopkins, and Marcus . . ."

"Already bought my Northwestern hoodie online!" he cuts in. "Shelled out the extra fifteen dollars for expedited shipping too."

I smile in a show of excitement for them but dig my nails so hard into my palms I nearly draw blood.

Yin throws her arm around my shoulder. "Just think: all this Monte Verde High stress and drama will be behind us in a few months."

"Not so sure about that," Leah groans, popping a tortilla chip in her mouth. "Premed's no joke. It might get just as intense."

Right about now, I'd kill for the opportunity to even be in that intense environment. I force a casual shrug. "You can always switch majors, can't you?"

They laugh like I've made some hilarious joke. Because, in truth, that's not an option for any of us. The last time Marcus broached the topic of pursuing a career in marketing, his parents called the school and had him switched out of his art elective mid-semester. Then they tried to get the art teacher suspended for poisoning young minds or something. It's funny now, but it sticks in all of our memories as reminders of what is and isn't considered success in our circles.

With my Delmont rejection, I'm further from this concept of success than everyone around me.

I'm lucky the others' laughter covers the falseness in mine. They all have somewhere to go, but I still don't. Until I get a letter of acceptance from one of the other four schools I'm waiting on, I'll have to bite my cheek, smile, and nod every time someone mentions Delmont. Because now, thanks to my bragging dad and too-loud Camilla, I've found that the pool of lies I've cannonballed into is even deeper than I thought, and staying afloat is the most I can hope for.

Mid-April, I get wait-listed at two colleges.

Mom and Dad console me with half-hearted assurances that it's those schools' losses for not wanting me to be part of their first-year classes. They rely on the one attempt at consolation that never fails to curdle my stomach: "At least you got into the dream school!"

I respond with a practiced smile so often that after a while the tears don't even prickle at my eyes.

Late at night, when my parents think I've long since fallen asleep, I hear their worries float up from the kitchen, where they anxiously swirl their glasses of wine: Only one school? What did we do wrong? Is it because Perlie's too young, not ready? Did you hear so-and-so's kid got into Princeton?

I use my slightly less judgy Bip and Bop bears as earmuffs to tune them out. I was the one who tipped the scales in favor of skipping grades: I'd been so enthusiastic, so sure I could do it and make everyone proud, that my parents couldn't say no. It's been rough out on the social scene, being both notoriously younger and unable to drive (this is California, after all). But despite occasionally shedding my share of tears in the privacy of Bip and Bop's company, I'm certain my age won't impact my ability to excel at any of the top schools. I just need to convince my parents of that too.

So I keep graciously thanking relatives and my parents' friends when they tell me how impressed they are about me going to Delmont. I check the other college admissions portals every day, as if my acceptance will magically appear even when no one else has gotten word either.

Then I get rejected from those last two colleges in one day.

I read those final rejections on an overcast Wednesday morning, seven minutes before we're supposed to leave for school.

All the stress acid simmering in my stomach since forging the Delmont acceptance bubbles up at once, volcanic, and I rush across the hallway to the bathroom not a second too late.

None of the nine top-tier schools I applied to want me. I worked so hard all these years, followed every part of the plan down to the last detail, and I have nothing to show for it. My dreams of going off to a prestigious university this fall dissolve and spill out of me with my breakfast.

Did I underestimate my competition?

Worse, did we overestimate me?

I stagger over to the sink and let the cool water run over my hands, drought be damned. I should come clean: about the rejections, about the forgery, about everything. People recover from much worse dishonesty than this. They apologize, they atone, they move on. Reality shows abound on this topic. Everyone loves a redemption story.

But not everyone has the expectations of a community, of generations on their shoulders like I do. Though Dad was born here and Mom's been in the US for over two decades now, the influence of their ancestral values clings to them like the pigment their skin products try to whiten away. The words for those values rarely trickle down to me, with my one language and clumsy pronunciation of anything else, and I find myself grasping for fragments of my own story in conversations with older relatives.

A couple years ago, I heard the phrase *utang na loob*, a sort of debt of gratitude. My grandparents and parents did everything to get me where I am today, so I have a cultural obligation to show my appreciation by being the smart, obedient, Perfect Perlie they want.

Basically, I owe them.

I know this is a simplistic way of looking at it, but this concept of a debt of gratitude is rooted in the close-knit communities my grandparents came from, where it was easier to rely on your neighbors and trade favors in kind. Those community ties snapped and frayed when our families moved to the US. Without anyone else to lean on, our values had to twist and mold themselves to fit into this new environment. We are seeds, alone on this side of the cliff, with no other trees to shield us from the elements.

Here, my community is my small family—with everyone else a competitor rather than a collaborator—and the only currency they'll take as payment for their sacrifices is my dazzling, spotless image.

Failing to get into any colleges means I'm dangerously delinquent on that debt.

I rinse the vomit from my mouth, then calmly descend downstairs, intent on faking a stomach bug so I can stay home from school. I'd prefer to think this through locked in my room, without Mom and Dad and the entire Monte Verde student population hounding me.

In the kitchen, Mom screws a lid onto her travel coffee mug: a blue one she bought from Delmont during our campus tour last fall. She's in tailored, dark wool slacks and a satiny green blouse that makes the brown of her skin pop. She lifts a perfect, microbladed eyebrow at me. "Where's your backpack?"

My outside must match how I feel inside because she circles the island to put a flawless, moisturized hand on my forehead. "Perlie, are you okay?"

I shake my head, not trusting myself to speak quite yet. The concern in her eyes makes me think I could tell her. She loves me, and though she'd be just as sad that I didn't get into any schools, we'd find a way out together. I lift my chin a little, hopeful, and meet her dark brown eyes.

But then she says, "You don't seem to have a fever. Get your backpack."

My hopes shatter.

Mom drops the hand that was on my forehead, and, for a moment, the child in me who wants a sympathetic smile and a hug misses the warmth. But I'm not a child anymore. These aren't broken toys or skinned knees. Nothing about my situation warrants any sort of positive attention from them. My parents aren't going to be the solution here, not when they're part of the problem.

Mom would be the first to admit she and Dad are tough on me but, in their minds, justifiably so. They both come from families who left comfortable lives in the Philippines to come here with little else but the dollars in their pockets and a whole lot of determination.

My grandfather, Dad's dad, was a school principal back home, but when he got here, American schools didn't accept his credentials: they thought these foreign institutions were lesser, that my grandfather therefore wasn't as smart. So he worked in cafeteria services and took night courses until he had the right qualifications to begin teaching again. According to Mom, he never told our relatives in the Philippines about this; he always said he "worked at a nice school," which is technically true. That set the strict tone for the very selective image our family has portrayed for generations.

Dad is the first American white-collar professional in his family, earning his JD at twenty-two years old and climbing the legal ladder two rungs at a time since then. Mom, who took a little longer to graduate college because she worked to help support her parents and sister, is one of the most sought-after cosmetic dermatologists in this area. And somehow, they expect me to top all that, and nothing less.

"My stomach feels off," I say, giving her one last chance to show me that she's willing to put Perla her daughter above Perlie the perfect-attendance dream.

Mom purses her lips, the makeup around her mouth caking slightly. Her successful dermatology practice requires her to look the part.

"Can't I stay home?" I ask.

I think I already know her answer. Last summer, one of her top clients invited the whole family to their Napa vineyard for a day. First of all, I'm too young to drink legally. Second, I don't have a license, so it's not like I can play designated driver either. Still, for the sake of showing off her perfect family to Mom's client, I spent the day sipping iced tea and smiling until my cheeks hurt. I was miserable, but when I'd pulled Mom aside to ask to leave, she said she was disappointed at me for complaining. She reminded me that our family's success requires sacrifice on everyone's part. I ended up ingesting so much black tea that day that my physically exhausted self couldn't sleep until two in the morning. But that client introduced Mom to more of her Napa friends, and the new income paid for my SAT prep classes and Dad's Lexus.

As awful as I felt that day after the vineyard, it's nowhere near how terrible I feel right now. But Mom has that same do-it-for-the-family glint in her perfectly lined eye.

"Are you willing to mess up your attendance record for this?" She steps back toward the island to pick up her travel mug. "You seem fine to me. I don't want you getting behind by missing class. I know kids think they can slack off senior year, but not you."

I shut my eyes and massage my temples. At the beginning of the year, I might have agreed with her. I've worked too hard to let myself slip, for even a moment. But I can't think of a way to defend myself that doesn't involve me laying bare the truth of my college rejections.

So next thing I know, I'm in the car, clutching a sleeve of saltines and a bottle of Pepto-Bismol. I know Mom means well—that attendance record really is a big deal at Monte Verde—but I can't help but wish I was still at home, sandwiched between teddy bears.

Her hand lingers on my shoulder a second longer than usual at drop-off. "Feel better, Perlie. I'll try to leave work early to pick up that chicken pho you like for dinner."

I nod and open the car door.

"Just focus on writing down everything the teacher says today," she continues, putting her hands back on the steering wheel. "You can reread it later, when you're well."

As I trudge toward my locker, my fingers wrap tight around the backpack straps at my chest. Graduation approaches. Signs plaster the concrete columns in the quad, reminding people to pick up their caps and gowns and finalize their names and schools for the printed program.

My stomach churns at the reminder that I won't have a school listed by my name.

All the seniors have somewhere to go in the fall, and they all think I'm going to Delmont. What's it going to look like if I don't go anywhere after all? What am I supposed to tell everyone?

"You could just tell them you're going," a voice says to my right.

"What?" I swivel to see who's talking, but of course they're not speaking to me.

Camilla, Edie, and Arnell sit on the other side of a concrete planter, a shrub between us.

Camilla shakes her head. "To the beach cleanup? It's not going to work, Edie."

Edie shrugs, her sweater sliding down her thin shoulder at the movement. "It will! You already told them you'd be out all Saturday morning. This is just a slight change of plans. Get dropped off at the cleanup site, and we'll pick you up. We'll get a fake number online to give your parents, in case they want to call the cleanup coordinator. It's not like they'll stay to watch you pick trash, right?"

There's a pause where an outright reaffirmation of the "it's not going to work" should be, but I guess this is where Camilla and I differ.

Arnell shoves Camilla on the arm. "Come on. They expect you're off being a wonderful person volunteering on the sand;

you're with us in my dad's boat on the water. Everyone wins."

Again I wait for a "no," but what I hear instead is an "I don't know. I'll think about it." To my surprise, she leaves that door open. Camilla Kang-Jansen may do something she's not quite supposed to.

The bell rings, and people begin to hoist up their backpacks to head to class.

I speed-walk away to avoid getting caught eavesdropping. Camilla lying to her parents? I start to tuck the info away in that mental file I keep for competitive edge.

I nearly trip over my own feet when the idea hits a different way.

Someone walking behind me stumbles aside just in time to avoid knocking me over. "Watch it!"

I manage a weak, apologetic wave with my sleeve of saltines, but my feet stay planted.

Camilla's parents expect her to be out all day at a beach cleanup. They'll drop her off with the other volunteers, but they'll have no reason to suspect she's doing anything different.

Everyone's expecting me to go to Delmont.

So what if I just go to Delmont?

No one knows I didn't get in, and I can keep it that way.

My four years at Monte Verde High have proved I somehow have the power of social invisibility. The Delmont staff won't even know I'm there. And if I'm on campus, I can research and analyze why I didn't get in so I can reapply with a stronger, targeted application.

When the admissions committee sees how well I fit their model of a perfect Delmont student, they'll kick themselves for not snatching me up the first time and offer me a place in their spring class. It's just like my grandfather, decades ago, who "worked at a nice school" but never quite told people precisely what that work was at first. I wouldn't be the first person in history who has fudged the truth a tiny bit to make themselves look good.

The best part is that I'll still get to graduate from Delmont: if I work my butt off and load up on classes, no one will have to know that my actual start was delayed.

Everyone wins.

The beginnings of a plan whip around my brain like leaves in a hurricane.

It's absurd, I know, and incredibly risky. I'll have to plan out every single detail, from what I'll bring to campus to how to stop my parents from sending tuition checks to the school. Every throw of the dice will have to land in my favor for this to go well. But paraphrasing my role model Albert Einstein, this is the only way I can achieve the impossible.

If Camilla and her friends can convince their parents that they're off saving the planet, if my grandfather could keep impressing his nosy town mates, then I can do this. I'll go to Delmont so that I can go to Delmont. If anyone's smart enough to pull this off, it's me.

I'm Perfect Perlie Perez.

That night, the scent of our pho dinner lingers in my hair as I tug out my hair tie and plop into my desk chair. Dad paces downstairs, still working. Mom concentrates on her ten-step skin care routine. I played up my fake sickness to head up to my room early, plotting out the next few months of my life with all the meticulousness of a heist at the Louvre.

My first stop is combing through the application I submitted to Delmont. Scrutinizing every word now feels awful, like watching myself on camera and noticing all the odd faces or hand gestures I'd made. But the only way I can crack how to get into Delmont is to first figure out why I didn't get in.

To my relief, I filled out every required line, checked every applicable box, and spelled all the short answers correctly. Then I get to my personal statement.

It looks great, like every other time I read it. I pull up the two rounds of feedback from my application coach, Raj. He'd come highly recommended from a man Mom met at a medical conference last year. Raj had coached the man's son, who is in his third year at Delmont now, double-majoring in chemistry and biology.

As I reread Raj's comment boxes on my documents, they practically scream at me tonight, much louder than they did when I first reviewed them.

More specificity. Tailor this to the Delmont program.

Make it more personal here. What does it mean to you to be a doctor?

This last part needs work. Why medicine? Really convince us this is your dream.

My mouth goes dry. I thought I'd addressed all of those

concerns, but now I worry that I didn't. Perhaps the admissions committee agreed with Raj that I needed more specificity and more heart. In my personal statement, I said I wanted to be a doctor; maybe they didn't believe me or I didn't distinguish myself from the herd enough. And maybe Raj just said I did a good job because our two-rounds-of-edits package meant he could take his money and go, whether or not my essay was fit for Delmont acceptance. How I regret giving him a five-star review and testimonial now.

I close my old application. Then I open a new spreadsheet, add unguessable password protection, and create seven tabs.

At the bottom of the first tab I type that favorite Albert Einstein quote. I'm going to need this much planning and more than a little luck to pull off this impossible task.

Part one: Learn about what it's like to be a first-year student at Delmont University. I can start this part now. It's never too early to know one's temporary adversary. If specificity was a deficiency in my application, this will solve it.

Part two: Find a place to stay on campus. This will be the trickiest. The rest of the parts will unravel rapidly if my parents have nowhere to move me into in September, and Delmont doesn't offer online-learning options for first-year students. Their old-fashioned requirement for physical presence on campus isn't a surprise, given that they still send out their admissions letters by mail.

Part three: Make a friend, but not a close one. This will be primarily for information gathering—maybe I can divine why they got admitted and I didn't—and it wouldn't hurt to have someone vouch for my presence in the dorm or the dining halls.

Part four: Figure out excuses to tell my parents to minimize mail and avoid visits. I don't need to worry about them casually showing up on campus, on top of everything else I'll be juggling.

Part five: Sit in a couple premed classes. I'm there to learn about life at Delmont and their premed program, aren't I? When I'm done with these classes, I'm going to write such a convincing argument about why I want to be a doctor that the admissions committee will think I already am one.

Part six: Revise my personal statement and reapply for the spring incoming class at Delmont. I'll channel everything I've learned through the previous parts into this, and I'll hit every note of Raj's feedback. The admissions committee will see how perfect of a fit I am for this school.

Part seven: Get in! Get that admissions letter, explain away this new "acceptance" to my parents as some minor administrative error, and lie low until spring semester starts.

I survey my plan for the next few months. In the coming weeks, I'll fill in more details to propel this plan from absurd to achievable, but the basic map to success is there, a glimmer of hope in the darkness.

"What do you think, guys?" I say over my shoulder to Bip and Bop, perched neatly on my still-made bed.

I take their silence as speechless awe.

I crack my knuckles and get to work.

FOUR

I smile for the thousandth time today, and the oversized graduation cap slips despite the bobby pins holding it in place.

"Say 'cheese'!"

Auntie Trish's lips, painted dark red to match the wrap dress hugging her curves, lift into a smile. She pulls me in for a tight hug once Dad snaps the picture. "So proud of you, Perlie!" She lowers her volume. "You like those farming kind of games, right? Picking turnips, milking cows? Got you something for summer break."

She winks at me and moves aside for the next set of family members, Dad's sister Silvie and her husband, my uncle Mario. I rearrange the orchid-and-dollar leis around my neck while Auntie Silvie finger-combs her hair into place.

Graduation day blurs by with smiles and school colors, scents of sweat and special-occasion perfume. All around us on the football field, people squeeze into photos with their grads.

I haven't been alone since the second I lumbered downstairs. Mom, with her designer ivory skirt suit and matching handbag, nodded approvingly at the sunflower-yellow dress we'd chosen months ago. Today, the color screams a cheerfulness I don't feel, but at least I can explain away the bloodlessness of my face as washout from this flashy fabric.

Before we left home, Mom gave me my graduation gift early so that I could wear it during today's ceremonies: a gold heart-shaped pendant with a golden South Sea pearl embedded in it, hanging on a delicate chain. It was my grandmother's, gifted to Mom decades ago, and now it's mine. I'd touched it almost reverently when Mom clasped it around my neck. As we stared at our jewelried reflections in the mirror—me with the family necklace, her with the thousands of dollars' worth of diamonds she'd bought herself—I'd thanked her profusely, biting back the flare of guilt at the fact that she probably wouldn't have handed me this heart if she knew I'd failed to get into Delmont.

Auntie Silvie scoots closer to me, and we all say "cheese" on command.

Dad nods in approval at his shot. "I'll post a few now."

I'd tell him to do it later, but I've been getting the feeling that a good portion of today is for family bragging rights.

Dad focuses on drafting captions for his Facebook post. Then he'll peek at his phone every fifteen minutes to revel in the comments from distant relatives and acquaintances congratulating us.

I've had more people talk to me these last few hours than during the entire school year. To be honest, it stung after I skipped grades and realized that people only seemed to notice me when I was doing something for them, when I had the potential to make them look good. Folks would say hi to me when we'd have a group project together, but then wouldn't move their backpacks from the bus seats next to them on field trips. I learned early on not to let it bother me too much; not everyone is purposefully mean. But neglect is a tough pill to swallow too. It'd be nice to be noticed and included because someone wants *me* and not what I can offer them.

Today, after the last diploma was handed out and we had tossed our caps in the air, people who had barely spoken to me outside of class assignments had patted me on the back or high-fived me and wished me all the best luck. I even ended up in a few group pictures with people who didn't pass me their yearbooks to sign.

I did get in a brief hug with my lunch crew though, spouting out some noncommittal "text me so we can hang out over the summers." Part of me regrets not being close enough to my own friends to confide in them, but they wouldn't understand what I'm about to do at Delmont.

"Perlie, you're living on campus, right?" Auntie Silvie asks. She pulls a red box of crackers out of her backpack for my three-year-old cousin, Hudson, who is kicking a hole in the grass beneath his light-up sneakers. "The junior accountant at my office just graduated from Delmont. I could see if she could give you some advice."

Auntie Silvie and Uncle Mario aren't as outwardly high-pressure as my parents, but the mandate to do well, to be successful and brag-worthy, emanates off them just as palpably. I feel for poor Hudson, who cheerily drops an elephant-shaped animal cracker in the dirt he'd unearthed.

She and Uncle Mario aren't exactly cheerleaders, who shake pom-poms and flip through the air no matter how the game is going. They're more like fair-weather fans, here to smile and pat me on the back when I'm winning and doing the family proud, but more than ready to disavow me and burn my jersey if I falter. If they were to find out I didn't get into any colleges, they'd tack up an unflattering picture of me at their house as a reminder to Hudson of "Study hard or you'll end up like that no-good Perlie."

I start dislodging the bobby pins in my hair. This graduation cap is stifling. "I'll be in the dorms, in one of the single rooms." I relay, word for word, the language on the Delmont residential hall website I'd pored over yesterday. Details about square footage, evening security patrols, social programming coordinated by RAs. The inundation of information is enough to send Auntie Silvie into mindless "uh-huhs" and "oh greats."

"That must be costing you," Uncle Mario says to Dad. "Those private universities don't come cheap."

Dad nods. "Perlie was awarded a generous grants package. Can you believe it? It covers tuition and room and board for the fall semester. They're even waiving the seat deposit: that's how impressive she is. And hey, it'll give me some time to win some poker tournaments to pay for the rest of those years."

I force a laugh to match Uncle Mario's.

The words sound true when they come out of Dad's mouth. I would've believed him, if I wasn't the one that told him those lies. I'd crafted some fake enrollment and housing forms, complete with scholarship and grant information, to conveniently leave in easy-to-stumble-upon places around the house. Google, the high school counselor, and eavesdropping at school told me all I needed to know about the enrollment and financial aid process.

"Wow, they want you so bad they're paying you? Way to go, Perlie," Uncle Mario says with a wink at me. "You won't be as bogged down by student loans as your dad and me. I'll probably still be paying those when Hudson here moves me into a nursing home."

The flush that rises to my cheeks is real, but it's more shame than humility. Today should be about triumph, but instead, I feel the opposite. My family gave up their whole day to sit wedged together on the crumbling bleachers of our football field, and I'm thanking them by lying straight to their faces.

The weight of their pride, and of the magnitude of my deception, sits on my shoulders, heavy and unrelenting. I shift, and the orchid-and-dollar leis rustle, my grandmother's pendant warm against my skin.

But I can't break their hearts with the truth, not now. I stick another knife in that part of me that rears its timid head and suggests I come clean. That part needs to be dead and buried like Hudson's animal cracker if any of me is going to survive the next four years.

Besides, this isn't lying entirely. I'll still be going to Delmont in September. And I'll get admitted into their freshman class, eventually. So what if the timing's a bit off? My family doesn't need to know that, and they won't care when I'm brandishing that gold-sealed diploma years from now. If my grandfather could fudge the details of his employment but still couldn't figure out texting until the day he died, then I definitely can do this.

"What are you majoring in?" Auntie Silvie asks.

"Biological sciences, to put me on track for med school." The answer is a reflex.

Auntie Silvie coos, clearly impressed, and Dad pats my back.

"Wow," Auntie Trish says. "So no more video games?"

I almost flinch, remembering my brief, slightly embarrassing middle school dream. "I still play. But it won't get me into med school."

Auntie Trish beams, like I'd said precisely the right answer. She'd come over for dinner the day back in middle school when we had an assembly speaker preaching the idea of finding something you love and making that a career. I spent the whole meal proclaiming my calling of something-to-do-with-video-games (design, testing, anything!). My parents had smiled at my earnestness, and then Mom and Auntie Trish reminisced about some old neighbor of theirs that flitted around from one low-level tech job to another before he finally went back to school for a nursing degree a decade later. Mom and Auntie Trish both knew his story because they'd recently accepted the guy's Facebook friend requests out of curiosity and a touch of pity.

Even in middle school, I knew I didn't want to end up someone's sympathy or sadism add on social media. It'd be like going to a cool kid's birthday party just because their mom made them invite everyone in the class. That settled it for me: gaming would stay as a hobby while I forged ahead to become a doctor. Later that year, when that gaming career fantasy had faded, we bought the red binder that would eventually house Perlie's Academic Plan: a tangible reminder of our shared dream.

"Aren't you worried you'll get overwhelmed, Perla? I mean, college is hard enough when you're eighteen, but at your age?" Auntie Silvie asks.

"I'll be fine. I've done this well so far," I say through a tightening jaw.

That response doesn't seem to satisfy my aunt. She turns to Mom and Dad instead. "Have you considered holding her back a couple years to mature? Gap years are common in other parts of the world."

Just like that, I'm shoved out of the conversation, relegated to the sideline as a kid too young to guide her own destiny.

Auntie Trish threads her arm through mine. She's almost a decade younger than Mom, and she catches on to these moments of exclusion more often. "Don't listen to them, Perlie. You'll do great," she says.

With my free hand, I adjust the leis around my neck, and Auntie Trish's eyes catch on the heart pendant peeking out from under my gown. "Mama's necklace. It looks gorgeous on you." Her eyes mist for a moment, and I'm reminded that even with this same internal debt she and Mom grew up with from their parents, there was love there too. "You know we're all proud of you, right, Perla? Your mom and I—our parents worked tooth and nail to put us through college. That was Mama's one special-occasion necklace, the one splurge she allowed herself, for only the most important family gatherings. I know that if your grandparents were still alive, they'd be so thrilled to see how far we've all come, especially you."

"Thanks. It means a lot that Mom gave this to me." The smile I offer her is genuine, despite the extra pressure Auntie Trish unintentionally added with her kind words. "And thanks for that farm game. I was going to use my graduation money for it."

Auntie Trish squeezes my arm. "Save that money for lattes. You deserve to do something you enjoy now and then!"

To have someone in my family say that out loud warms me, even if she did add "now and then."

It takes me a second to realize the Kang-Jansens have joined us. Ms. Kang and Dad launch into shop talk, and Dr. Jansen and Mom trade forced compliments about each other's skirt suits.

Camilla's already ditched her cap and gown, and her dark red sleeveless dress flatters her. Her hair, once as long as mine, has been cut into a sophisticated bob. She stands two inches taller than me—four, thanks to her wedges today—with all the poise of a ballet dancer. And how did she manage to take all those honors classes, win academic decathlon trophies, and learn how to do perfect cat-eye eyeliner? I take a step to the side, putting some distance between us. I must look like a middle schooler standing next to her.

"Congratulations, Perlie," Ms. Kang says with a smile. That smile would look genuine if I didn't know her better from years of competition with her daughter and her purposely using my cutesy family nickname, which makes me sound like a yappy Pomeranian. Though the Kang-Jansens may be happy for me, they'd be happier if they had something to gloat to the Perez family about. But for once, we're celebrating the same milestone, and Camilla and I are equals.

"Thanks. And congratulations to you too, Camilla. We did it!" I lean in for the kind of head-off-to-the-side-and-two-pats-on-the-back hug I've become a pro at today. Camilla knows the drill.

"I hear you're heading off to Delmont," Ms. Kang adds. "Such an accomplishment, for your age."

I return a fake, gracious smile of my own. So today isn't a truce day after all. That qualifier of "for your age" is downright insulting every single time. I'd never tell Ms. Kang she looks good, for her age.

"Perlie's more than prepared," Mom answers, saving me from having to spin another lie. "She's got a whole list of summer reading she's already started on. A few highly recommended college prep books too."

That reading is all for my seven-part plan for getting into Delmont. I've got thousands of pages of material on college success to get through in the next few months, and the thought almost makes my eyeballs ache. To make this all a little less serious, I've started thinking of my Delmont plan like it's a video game, a challenge that will require all sorts of skill and strategy to conquer. I've got my objective of getting accepted for real and all sorts of quests I must complete first. My spreadsheet is my way of preparing for the trials ahead. Some people meditate, others exercise: I make spreadsheets.

Under part one, learning about what the first year at Delmont is like, I have a side mission of talking so much about Delmont at home during the summer that my parents assume this is excitement. Mom's mass purchase of prep books stemmed from how well I've acted this out. For her and Dad, money is easy to part with if it means my success.

"College prep books. That's very smart of you," Ms. Kang says in simultaneous approval of me and wonder as to why her own daughter isn't doing the same.

Camilla throws me a kind smile. At least she got the memo that we're supposed to be nice to each other today. "Anything fun on that reading list? I finished this amazing sci-fi one, and I was hoping—"

"Then I'll get you a book like Perlie's," Ms. Kang says. "Maybe if you prepared like she did, you could've gotten into Delmont too and not wait-listed."

Camilla's face sours, and we're suddenly back to being competitors on a day I'd hoped we'd be friends. If she doesn't already, Camilla will loathe me for getting into her dream school when she didn't. I can't do anything to make her feel better about it either, not without running the risk of outing myself. It's for the best that we won't be at the same school. It'll make keeping my cover that much harder.

I slide off my graduation cap, letting the sun warm my face as Camilla and her parents trudge over to the next group of family friends. The breeze sends wisps of my newly freed hair tickling my face, and I try to ignore the thought that, of all the people I'm lying to, I hadn't expected to feel this guilty about Camilla.

On PicLine: my black cap and gown draped over the brown leather couch in the living room.

Caption: Goodbye, Monte Verde! #Graduation.

Eight likes.

FIVE

I cold-sweat enough to fill a kiddie pool during our seven-hour drive to Delmont. The early Labor Day weekend traffic makes our Thursday trip a whole excruciating hour longer. Dad drives, Mom texts her office manager, and I slouch in the back seat next to my bed-in-a-bag comforter set and toy nervously with my heart pendant. I couldn't get out of my parents' expected move-in road trip without setting off some big alarms in their heads. Besides, without a driver's license, I actually do need a ride to campus with my stuff.

Now that we've arrived at Delmont, the probability of me being found out increases exponentially, and so does my anxiety. Dad oohs and aahs at a *Welcome* banner hanging on the carved stone arch above the campus's main driveway. Blue and green balloons flank the road, and at the front of the line of cars ahead, volunteers lean casually into windows, chatting with new Delmont families. On the sidewalks, students with their belongings Tetrised into plastic wheeled carts weave past each other and the plush dragon mascot dancing in his oversized Delmont basketball jersey. The excitement of newness infuses everything and everyone.

Everyone except me. I should be thrilled. This should be the day that my life as a Delmont student begins. But I don't feel anything but gray, bone-deep dread.

Dad eyes the dorms ahead. "Which hall are we looking for?"

"Keith Hall."

One of the original halls on the edge of the residential part of campus.

Part two of my plan is the trickiest: find a place to stay. I'd scoured the school website and social media posts for any info about move-in and getting in and out of the residence halls. Thanks to a five-year-old petition I'd dug up on a student page, I'd learned that the school relaxed the requirement for first-years to live on campus due to student financial and health concerns. This, combined with all those expensive new dorms closer to the classrooms, means that many of the old ones like Keith Hall sit empty as students search for cheaper, more spacious off-campus housing.

I'll have a better chance of finding an unused space to ditch my things in at Keith Hall before sending my parents off. Maximizing my chances is important. I won't even get to the other parts of my plan if I can't convince my parents to leave me in a nice, secure dorm room. All residence halls operate on the same keycard system thanks to a big, donor-funded upgrade a decade ago, so once I crack Keith Hall, I can use that knowledge for other buildings too, as needed. Though if all goes according to plan, "as needed" won't be an issue.

Stuck behind a dining supply truck, we crawl up the hill toward Keith Hall. The building looms into view: twelve floors of single rooms, communal spaces, and shared bathrooms.

I sit up as we approach, my stomach churning with acid and anticipation. Ahead, blue-shirted volunteers surround rows of check-in tables full of clipboards and stacks of paper. The intricate strategies I'd run through all summer swirl in my head.

As Super Mario says, *Here we go!*

"You find parking. I'll check in on my room." I don't wait for an answer. My hand's on the door handle and my feet on the pavement in a matter of seconds.

I spring toward the registration table. Mom calls an "Okay, we'll meet you at the entrance!" at me as a volunteer in an orange vest waves their car forward.

I slow a few feet away from the table and scan the faces of the volunteers. Many are up on their feet, energized and approaching any lost-looking students. I notice one white guy, his acne-dotted chin propped up by his hand, his eyes half-asleep. Exactly the kind of volunteer I'm looking for.

I stride toward him. "Hi, checking in."

He blinks slowly. "Last name?"

"Reyes," I lie.

It takes him much longer than it should to find the "R" part of the alphabetized list. How did he get into Delmont and I didn't?

"First name?

"Michelle."

I pray there isn't a Michelle, and I'm rewarded by a brow-furrowed look seconds later.

"I don't see you on here."

Perfect.

I draw on all that A-minus drama class experience and throw on my most impatient look. "What do you want me to do? My parents are already parked. That one-hour meter is ticking."

"I—"

"They've got to be back at the airport soon. Do you know how much it is to change an international flight because someone took too long moving in?"

He blinks slowly, barely registering my words.

"Here, I'll find it." I snatch the list out of his hand, and he makes no move to grab it back. I picked a winner.

The columns at the top of the spreadsheet break into last name, first name, student ID number, room number, assigned move-in date.

I pin my finger to the move-in date column and quickly read down. Most people are arriving today. But then I see them: a few rows printed in red, as special exceptions. One girl, Samantha Simon, is missing her assigned arrival date and moving in on Friday, a whole week from now, a few days after class starts. Why would someone move in so late?

A news story I'd linked in my spreadsheet shuffles to the top of my mental stack. I'd read that staff shortages and changing immigration policies have been increasing visa processing backlogs. The politics of it aren't as important to me as the fact that some international students have been experiencing delays getting their student visas in order. I saved this story because frustrated foreign residents may drop their Delmont dreams altogether, and one of those open spots could be mine in spring. In fact, Samantha Simon's name is on a list of a dozen move-in-weekend exceptions and any one of these rooms will work for what I've got planned.

This girl's late arrival gives me a couple more days to find a more permanent room. My parents will still be able to see me moved in before they make the long drive back home, chatting teary-eyed about how proud they are of me. Probably.

"I'm in room 217," I say, letting the papers flip back down. I shove the clipboard back at him.

He calls the number behind him, and an East Asian girl reaches into a heavy-looking file box and pulls out an envelope. "This key's for your room only. You'll need your student ID to get in and out of the residence hall itself. You want any help with your bags?"

I shake my head, already walking away. Through the thin paper, I feel a plastic card. My room key. Or rather, Samantha Simon's room key, for when she arrives next week. A thrill at this first success hums through my veins, like I aced a pop quiz or beat a mission on expert difficulty. I almost skip back to my parents.

At the car, Dad fills a cart with my new stuff: a fluffy pillow, my bed-in-a-bag set we'd picked up at Nordstrom last week, a roomy laptop backpack. Mom taps her manicured fingers on the handle of my one rolling suitcase of clothes. I had purposely packed light, knowing that it may take me some time to find an empty room to settle in.

The doors to the residence hall are propped open for move-in hours. I lead my parents past all the volunteers with their walkie-talkies and lists. We cram into the elevator, arranging ourselves around the cart.

Seconds later, the doors open to a gray-patterned carpeted landing, bordered by white walls that look like they've been painted over a hundred times. Thanks to a Pinterest board of an RA from last year, I knew how seriously the staff took Welcome Week door decorating, and sure enough, construction-paper dragons featuring the resident's name are taped on each door.

I practically sprint out of the elevator, leaving Mom and Dad to maneuver the wobbly moving cart through the elevator doors. I make it to room 217 first, and a green "Samantha" dragon stares at me. From the elevator, this is one long hallway with a clear line of sight, so my parents would notice me tinkering with the decorations. I quickly swipe the room key into the door's card reader. It blinks green, and the lock clicks open. I bite back a sigh of relief, but not before swinging the door open and tearing down the "Samantha" dragon now hidden behind me. I make a note to replace it or pull down some other dragons so my room's not so out of place later, but for now, I'm hoping there's not some surprise *This is Samantha Simon's room!* banner strung between the walls inside.

The room is thankfully bare, and when my parents wheel our cart over, we gaze into the tiny space that's supposed to be my home for the next year.

Dad purses his lips and exhales through his nose. "At least

we're not paying for this."

If they notice the personalized door decoration missing, they don't mention it. My parents are more focused on the fact that there's just enough room for the bed and the desk, and I doubt we can have the cart and all three of us inside at the same time. Dad parks the cart right outside of the door and grabs the bed-in-a-bag set.

Mom angles the handle of my rolling suitcase toward me. "You'd think a school with an endowment the size of Delmont's could upgrade its student housing." Her eyes fix on a streak of rust on the door hinge, and her lips dip into a frown.

"It's . . ." I struggle to spin this. ". . . cozy."

Mom and Dad exchange a glance, but I cut off conversation by grabbing my suitcase and heading inside.

This room, the size of my parents' walk-in closet, feels smaller and smaller as we unload the cart's contents. It's not spacious or state-of-the-art or even that clean, but it checks every one of my boxes: it's private, empty, and, best of all, on the Delmont campus, a six-hour drive from Monte Verde.

When the cart is empty, Dad brushes his hands off on his dark jeans. "It's a good thing you left Bip and Bop at home. There's barely enough space for you."

I'm about to remind him that I don't need to bring my childhood teddy bears with me everywhere I go, but then I'm hit with a pang of regret. I actually miss the two fluffy faces, judgmental as they may be.

"Are you sure this room is okay, Perlie?" Dad asks. His hand lingers by the phone in his pocket, as if he's willing to look up and call every Delmont dorm authority possible to ask for a room change, if I wanted it. Only the best for Ernie Perez's family.

I toss my pillow onto the bed and smile as I assess my new dorm room. "It's perfect."

I usher my parents out of Keith Hall as the next batch of students moves in.

"You call when you're all unpacked, okay? We can mail anything you need," Mom says, her hands still on my arms, as if she's not ready to break the hug yet. She smells of freesia and vanilla, a high-end perfume that a top client complimented and that she now wears everywhere. Mom had originally wanted to spend a few days helping me settle in, but thankfully, Dad has to be back in Monte Verde for a trial tomorrow.

"I will."

"We're only six hours away. Five, if I drive."

"I know."

"So if you need anything, you just—"

"Lina, let's go," Dad cuts in, one hand on the steering wheel, the other fiddling with the navigation app on his phone. "She knows how to reach us. And she has our Amazon password."

Mom finally drops her arms and joins Dad.

The closing of the car door rattles a piece of my courage loose, revealing a hint of regret that wasn't supposed to be there. I want to jump back into the car. I want to rewind.

I lock eyes with Mom, and, for a moment, her gaze softens, like there's something important she wants to say but she's struggling to find the right words.

What comes out is "Study hard, okay, Perlie? No distractions."

"And no boys," Dad adds with a joking-but-not-really smile. "Only As."

I nearly laugh at how far from a made-for-TV-movie farewell this is. This is their heartfelt way of saying goodbye, and their predictability is actually comforting: of course they'd take these last seconds to remind me that their rules and expectations stretch all the way down the coast.

I wave goodbye and spout out a few more assurances of "I'll be fine, really"; then they join the row of cars disappearing down the hill. I watch them go, shielding my eyes against the Southern California sun that keeps the air summery hot. I don't know how September came so fast. One day I was handing Dad a freshly printed admissions letter, then suddenly I'm standing in front of one of the oldest residence halls at Delmont, wondering if he looked back in the rearview mirror at me one last time.

A cart crashes against my side.

"Sorry," a Latina girl with purple hair says. It's shaved on one side, and the other side hangs long, obscuring her vision. I rub my hip, where a bruise is sure to bloom.

The woman next to her, her mother judging by the same wide face, reaches out to help the girl with the cart. "Careful, Tessita!"

"Mom," the girl pushes out through clenched teeth. "Tessa, please. And I got this."

"All right, Tessa. But you're going the wrong way. The volunteer said the elevator's in the other direction."

"I can show you," I offer. I don't want to stay out here amid the tears and goodbyes much longer anyway. Plus, the more I go in and out of the building, the more people will accept me as part of the Delmont scenery. That's what I need to be if I'm going to stay here long enough to apply for the next semester: someone who's familiar enough that you let me into a building without swiping a student ID but who's unremarkable enough that you don't ask where I'm going.

Tessa's mother rewards me with a gleaming smile and a story about their parking troubles as we weave our way to the elevator.

"Which floor?" My finger hovers just off the brass elevator buttons.

Tessa plucks the envelope from the back pocket of her torn jeans. "Two, please. I'm in 210."

"We're on the same floor," I note.

Tessa could be a good candidate for my part three: make a friend, but not a close one. I'm trying to learn about Delmont and other admitted students so I can use it to my advantage when applying for the spring class, and what better way than to pick the brain of someone who's here with me?

Making friends has never been one of my strengths though. My Monte Verde yearbook is proof of that. It's why I included in my spreadsheet six links to articles on small talk and how to generally be a social, unawkward member of the community.

I push the 2 button. "I'm . . ." It occurs to me then that no one here knows me as Perlie. I can shed my cutesy family nickname, finally, like this Tessa girl is trying to do with Tessita. ". . . Perla Perez."

"Nice to meet you, Perla. I'm Belinda Rivera, Tessa's mother." Belinda reaches her hand out to shake mine, which I do, awkwardly, holding the handshake a second too long. I don't remember the last time I shook someone's hand—maybe the principal when I got my diploma? Nor do I remember the last time I was formally introduced to someone new. I should probably practice. Delmont is chock-full of someone-news, and I don't want to be remembered as the weird girl who doesn't know how to properly shake a hand. I wish I'd reread some of those articles on small talk on the drive here.

The elevator chimes and the doors slide open, distracting both mother and daughter. I let them exit first, and they're so preoccupied with finding the right room that they don't notice me slip by them.

I close the door to my room and blow out a breath. I force my hands to unclench. I hadn't realized I was wound so tight.

I'm here. I'm finally at Delmont.

Exactly where I'm supposed to be and not supposed to be.

The thought dynamites the emotional dam holding back my tears. They flow free. I crumble down onto the floor, my back against the cold door.

Since the day I'd forged the admittance letter, the guilt bubbled in my stomach. But with each proud smile from my parents and their offhand mentions to everyone who'd listen that their daughter was going to Delmont, that guilt began to clear. In its place grew a determination to succeed, and when I'd opened up the spreadsheet last night to finalize some plan details, I thought the guilt was all but vanquished. No, it was still there, weakened, but waiting.

I let my head hang, the heart pendant gleaming below my chin. I grip it tight, the shape of the pearl imprinting into my palm. Part of me isn't surprised I let the lie get this far. The Perez family is supposed to be the best: the models of success, intelligence, and new wealth. I can't be the failure in the family, the one our friends and family will whisper about, with their "sayangs" and "she had so much potentials." I refuse to be, because I know I'm exceptional.

Every deviation from the infallible Perlie's Academic Plan is a crack in the family's polished veneer, and heaven forbid anyone look close enough at the Perezes to see that.

A tear drops onto the gray carpet beneath me, joining a growing splotch. It's too late to tell my parents now. I can't imagine the anger this level of deception would incur. Or maybe my parents would dole out an even worse punishment: go quiet, then let the thick disappointment smother me.

I lift my head and stare into my new room.

I earned this, no matter what that admissions letter said.

Delmont's the one that made the mistake, not me. My reapplication will give them a chance to recognize their error and remedy that.

I drag the bottom hem of my shirt across my face to mop up the tears. I am determined to see this through. I have every detail of this plan spelled out and spreadsheeted. This time next semester, I'll be moving into a tiny dorm room with my name rightfully on it.

I haul myself onto my feet and dig through my backpack for my new MacBook: a college gift from Dad. On this hard drive hides a copy of my password-protected seven-part-plan spreadsheet. I've got work to do if I'm going to make myself a part of Delmont, use what I learn about the campus to tailor my application and personal statement, then resubmit the whole package at the end of November for the next incoming class.

I slide the window open to let in some fresh air to clear my mind. A massive tree branch sits right outside my window, its leaves tickling the flimsy screen between us.

Keith Hall sits the highest on this hill, and a steep, tree-covered slope drops down to the next hall, affording me plenty of privacy. My window looks out at a thick covering of trees rather than straight into someone else's room, like the more crowded dorms at the bottom of the hill.

Off in the distance, the Delmont marching band starts practice. The faint vibration of drums flows into my room with the breeze.

There's a knock on my door, and I swipe my hands under my eyes to make sure the tears are gone. I ignore the alarm in my chest—I'm supposed to be in this room after all; Samantha Simon who?—paint on a smile, and answer.

Tessa stands in the hallway, her hands stuffed in her pockets. A lighter line circles her brown wrist, like she was out enjoying the sun all summer and a watch got in the way.

"Hey, Perla, right? I didn't get to thank you for showing us the elevator. And for not being super weirded out when my mom shook your hand like she was trying to sell you something. She's got her own consulting business, and she doesn't know how to introduce herself to normal people."

She grins as she apologizes, and I match it.

"Thanks for thinking I'm normal."

"Anyway, want to grab dinner later? It'll be kinda like a mini support group from being traumatized by my mom's aggressive friendliness." She juts a thumb down the hallway.

I ignore the part of me that wants to wallow alone in my stolen dorm room and pore over my plan. My feelings are still too raw. If I stay in here, I might be tempted to call Mom and Dad and ruin everything I'd painstakingly constructed. A dinner can't hurt. And I can use this to gather more information for my plan.

"Sure, text me when you head out." I don't need any more surprise knocks on a door that isn't mine. After dinner, I'll come up with more ways to hide my temporary residency, to minimize the noise and even light leaking out of the room.

We exchange phone numbers, and as Tessa leaves, I close the door and smile into my tiny dorm as another breeze blows in. The leaves rustle and brush my window.

Parts one, two, and three of my plan already in motion? I'm impressed at my own progress. This is precisely the kind of intelligence and maturity my parents would be proud of—if they knew, which they never can.

So why can't I shake the worry deep in my chest that these small wins are simply Band-Aids over broken bones?

SIX

The sun is barely starting to set by the time Tessa and I spill out into the cul-de-sac. Most of the cars are gone, so the two of us can walk free on the hot black asphalt. Cleared-off registration tables, dying balloons, and abandoned carts block the sidewalks.

Tessa peers down at her crumpled campus map. I don't need one. I'd spent a few hours over the summer memorizing the layout of the residence halls, figuring out the best routes for getting places fast and, most importantly, undetected.

"There are four dining halls. Any preference on where to go? I knocked on the RA's door to try to introduce myself and ask for recommendations, but she was on the phone. Not exactly the warm Delmont welcome spelled out in all our materials."

"Word on the street is that the best dining hall is in Godwin Village," I offer. I'd come across a ranking of the dining halls on a student blog.

Tessa bites her lower lip and scans her map. "It's at the bottom of this hill."

We gaze down the steep hill that my parents' car had made effortless earlier.

"Your intel better be correct, Perla. You want me to walk all the way down there and back, on a full stomach?" With a smile, she tucks the map into her back pocket. "It's good thing no one else took me up on my dinner offer. You'd be outvoted."

We walk to the campus soundtrack of cars, people, and far-off lawn mowers. I instantly like Tessa. We've spent a total of ten minutes together, and she hasn't tried to play the "I'm better than you because" card once. This isn't like Monte Verde High at all: we're not jockeying for a higher position than anyone else. She doesn't care—or know—that I'm younger and treat me differently because of it. She doesn't associate me with the flawless Monte Verde Perezes, conjecture about my GPA, or seem to strategize about the best way to use me.

We're all new and trying to figure this place out.

It's refreshing.

Mid-conversation about majors, Tessa grabs the door handle, and we find ourselves in a long line to enter the dining room. I peer at the front, trying to figure out what the delay is.

Someone is scanning student IDs.

Which I don't have.

A lump hardens in my throat. A recent grad's blog assured me that most campus dining establishments take cash. Apparently not this one though: there isn't a cash register in sight. Just an older white woman in a wheelchair and a dark blue apron, monitoring the card scanners on either side of her. There's no getting past her without swiping a student ID.

They're going to find me, the non-Delmont Delmont student, before I've even unzipped my suitcase. The panic bangs around in my chest like a pinball.

"—which I think will be interesting, but my mom will probably say something like she doesn't know what jobs will come out of it." Tessa pauses. "You okay, Perla?"

Somehow, we've made it to the front. I don't even remember moving my feet.

Tessa swipes her ID into the scanner, and the attached monitor flashes "20 meals left" in bright green.

I stagger back a step, my new Adidas scuffing the shoe of someone behind me. I can't believe I missed that there's a meal plan required to eat in this specific dining hall because I'd gotten caught up in the fuzzy feeling of someone wanting to befriend me. I've been here less than half a day, and I've already jeopardized my whole plan.

"You're up," the Delmont staffer says, pulling me out of my spiraling thoughts.

I gulp, my mouth bone dry. I need to find a way to get out of line and out of this dinner.

"I . . ." I don't have an inkling as to how to end this sentence.

Tessa frowns. "Oh no, did you forget your ID?"

I nod slowly at the suggestion. It's believable. It could work. "Yeah, I think it's still on my desk."

"All the way up that hill?"

My confidence flares slightly at the fact that Tessa hasn't out-right dismissed me. Each unchallenged lie boosts my energy like a game power-up: a super mushroom, a healing spell, a heart container. She doesn't suspect that something's off, that I don't belong here. At most, she thinks I'm a little flighty, which I don't love either, but it's better than being chased off campus with torches and pitchforks.

"I guess I can go back and get it." My eyes drift past the increasingly impatient line of people behind us to the dining hall doors. "Unless I can come in just this once?"

Back at Monte Verde High, teachers and administrators afforded Perfect Perlie Perez a tiny bit more leeway. They overlooked dodgeball near misses and let me stay in the game or manually overrode the due date on library books returned a day late.

But this Delmont staffer is immune. She shakes her head. "Sorry, hon. No admittance into the dining hall unless you have your student ID or someone swipes you in."

Tessa brightens. "That's an option? Psh, Perla, I got you. I have the Dragon-plus meal plan." She swipes her card again and the monitor flashes "19 meals left."

"Wow, thanks." I wonder then what she wants from me, how she's going to somehow use this mistake against me. "That's too nice of you."

"Don't worry about it," she says over her shoulder as she strolls ahead. "You can get me later. Or carry me back up the hill to Keith Hall. We'll see how I feel after we hit up all these food stations."

Yet another reminder that this isn't Monte Verde High. Not everyone here is out to get me. Tessa may actually just be a decent person.

I follow her in, my legs still weak from the narrowly avoided misstep. I promise myself I'll spend an extra hour tonight memorizing the dining options tab of my spreadsheet.

The second that oil-and-yeast smell of pizza hits my nostrils, my legs suddenly feel renewed. We lose each other in the bustling, hungry crowd, and by the time I regroup with Tessa again, we take one look at each other's overloaded trays and laugh.

A bowl of steaming pasta pomodoro overlaps onto a plate of chicken pesto pizza on my tray, and a paper cup of simultaneously crisp and mushy-in-the-right-places french fries takes up any remaining space.

Mom has carefully monitored my diet since I hit puberty, because apparently my size is another aspect of the perfect Perez family that her more superficial, appearance-obsessed clients may see and judge us for. She definitely would have commented on the level of carb wonder in front of me. I'm determined to savor every crumb on this tray tonight.

My first bite of the chicken pesto pizza is cheese-and-basil heaven. I could get used to this.

"You've got to try these mozzarella sticks," Tessa says, pushing the bowl off her tray and onto the table between us.

"Only if you take some of these fries." We trade, and after a bite, the melted cheese strings almost the length of my arm from my fingers to my teeth.

I'm winding the cheese closer to my face when I hear, "Perlie?"

I shove the rest of the mozzarella stick into my mouth, and, to my horror, Camilla Kang-Jansen stands next to me, tray in hand. She has a sensible salad—dressing on the side—and a glass of water. Dr. Jansen is as extreme about portion regulating as Mom is.

"Hi, Camilla." I blink again, hoping this is a pizza-induced hallucination, but she's still there. "I thought you were going to NYU." Out east. Miles away from here.

"Got a wait-list spot just last week! It was a whole mess. We barely worked it out in time before move-in." She has shadows under her eyes, and years of knowing her parents gives me some insight into just how hectic her last few days must have been. They probably had graduation program correction notes printed and sent out to their friends.

"That's great." I hope there's enough sincerity in my voice to mask the nerves. Only a handful of people at my high school had enrolled at Delmont, and I wasn't close enough to any of them to care about them poking into my story. However, Camilla's family intertwines so closely with mine that our parents will almost certainly swap kids-in-college stories over dinner.

"Are you in Godwin Village too?" she asks.

I shake my head. "Up the hill, in Keith."

"Yikes, that's a hike. You're going to end up with quads of steel by the end of the year."

I'm too surprised to laugh. Did she just joke with me? And in front of other people?

"Do you know what group you're in for orientation? It's in the welcome packet."

"Oh, I . . . I don't remember." I shrug as casually as I can to disguise the fact that I hadn't even opened my—Samantha Simon's—welcome packet yet. I had been too busy convincing my parents I'm fine and then working through the ensuing crisis of conscience.

Camilla's head tilts ever so slightly. Perfect Perlie Perez of Monte Verde would never skip over instructions or forget a detail, but I didn't think Camilla had paid enough attention to me the last few years to remember that. Does she suspect something's off? The pizza cheese curdles in my stomach.

Before she can question me, an arm snakes across her shoulders. "Hey, babe, need a hand with that?"

I blink up at the tall white guy with short sandy-brown hair and a dazzling white smile that must either be genetics or thousands of dollars in orthodontics.

He holds his own pizza-laden tray one-handed and smiles at me. "Hi, I'm Rich."

"Babe," I whisper before gathering my thoughts and manners together enough to respond politely. "I'm Perla, and this is Tessa." Tessa, mid-mozzarella-stick-bite, nods in greeting.

"So, you're Camilla's boyfriend?" I throw the guess out wildly, fishing. If they are dating, it'd make sense that Camilla would want to go to the same school as her secret boyfriend. The fact that Delmont's got a stellar rate of graduates who get into law school? That's the cherry on top.

He blushes. "We don't like to put labels on it."

Camilla's cheeks redden too, but the missiles that explode behind her eyes tell me it's because I've stumbled upon a secret of hers. Maybe not as life-ending as mine but definitely destructive enough that a word to her parents could utterly ruin this small piece of independence she's carved out for herself.

Because at the top of the pyramid of our "focus on school" rules is "no dating."

Everyone at Monte Verde High with our style of parent knew this. Networks existed to cover for one another while couples were out on dates. Some people had been seeing the same folks for years but would easily disavow any knowledge of their long-time partners if their parents asked.

I return Rich's smile. "It's so nice to meet you." I glance back at Camilla, and her lips are pinched like she's bitten into a lemon. "Do you go here too?"

Rich shakes his head. "Nope. I'm over at Cal State. I'm just checking in on our Delmont girl here before my shift at Bartleby's." The sheer admiration in his voice is rom-com-lead-worthy.

"Oh." I barely manage to hide my surprise, but I'm sure that one syllable was a note too high. I went fishing and ended up with enough to feed an army. Camilla not only has a secret boyfriend, but he doesn't go to parent-approved Delmont? Instead, he works at the Bartleby's, which we drove by on the way in. It's a knockoff of chains like TGI Fridays and Applebee's, and now that I take a good look at him, he's even wearing the signature blue-and-white-striped Bartleby's polo shirt.

"I love Bartleby's!" Tessa cuts in. "Their buffalo ranch dip is the best."

She and Rich go back and forth about the merits of this dip while Camilla, lips still pressed together, locks eyes with me. I mouth silently to Camilla, "Boyfriend?" Then I see the silent plea in her gaze: Don't say anything to my parents, all right?

It shouldn't surprise me that Camilla has a boyfriend. It's not like we hung out enough back home for me to stay current on her dating life. But this, combined with the way she snuck out for that boat day with her friends, gives me a glimpse of a side of her that I had no clue existed. It's unnerving, to experience firsthand how the tip of an iceberg is only a hint of what lies beneath. It makes me wonder what else I'd failed to see in others and even myself over the years.

Camilla and I may be competitors, but we're not enemies. I give her a slight nod to let her know she's safe.

Camilla's shoulders slump with relief, then she coughs to interrupt her boyfriend. "Come on, Rich. Let's let these two eat. See you around, Perlie."

The thankful smile she gives me is so genuine that I forget the sight of her here almost made me choke on a mozzarella stick.

"Who's that, *Perlie*?" Tessa asks once Camilla's gone. She teases out the "Perlie" into an almost giggle.

I snatch a curly fry off her tray. "Just someone from my high school, *Tessita*." Two can play at this game, and Tessa's wide-eyed glare tells me she's surrendering. Tessita and Perlie don't exist here. They're back in high school, stressing about standardized tests and minutes in between bells and whether they should rat out the folks paying others to write their personal statements. Delmont's only got room for Tessa and Perla.

Though technically, Delmont didn't have room for Perla either, but I'm going to choose to ignore that and not let anything further ruin my pizza.

On PicLine: my suitcase, unzipped, with a neat stack of clothes artfully laid out next to it.

Caption: All moved in and unpacking! I have a walk-in closet! (as my entire room) #collegelife #Delmont

Fourteen likes.

Comment from WestPinesCredit: Need student loans? DM us for more info!

SEVEN

I fade to the back of Samantha Simon's assigned orientation group, eyeing the orientation leader in the middle of our circle. Hundreds of other students mill around on the football practice field. Hand-labeled sandwich boards dot the grass, sorting us into groups named after local flora and fauna. Samantha Simon is in Sycamore, and therefore so am I. Across the field, someone directs the Manzanita and Poppy groups via loudspeaker to their first sessions. I think I spy Camilla in the Poppy group, but thankfully, she's too busy chatting to peer my way.

I try to keep my posture relaxed, but my muscles keep revving up to flee. Last night's dining hall surprises still rankle me. I considered skipping orientation, but it's to my benefit to take a crash course in Delmont University life. A formal introduction might help fill in some of the wide gaps in my research. There's no way I can cross this tightrope of a semester if I keep nearly plunging headfirst into these canyons like I did yesterday.

A pair of students joins Sycamore group, shuffling in front

of me and partially obscuring my line of sight of the orientation leader. I let them.

The orientation leader is in a forest-green volunteer T-shirt, with a matching green Delmont ball cap taming an uncombed mop of dark brown curls. He smells of stale beer and smoke, like our garage after one of Dad's poker games.

Last night, after tearing down a few more door dragons on my way back to my room, I researched to make sure there wasn't a strict ID check to join these tours. I'd prepared and practiced a whole cover story about losing my wallet. But this orientation leader didn't even second-guess me when I checked in as Samantha Simon and oh-so-casually mentioned I actually go by my childhood nickname, Perla. He waved off my explanation and simply marked boxes on his clipboard, then beckoned the next folks over. Once they checked in, he fished out two loose pills from his pocket, popped them into his mouth, then downed an entire blue Gatorade in one go.

I take a step closer into the Sycamore herd, relieved that the orientation leader clearly isn't running at 100 percent this morning. I missed a few hours of sleep over nothing. Better to be overprepared, Mom would say. I'd taken so many practice SATs junior year that I could recite the multiple-choice questions like they were lyrics to a song.

The orientation leader gives one loud clap to get everyone else's attention.

"All right, twenty of us. Looks like we're all here, Sycamore." He waves a hand circled with faded rope bracelets. "I'm Charles

Worthingham. Welcome to Delmont University, home of the Dragons!"

He pauses to let people clap or whoop in excitement or whatever, and no one does. "We're standing on what was a field of orange groves a hundred and fifty years ago, until Eugene Delmont . . ."

I take out my phone to jot down a couple notes. Knowing the history of Delmont helps. Maybe I can work something about the bold spirit of Eugene Delmont into my personal statement. I have two months until the spring class admissions deadline, and I hope that's enough time to research the specifics of why Delmont accepted everyone here.

Other Sycamore members have their phones out too. One girl at the far end of the circle holds out her phone an arm away, batting her eyes and whispering commentary for whoever is watching her livestream. Maybe I needed to have more of a social media following and mention it in my statement? I bat that idea down. I'm only on PicLine, and I'm carefully managing that to align with my cover story, in case anyone back home—like Auntie Silvie, who is trying to stay connected with "the young folks" but may also snitch on me to my parents—is watching.

Charles claps his hands once again, like it's an audible hard return before his next spoken paragraph. "Before we move on to Wu-Paulson Auditorium, let's go around and introduce ourselves, yeah? Name, where you're from, and last TV show you marathoned. Anyone want to start?"

I pretend to look anywhere else but at him, and it works. An

East Asian girl with a black shoulder-length bob speaks. She says she's not from anywhere, having moved around often thanks to her father's shifting corporate role, and she proudly declares she juggled three true-crime documentary series in the last month. I make a mental note to stay away from her. She probably knows the A to Zs of disposing of a body.

The number of people between Ms. Murder and me dwindles until it's my turn.

I cough to clear my throat, uncomfortable at the number of eyes on me, as if they could see instantly that I don't belong.

"Hi, I'm Perla"—I purposely leave out my last name—"from up north, near the Bay." I send a shy wave at the three other Northern Californians who have introduced themselves. "And the last show I watched was . . ."

I can't say *She-Ra*, can I? Dad thought I'd earned a summer "break" and let me watch while Mom was at work, but I really don't want to explain the messed-up dynamics of that to anyone here. A white guy in a fully buttoned-up long-sleeve shirt had already ended his introduction with a snooty-sounding "I don't watch television," complete with looking down his nose at us and saying the full word "television," and he'd earned some eye rolls from the group. It strikes me that icebreakers are a way for setting the stage of exactly how you want people to see you. Everyone curates their answers to show off what they think are their best selves. I can reinvent myself with each new introduction.

I reach for something that's relatable but slightly more adult than a cartoon. ". . . *90-Day Fiancé*. It's a good break for my brain."

A couple folks laugh in understanding, and the group moves its attention to the next person. A stocky white guy with glasses tries to whisper something to me about immigration reform, but I politely pretend I'm focused on the intros instead. I don't need any follow-up questions about a show that I only caught when sneaking past Mom to the kitchen for a late-night study snack.

Aside from glasses guy and the cluster of people who seem to know each other, the rest of the group seems as content as I am to say the required info, then shut our mouths and stick to ourselves. No extra digging, no sizing me up as academic competition, no pressure to tell anyone where I see myself in five, ten, fifteen years.

Then I creep back to the fringe, far enough that Charles doesn't have an eye on me but close enough that I hear every rehearsed bit of history he spouts out. I type away on my phone to save as much of it as I can for later.

The sun rises higher as we traverse the campus, all stately brick and towering trees, which I'm not sure are the best architectural choices in earthquake territory. This whole area is supposed to be desert, but it's been carefully manicured to conjure the look of an elite East Coast campus. Even Delmont is faking it till it makes it.

My stomach rumbles as we pass a café radiating the scents of bacon and brewing coffee. My body begs for something other than the sugary granola bars I'd tucked into my suitcase as study snacks. But I can't freeload swipes off my new dorm friend for every single meal.

I peer in as we shuffle by, and my heart somersaults when I spy a real cash register and not just an ID scanner. Charles drones on about some 1950s benefactor of the school when I back away from the group and duck into the café. I grab an oversized blueberry muffin and bottle of water and hand over a crisp ten-dollar bill fresh from a graduation gift envelope. I frown at the meager amount of change the cashier slides across the counter to me.

With my cover story about tuition, room, and board being covered—I couldn't exactly have my parents writing checks to the university without life-ruining questions on both sides—I only have years' worth of birthday and holiday money to keep me afloat for the next few months. Based on today's purchase, my savings might ebb away faster than I'd calculated. I'll need to add a tab to my spreadsheet for this when I get to my room.

Charles is still monologuing when I rejoin the group. I peel back the plastic cling wrap on my muffin. Some of the brown-sugar crumble topping sloughs off onto the ground, and I almost whimper aloud. That's probably twenty-five cents' worth of muffin right there.

"And here's the Wu-Paulson Auditorium, flanked on either side by our arts buildings." Charles sweeps his arm toward a massive brick auditorium, complete with imposing columns and leafy vines blanketing one side. "If you're thinking of any of the arts and humanities majors, Delmont's are some of the best. This past year's National Book Awards counted two Delmont alums. And if you're undecided, the university is piloting an interactive entertainment major so students can stay competitive in the growing gaming market. The major combines all the nerdiest parts of computer science and, surprise, literary analysis."

A few people laugh, but I ignore his condescension. Some of my favorite games' story arcs rival the classics imposed on us at Monte Verde. Something prickles at the back of my neck as I gaze up at the brick building, with its swirling carved embellishments and grand sweeping archways. I could see myself leaned up against one of those columns, a book tucked under my arm, a phone in hand as I text some dreamy, dark-eyed philosophy major to meet me after class for a likely overpriced mini cup of espresso.

"Gorgeous, isn't it?"

I peer over at the petite olive-skinned woman next to me, and even though she's in a severe-cut black blazer and pumps that scream icy board room, she offers me a warm smile with her glossy mauve lips. She dresses and acts older than the students around me, but not by much.

"Yeah, it is."

She tilts her head slightly. Her long black waves sway with the movement. "You know, you practically lit up when he mentioned the interactive entertainment major."

I spy the Delmont pin on her lapel. She must be university staff. I remind myself to guard my naked reactions more closely, but my curiosity gets the better of me now. "Are the classes here, in these arts buildings?"

"Some are in the Alder Engineering Hall, and I believe a few are usually held there." The woman points past one of the massive green trees. "The Muses."

It isn't even called a hall or an auditorium or a wing. It's the Muses. I could topple over in love.

"I can tell you more about the program, if you'd like."

"I'm signed up as bio sci, but interactive entertainment does sound fascinating." I don't blink as I both lie and lay my dreams bare. To be honest, I didn't even know that gaming dream still lived strongly enough in me to form those words. Middle-grade Perlie would've peppered this woman with a dozen questions, trying to figure out if the process of creating games is anywhere near as fun as playing them. What kinds of roles are out there for someone who loves spreadsheets and structure? What subjects do I need to load up on to succeed? What do they pay?

But it's been such a long time since all that was squished under the giant red binder like an unwelcome bug. We want me to be a doctor. That's why I'm here.

The woman nods, as if she's heard this sentiment before. She pulls an embossed business card out of the pocket of her blazer. "Here, if you ever want to talk about your academic future, what classes to take and all that, come by."

I glance down at her card. Nicole Ali, Academic Adviser.

She strides away on her too-high black pumps, and I like her. In another world, I could just waltz into her office, plop into an overstuffed armchair, and talk about how I can take a few fun classes or even minor in Interactive Entertainment without derailing my path to medical school. But I can never speak to her again.

When I get into Delmont for real, I'll have such a packed schedule trying to make up for a whole missed year that I can't even dream of taking a class not directly related to my major. And as I follow the group to the electrical engineering department, I realize there's a small hollowness in my chest where my excited, unquestioning pursuit of medical school used to be.

EIGHT

Between the towering residence halls and the stuffy academic part of the campus sits the Boulevard, the main artery of Delmont. Trees and old-timey LED lantern holders line the expansive brick walkway, and so do tables propped up by campus clubs and vendors. Orientation isn't over yet—I skipped out before the academic advising sessions—and the Boulevard already teems with people.

"Delmont Democrats?" a redheaded girl asks, thrusting a yellow pamphlet in front of me. I take it, and she rewards me with a grateful smile before lunging at the next passerby.

"Spirit Squad? Tryouts start next week!" shouts another. I can barely touch my toes. What in the world makes her think I possess the ability to leap up and trumpet school spirit? I stride by her.

I grab a few more pamphlets and flyers from the Coalition for Animal Justice, the Filipino American Student Alliance, Model United Nations, and ten other groups I was too polite to say no to, especially after my hands were already crammed full of multicolored paper.

I speed up on my trudge back up to the residence halls, if only to avoid having to disappoint these eager flyer peddlers.

"Need credit? Sign up for a card today and get a free T-shirt!"

I pause. Credit. That'd be the answer to my cash flow problem. My mouth waters at the memory of this morning's blueberry muffin.

If I call home for cash too often, my parents will wise up to my nonexistent scholarship situation. This way, I'll be able to lie low until my Delmont application gets accepted.

I swivel to face the credit card table.

The lanky, ponytailed white guy who had yelled looks like he's barely out of college himself. He stands out in his sunshine-yellow First Cal-Am Credit polo shirt, and he smiles wide, revealing a gap in his teeth, when he sees me eyeing the table.

"You look like you could use a new credit card, and hey, we all could use some free T-shirts, am I right?" He points, his hands posed in finger guns, at the stack of white shirts. "And all our student cards have cash back!"

I pick up a glossy brochure and pretend to read. "I'm not eighteen until January though," I say, with a forced wistfulness, leaving out the fact that I technically mean January almost two years from now.

I hadn't fallen for this guy's stoner smile for a second. He's a financial predator. The dollar signs gleam in his eyes, and in fact, I'm counting on the greediness.

Guilt doesn't even brush my conscience as I plot. When I'm

gaming, there's no room for feeling bad for the troll I steal magical armor from because, without it, I'll be decimated by the sorcerer on the next level. This is practically the same thing.

"That's not a problem." He pulls a pink form from behind the desk and hands it to me. "We'll need a parent or guardian to sign this form, but you can still walk away with a T-shirt today. If you're approved, your card will come in the mail in a week. Rad, right?"

Good thing I've had years of practice with Mom's and Dad's signatures on permission slips, parent/guardian authorizations, and all manner of liability waivers.

I take the forms. "Rad."

By the time I get back to my dorm room, slinking in behind a group of laughing guys who don't even notice me trailing them, I've got a dozen flyers, a campus map, a course catalog, Ms. Ali's business card, a large-sized First Cal-Am Credit T-shirt—the only size they had left, but I wasn't leaving without my free T-shirt— and a route to a monetary lifeline.

I plop onto my stomach on my plain ivory twin-XL sheets and spread my fingers wide over the cool fabric. It'd been a battle to avoid the ultra-pink floral print sheets Mom had wanted. "These are like the ones you have at home, Perlie!" she'd argued. Which is exactly why I hated them.

We settled on these new sheets, which are more Delmont Perla's style. Sophisticated. Smart. New.

I grab the thick course catalog and peel open one of the free granola bars I'd snagged on the Boulevard this afternoon. I'd feigned a massive headache so that Tessa wouldn't drag me to dinner that she'd end up swiping me in for. I need to come up with some better excuses for skipping out on dinner, unless my new friend is fine subsidizing my life for the next few months.

A burst of unpleasant, chewy sweetness hits my taste buds: this granola bar has raisins. I contemplate throwing it out, but my food options are limited, so I pinch my nose shut and force myself to take another bite.

I tug my laptop over and open my spreadsheet so I can fill out part five: sit in some premed classes. That's where this giant course catalog comes in. Creating a believable schedule around these classes and memorizing details about the times, professors, and locations is key to pretending I'm a real Delmont student. I can't just fake that I'm taking one class: I'm going to have to be able to talk about a whole fake course load to fit in. Plus, I can use this to ramp up the specific-to-Delmont love in my personal statement, as Raj the application coach had noted on an early draft. I'll mark ones with big, spacious lecture halls I can disappear in, if anyone comes looking.

The most recently opened tab was for part two, finding a place to live. It reminds me that, with only a week until Samantha Simon moves in, I've got to find alternate locations to sleep and store my belongings. Most residents have moved in, and while all the first-years were out at their academic advising sessions, I scouted a few empty-looking rooms, a storage room with a faulty lock, and even a comfy student lounge couch or two on some of the quieter floors. As glorious as these sheets are, I wish I hadn't brought the whole bed-in-a-bag set. It's just more stuff to pack up and move to avoid detection.

My staying here at Delmont hinges on simultaneously looking like I belong in this building and not having my squatter situation appear too obvious. The only things I'd unpacked in the last day were my laptop, towel, and bedding. Everything else is stashed in the closet or still rolled up in my suitcase, which lies against the bottom of the door to block light from escaping.

My phone rings, and I slide my hand across the bed to it and answer.

"Hi, Mom."

"Hi, Perlie! How's everything?"

Not any different than the two other times she's called in the last twenty-four hours. I want to be annoyed, but I find it a little sweet that they miss me.

"It's great. Everyone's friendly, and the food's decent." If only I could be eating some of that decent dining hall food instead.

"You eating your fruits and vegetables?"

I frown at my raisin-infested granola bar. "Yup."

"Good, good. Have you been making friends?"

"Yeah, a few people on my floor." I tell her about Tessa and one or two fake, nameless "girls down the hall." I leave any mention of guys out altogether. Not that she doesn't know that this is a co-ed dorm, but the last thing I need is to remind my mom that, yes, guys exist in close, unsupervised proximity at Delmont. I currently don't have the energy for a birds-and-bees talk.

"Tessa sounds nice," Mom says. "By the way, your dad felt bad we had to rush back to Monte Verde for his trial, but we can come visit next weekend if you need anything."

"Mom, no!" I wish I could kick myself for how painfully panicky my outburst had sounded. I shift my weight on my elbows and tone down the emotion in my voice. "You don't have to come down here so soon. Really. It even mentions it in the welcome materials, like how it's important for adjustment to campus life. But . . ." I throw a tremble of uncertainty into my words.

"But what, Perlie? Do you need more cash for textbooks? School supplies?"

Bingo. "It couldn't hurt. I could save some money by checking the textbooks out at the library, but if someone else gets to them first . . ."

"I'll mail you some money. Text me your address, okay?"

"I will," I say, already clicking to the fourth tab of my spreadsheet: part four, figure out excuses for parents to minimize mail and avoid visits.

In the meantime, I give her Tessa's room number. I'm banking on the likelihood that, with the franticness of moving in and beating the parking meter, my parents neglected to take note of my exact room number, and thankfully, Mom doesn't argue when I give her something other than Samantha Simon's 217. I'll explain the "mix-up" to Tessa later, but by then, I'll have Mom's envelope in hand.

A few sensationalist news stories made Mom wary of the world of transferring money via app. Plus, with my parents still paying for my phone, they'll get notifications of any apps I try to download on it. I have no interest in talking them through the terms and conditions and what I'm planning on using the money for and why. Cash is easier. Mom can't attach strings to it from all the way up in Monte Verde.

"Oh no, I just saw the time. I'm not keeping you from dinner, am I?" Mom asks.

"Already done." I toss the granola wrapper at the brown plastic trash can and miss. "I'm checking out the course catalog. Most of our first semester's set up with required classes, but I get to choose an elective." I turn the page quickly, to make sure she hears the paper flipping.

"Choose something in biology. Get ahead, go for credits toward your major now."

The lingering sweetness of the granola bar on my tongue sours. I don't even know why this grates me. I'm not actually taking classes. The idea of her not trusting my decisions makes something ugly flare up in me, but why waste my anger and energy on something that literally doesn't matter? I go for brownie points instead. "I can probably knock out the general education math requirement," I muse.

As expected, Mom mm-hmms approvingly.

Half an hour later, after reading through a couple course descriptions aloud and weighing pros and cons—Mom's idea of a good time—we wind up our conversation.

"I'm glad you're taking college so seriously," Mom says, and my chest tightens. Did she not think I was taking school seriously these last few years? That's a little insulting. "If you keep this up, you'll have your pick of med schools. I'd better work through that huge pile of papers on my desk so I can make room for you in my office right away."

She means it to be complimentary, maybe even a show of pride that I'd normally glow over, but her words don't meet their mark this time.

"I . . . Thanks, Mom. Good night."

I stare at the dark screen of my phone a while after she hangs up, uselessly upset. A sole focus on studies, prestigious medical schools, becoming a doctor in record time: distance does nothing to blunt the crush of these expectations of excellence.

Then I chuck the course catalog against the door. It nicks off a chip of gray paint and crumples to the ground. I curse at myself for making such a loud noise in a room that's supposed to be vacant. I shouldn't even have taken Mom's call from in here. I'm lucky that there are enough loud relatives still knocking around this building, rearranging their students' furniture, but when move-in quiets down, this kind of carelessness is going to get me discovered faster than I can click between spreadsheet tabs.

I bury my face in my pillow, blaming the unwanted raisins for the acid clawing at my throat.

NINE

The overly chipper alarm on my phone drags me out of bed after my fitful night of sleep. It's a little after seven o'clock in the morning, and the world outside my door is quiet.

I spent the weekend exploring the campus and hiding in Samantha Simon's room. The swarm of students and families finishing their move-ins and goodbyes helped disguise my coming and going. To my pleasant surprise, more than half the doors on my floor are without door dragons: some by my doing, the rest from folks who either messed them up during the move or didn't love the personalized decor.

The bustle settling down brings its own challenges. People are becoming familiar with their neighbors. They're learning faces and names and backgrounds. I have to be careful no one becomes too familiar with me.

On Saturday, I skipped the RA's all-floor ice cream social by making some excuse to Tessa about helping trusty-high-school-friend Camilla with something urgent. I've managed to dodge the

RA entirely so far. It helps that she doesn't think to knock on the door of a room she presumes to be uninhabited, and, according to Tessa, the RA has had late-night phone arguments with her out-of-state boyfriend the last two evenings. As warped as it is, anything distracting university authority figures is a blessing.

When I'd set my morning alarm—next to my face, on the lowest-possible setting—last night, I'd hoped it was early enough that not too many of my floormates would be awake. Then I'd be able to slip in and out of the showers unnoticed. It's the first day of the semester, and I have a class to go to.

I grab my plastic bathroom caddy and my new plush yellow towel. The yellow is much too cheery for my mood this morning, but I'm an expert at living with things that don't suit me. The hallway's clear. When I bump the girls' bathroom door open with my butt, the door smacks into someone.

"Hey, watch it!" someone snaps.

I peer into the mirror at the same time Tessa does.

Her makeup-less face brightens. "Perla! You totally missed out at dinner last night. I tagged along with Erin and Casper, down the hall. Have you met them? I think Erin's from NorCal like you. Anyway, the fried chicken was to die for." She glances at my bathroom caddy and starts to free up some counter space by centralizing her mass of bottles and brushes.

I set the caddy down on the water-spotted metal shelf above the sink, completely uninterested in delving into the personal lives of people on this floor, especially those who may have grown up even remotely close to Monte Verde. God forbid they dig into mine.

"You heading to class?" I ask instead.

"Yeah, Cellular and Molecular Biology, with Desai. Believe me, if I didn't have a class this morning, I wouldn't be up this early. I think there's two hundred people in this class, so I can probably hide behind someone and fall asleep."

I stifle a laugh. Seven thirty a.m. is not early by Monte Verde High standards. Perlie back home would be up at six to get to school for that extra class period. But Delmont Perla? I'm supposed to grumble about any wakeup before nine. And I'll probably show up to those morning classes in leggings and a shapeless hoodie Mom would be mortified by.

"Ugh, I know." I mimic her whine, and she smiles. "These morning classes are going to be the worst."

"What do you have?"

"Same as you, biology with Desai," I venture. Another piece of my seven-part plan clicks into place.

It's from my careful catalog work the other day under part five. Thanks to the granola-bar-fueled reading session, my spreadsheet tab has a list of a few classes in the biological-sciences track that I want to peek into or ask folks about, as research for my reapplication.

By design, this also coincides with part three: make a friend. I've already learned, from my short time here, that it's important I take at least one noticeable-to-the-people class to make my presence here believable. Most of the conversations I've eavesdropped on have a healthy dose of first-day nerves and what's-your-schedule? questions. Sitting in on one, gigantic class populated with first-years from my dorm could be a good way to blend in and inject some tailored detail into my Delmont personal statement, killing two birds with one stone.

I shove my toothbrush into my mouth to ward off any follow-up questions. To the relief of my pounding heart, Tessa seems to buy my answer.

"You can make sure I'm awake in time for it, then. I am not a morning person." She slings her towel over her shoulder. "Want to grab breakfast to go before we head to class?"

"I . . ."

Tessa frowns at my hesitation. "Come on, you've got to get a good start for your first day of school!" She bumps her shoulder against mine.

She has an air about her that comes off relentlessly friendly, and it's easy to get wrapped up in her enthusiasm. "I'd love to, but I can't. There's some issue with my student ID, and my meal plan isn't activated yet." The lie spins forth from my mind as I speak, but I'm too focused on my cover story and getting fed to feel guilty.

Genuine concern scrunches her brow. "That sucks. I can swipe you in again."

"I can't ask you to—"

"Come on. Twenty-one meals a week, and I won't even be getting up early enough for breakfast on weekends. I'm going to have a ton of meals left over at the end of the semester. I'd rather you have a couple than for me to waste it on midnight cheese fries. Until your meal plan kicks in, okay?"

I could almost hug her then, this purple-haired girl who I'd just met and has already proven nicer than most people back at Monte Verde High. I wonder if it's wise to get myself indebted to her like this though. My seven-part plan calls for me to make a friend but not one close enough to question who I am and what I'm doing here.

I want to say yes. From all those business dinners with my parents' colleagues, I know not to accept her offer too quickly. Being perfect requires me to be gracious even if I'm starving. "Paying for my meals? That's so much. I couldn't ask you to."

"Well, think of it this way: I'm probably going to bother you for bio notes every now and then because of unplanned or planned oversleeping. This can be how we settle the score." She squints into the mirror and presses her fingers against the bags under her eyes. "I'm worried this early-morning-class thing isn't going to work out."

A fair exchange of meals for notes; that'll work. I eat, and two parts of my plan stay in motion.

"Fine, fine. If you're going to beg, then yes, I'll have breakfast with you." I exaggerate my eye roll, and she laughs easily, like she didn't just do me the huge favor of keeping me fed and alive.

Students stream into the classroom doors ahead of us, like ants in a line. I shift my nearly empty backpack around on my shoulders, and my laptop thunks against my back.

"We're not late, are we?" I glance down at my phone: 8:23 a.m.

"No, we're right on time. Everyone's just early. Overachievers."

Tessa casts a smirk over her shoulder at me, as if she could never imagine us being one of those early arrivers. Perfect Perlie Perez of Monte Verde would be. She'd be right up front, nose to the door.

We jostle past the doors into the cavernous auditorium. Dozens of rows of green plastic-backed seats sweep down to where the professor stands at the front of the class. Most of the seats are already taken. People mill at the top of the auditorium, looking for a friendly neighbor to wave them over or, at the very minimum, make room for them to slide in.

I point a few rows away, at two seats tucked up against the wall. Tessa catches my meaning and shimmies past a few backpacks to free us from the doorway clog.

Tessa goes in first with her "excuse mes" and "I'm just trying to get over theres." We're almost to our seats when my foot catches on a backpack jutting out from under a chair. My hand goes out to Tessa's shoulder to keep me from toppling over into the row below. Someone grabs my other arm. Firm, steady.

"Careful." The voice swims around me.

I follow the strong, light brown fingers on my arm to their owner. Short black hair, a little long and wavy on top, mussed in the right places. Warm brown eyes that hint to East Asian heritage, a deep tan that speaks of hours kissed by the sun, and an effortless smile. My legs almost fail me again.

Tessa takes her seat and gives me a wide-eyed sit-your-butt-down-girl look, so I wobble the few inches left to my seat and plop down, like a salmon smacking against a riverbank.

"Hey, I'm Brand," my hero says.

I have to remember to look friendly, which means banishing the usual pained half smile I plaster on when I'm feeling awkward. I'm 100 percent sure I have that half smile on my face right now. "I'm Perla."

There's a second of silence, and Tessa coughs, so obviously they can probably get her signal in space, as she digs her laptop out of her backpack.

All this does is make me more self-conscious about how I'm acting. I try to find something, anything, to keep conversation with this guy going. Completely unbidden, my eyes brush down to his fingers. "You're taking notes by hand?"

He twirls the pen in a deft move. "I prefer to. I know it's a little old-school, but it works better for me. I've heard some professors even require it. You think it's weird?" He gestures at the many laptops starting up around us.

"No, I think it's . . ." Hot. "Smart." My eyes move to the margins of his notebook where a mess of triangles and a sketch of a boomerang-wielding Link fill up the space. "Are those Triforces?"

He nods. "Yup. You a Zelda fan?"

Did I beat *Breath of the Wild* for the dozenth time on an emulator last week to calm my coming-to-Delmont nerves? Did I also have a completely unrealistic, embarrassing crush on this pointy-eared, green-clad video game character a few years ago? In my defense, real-life crushes were even less acceptable to my parents. "Yeah, I play now and then," I offer casually. "That character sketch is pretty good."

"Really? Thanks!" His enthusiasm is as earnest and endearing as a kid who pulls off a spectator-drenching cannonball at a pool party. "I have to take a few beginner art classes for my interactive entertainment major."

As if the universe is dangling that interactive entertainment major in front of me.

"That sounds like fun. I'm bio sci, and my class schedule's going to be too packed to take on any fun-sounding interactive entertainment classes." Especially because I'll be starting in spring, a whole semester after everyone.

"There's a club on campus. It's supposed to be for careers and networking, but apparently they just order a lot of pizza and game. I saw flyers outside about the first general meeting."

A gaming club? I'm about to ask more when the TAs start passing stacks of paper down the rows at the front of the classroom. I tug my shiny new MacBook out of the padded sleeve in my backpack to at least make a show of being an interested student.

Brand taps my laptop lightly with his pen. "I can't lug something that expensive out surfing with me. My parents would kill me if I lost it."

Of course he surfs. I can see it in his arms and the taper of his chest. I gulp and force my eyes back to my MacBook.

I focus on opening up a blank document on my computer and not on how closely crammed together we are in these seats. "I type faster than I write by hand."

I nearly wince at my own words. What am I doing, applying for a part-time job?

Brand doesn't seem to notice the internal screaming I'm doing or, if he does, he's politely looking past it. "My handwriting's pretty atrocious, so I might bother you to help me fill in the illegible parts with those fancy typed notes." He winks, and I'm not even angry that I've somehow become the designated note taker for both him and Tessa in the span of one morning.

A boldness infuses my veins. "And I might bother you to bring me to one of those pizza-filled gaming club meetings. Or teach me how to surf." Which I've never had any inkling to learn, up until now.

His smile widens, and he's somehow more gorgeous than he was a minute ago. I remind myself to blink so it's not so obvious I'm staring. Gorgeous guys never talk to me.

Actually, that's not true. Sometimes they say "watch out" or "move."

"I can do that. Spent a summer teaching tourists back home. With a name like Perla, the water would be just your style. We should skip outta here right now."

An impulsive part of me wants to scream yes, when a voice booms a "Good morning, class" over the speakers overhead, drawing me back into reality. Hold it together, Perla. I'm in my first college class, and I can't go falling head over heels over the first guy I almost literally fall head over heels in front of. There isn't a tab for crushes in my spreadsheet.

"Good morning, class," the professor says again, and this time, conversation withers away. The professor is a bald South Asian man with a microphone clipped to the collar of his buttoned-up shirt, and he stands at the front of the auditorium with a confidence that demands our quiet.

"Welcome to Cellular and Molecular Biology. My TAs are passing out the syllabus now. As you can see, we'll be moving at a fairly rapid pace, but you should've expected that at Delmont. You're at a top-tier school because you are top tier. And if you don't think you are, the door in the back is open if you want an easier diploma. The state school just down the 5 freeway needs the cash, so they'll take almost anyone."

A few chuckles float around me, but my mood drops. I'm at a top-tier school, but I'm not, in fact, top tier. Tessa is, and Brand is, but me?

I inhabit a seat that doesn't belong to me, and a couple enrolled students mill around by the doors, scanning for a place to squeeze in. State schools weren't even a consideration in the creation of that school list at the front of Perlie's Academic Plan.

"That's kind of a messed-up thing to say, right?" Tessa whispers to me.

I angle to look at her. "Wait, what is?" I'm still too shaken by the professor's talk of being top tier.

"That jab about the state school. My sister graduated from there." Her eyes narrow, like she's already decided she doesn't like this class.

"Delmont is a top school." The state school isn't. Professor Desai's not wrong. I struggle to understand what got Tessa so riled up. Fellow Monte Verdans would agree with me that Delmont is shiny and elite in a way that state schools aren't, but judging by Tessa's glare at the professor, perhaps not everyone sees it that way.

Monte Verde Perla wants to pull out statistics and rankings to dig into why Tessa's defending the state school, but I don't even know how to ask those questions.

"Never mind," she whispers before shaking her head.

The professor goes over the rigorous semester schedule, complete with exams and papers and required reading, but his voice rises into an unintelligible roar in my ears.

My fingers pick through the papers the TAs hand me. I force the panic down with easy breaths and a visualization of my spreadsheet. I need to stay in this seat: so many parts of my plan depend on it. Not only does my presence in this auditorium align with my story that, yes, I am indeed a Delmont first-year, but it's also the best way I can get enough of a feel of this university's premed track to tailor my application perfectly and reapply. It doesn't hurt that I'm wedged between someone I'm starting to consider a friend, even if I don't understand her completely yet, and someone who looks like the chiseled love interest in a high-end perfume ad.

A pen taps my forearm. Brand leans in to whisper, and I catch the slight scent of salt. "This class sounds like it's going to be a lot of work. We should've gotten outta here when we had the chance."

I smile at his joke, a little flattered that I'd be considered for partner-in-crime status. But I've already put in too much work to even get my butt into this seat.

I'm staying.

TEN

I stay out on the academic side of campus for the rest of the day, wandering in and out of these esteemed halls, reading the free *Daily Dragon* newspaper over my $4.25 drip coffee. After picking up the hundred-dollar used biology textbook with Tessa, I linger on the grass near the library until it's late enough that she'd be off to dinner with other folks on our floor, without me. A cheap bag of preservative-laden chips from the vending machine will tide me over until morning, when the "how do you like your classes?" questions will have hopefully subsided.

Lying on the manicured grass with my backpack scrunched up under my head as a pillow, I watch the student body drift by. Hundreds of students march up and down the Boulevard with purpose, confident in their right to be here. Back at Monte Verde, I was one of the best of the best: so much so that I, almost a whole two years younger than others in my class, earned that annoying "Perfect" modifier to my name and all the loneliness, side glances, and tapered-off conversations that go with it. Here, I'm simply one of a couple thousand first-year Delmont students trying to figure this place out.

No, I remind myself. I'm not even a Delmont student yet.

The potato chips go stale in my mouth.

It's past seven o'clock, and the sun lowers toward the horizon, stretching the shadows of the Delmont statues. The last of the tablers on the Boulevard pack up their banners and pamphlets. I haul myself to my feet and trek slowly up the hill to Keith Hall, taking the longer back way through the woodsier area to avoid any run-ins. It's been a few days since I've seen Camilla, and I'd like to avoid that reminder and threat of my Monte Verde life as much as possible. As I'm about to emerge from the trees, I catch Tessa's voice. I freeze.

"My phone's charging upstairs. I'll just go grab it and knock on Perla's door to see if she wants to join us. I thought I saw her walking up here earlier. You guys will like her, promise."

I step back into the woods and slink behind a massive tree trunk. I missed dinner, but apparently there's some other function people want my company for. This is a first.

I consider staying in hiding and letting Tessa knock on an unanswered door. But she saw me come up the hill to the residence halls. She knows I'm here somewhere, and if I'm not in my room, she might start asking questions, and questions are not the friend of a fraud. She's going to assume I'm avoiding her. Which is correct, but for reasons she'd never suspect and I'd never explain.

I can't afford to lose the few friends I've started making. The different parts of my plan require me to tease out not only

Delmont premed track nuances, but also people's experiences at this university for my reapplication. Equally as important, friends would let me sneak behind them into the residence halls. Hanging out with other students makes me look like I belong here, and I can't jeopardize that.

I peek around the tree and frown. I can't very well stroll in through the main entrance with Tessa's new friends standing watch. I need to get up to my room so I can answer the door when she shows up.

Staying in the cover of the trees, I slink over to the side of the building where my room is. I scan the thick limbs of the tree next to the building, its branches reaching up and beyond my room. The second floor isn't too high off the ground. I can probably make it up there. I tighten the backpack straps over my shoulders, fill my lungs, and leap for the first branch.

I haven't climbed a tree in years, and my muscles scream at me for it. I struggle to launch myself up onto one branch and stretch out to reach another. My breathing quickens. Once I'm on a branch almost parallel with my window, I scoot across to get closer to my room.

In the distance, the elevator chimes. That must be Tessa.

I'm across from my window now, and I reach out with my fingertips to push in the grimy screen. Thank God I'd left the glass pane the tiniest open to let in that musty-smell-dispelling breeze this morning.

A few heavy knocks on my door. "Hey, Perla, it's Tessa."

She's already outside.

I need to get through this screen.

I grab for the pen in my pocket. I jab it straight into the screen and slash it open. I wince, hoping Tessa doesn't hear the rip.

A few more knocks. "Perla? You in there?"

"One sec!"

The hole looks big enough for me to fit through, and if it's not, it'll just have to make room. I balance on the balls of my feet and place my hands on the windowsill. I hoist myself up and in and, louder than I'd like, drop onto the floor.

Another knock. "You okay?"

I slide off my backpack and dash to the door.

When I swing it open, Tessa's already got her phone out, like she's going to call campus security for a wellness check.

"Hey, Tessa, sorry. Was moving some furniture around."

It's easier to lie when the alternative is getting caught climbing into a room that isn't actually mine, and all the chaos that comes with it.

She lowers her phone. "A few of us are going to head down to the practice field for the free outdoor movie if you want to join. I texted you about dinner, but—"

"I was out trying to buy some more textbooks, and my reception is just so bad on campus. Then I got wrapped up in redecorating." My words huff out after that unexpected physical activity. Thankfully my furniture-moving cover plays into my story.

She nods, and the fading sunlight glints off her gold hoop earrings. "Gotcha. So, you in?"

"Sure. Give me a minute. I'll meet you downstairs in a few."

The elevator chimes and whisks Tessa away.

Once I'm sure she's gone, I let the casual mask drop off my face. That was too close. I slide the curtains over the mangled window screen, grab my keycard, my phone, and a sensible sweater—some Perfect Perlie Perez habits die hard—and dart down the hall, pausing only to fish a chip of bark out of my shoe.

Between the patches of blankets and towels, the grass on the field lays trampled from the marching band's afternoon practice. Snippets of conversation and the buttery scent of popcorn hover in the air, and the sky has darkened enough for someone to fiddle with the movie projector.

Erin, a white pre-law major with thick eyebrows and wavy chestnut hair down to her shoulders, lays out a striped beach towel. The four of us from Keith Hall cram onto it.

On the way here, I'd asked Erin a few questions about her major. Her brutal assessment of her experience so far—including a review of a professor drier than burnt toast—along with what I've seen Dad and Ms. Kang go through affirmed that law isn't for me.

"What's the movie?" I ask, setting aside my phone after spouting out a couple checking-in texts to Mom and Dad.

"One of the Spider-Man reboots. I honestly forget which one though," Erin says.

I snicker to myself, remembering when I'd finished my SATs and my parents declared a relaxing movie night. Veggie pizza, frozen yogurt, Spider-Man, Mom's constant praises of Aunt May's Hollywood-flawless skin, and Dad's constant accompanying shushing. Something hot starts to gather behind my eyes—a tear? Do I miss them? Stripping away the layers of pressure and expectations that they slathered on me like sunscreen at the beach, then yes, I guess I do. I'd been so caught up in the plotting and cover stories that the emotion of the separation hadn't caught up with me until now. I quickly blink away the tear. I'm here at Delmont not only for me, but for them. This is for all of us.

Erin drags her leather purse over and dumps out a half dozen Reese's and some full-sized Hershey's bars. "But I did remember to bring candy. I can't watch movies without them. Lucky for us, I picked up a ton of these on the Boulevard this morning. Clubs are just handing these out like, well, candy."

I reach for a Reese's, my mouth already watering. I make a note to do a few more strolls down the Boulevard to replenish my dwindling dorm-room food stash. I need to find a way to eat while I wait for Mom's money and my credit card to arrive in the mail, and thankfully no one's around to tell me sugar isn't a food group.

Casper, the lone male in our group rises, towering above us. He's a tall Indian guy with close-cropped hair, thick black-rimmed glasses, and the jawline and build of a teen drama heartthrob. "I don't do chocolate. Anyone else want popcorn?"

We all raise our hands, and he disappears in the direction of the popcorn machine.

"Too bad he's got a girlfriend," Erin says, her eyes following him into the crowd.

Tessa shrugs and reaches for a Hershey's bar. "You think it's going to last? Her being all the way in Chicago and all."

I feel like I'm jumping late into a conversation, like there's so much background I've already missed because I've been purposely keeping my distance from most people. I unwrap my Reese's and pretend to be interested in the conversation anyway.

Erin pauses. Casper's chatting with the popcorn vendor, and the vendor's handing him cup after cup. He tries to juggle four—one for each of us—and he's leaving a Hansel-and-Gretel-style trail behind him. "I give it a month."

I bite into a peanut butter cup. My Monte Verde lunch crew didn't talk romance and dating all that often. Sure, there were the occasional crushes and a few dates (for the other folks, not me). Our parents shared the no-dating-until-you're-thirty-type rules, and after someone's ex revenge-formatted her laptop's hard drive before finals, I swore off even daydreaming about any Monte Verde rivals. I wonder if Camilla purposefully sought out a partner who isn't caught up in the competition hamster wheel.

But this sitcom-style banter with Erin and Tessa—is this what having close friends is like? I don't have anything to contribute, so I keep my mouth shut and reach for another peanut butter cup. I want them to like me, and the possibility of me saying the completely wrong, unexperienced thing right now is high.

Tessa rocks over and shoves her shoulder against mine. "Well, this one met a hot guy in bio this morning."

Erin's eyebrow rises and so does my temperature.

"It was nothing. He just kept me from squashing the people in the row below us. And he told me about this student gaming club I should check out. He's nice." The unplanned peanut-butter-scented words just spill out of my mouth.

Erin winks at me. "Right. Nice." The smile on her face spreads to mine and Tessa's, and we still have them on when Casper returns, clutching four half-full cups of popcorn.

"What'd I miss?"

"Just talking about classes," Erin says, with a conspiratorial glance at me. She reaches up for a cup from Casper, and a few kernels of popcorn scatter onto the beach towel beneath us. "What else are you all taking? I signed up for a once-a-week seminar on nineteenth-century German philosophy, and once a week already seems like too often to be discussing this. I'm probably going to drop it. I'm looking for another class if anyone's got suggestions."

She looks straight at Casper then, making it uncomfortably clear that she's really only digging for suggestions from him. Tessa and I share an uneasy glance, but Casper doesn't seem to pick up on Erin's attempt to force her way into his schedule.

"You could actually sign up for a math class," Casper says, tossing a kernel in the air and catching it in his mouth.

Erin scrunches up her face. "No, thank you. I'm saving that for second year, when I can count on first-years to drag down the curve." A slight cloud of frustration in her eyes, she turns to me instead. "What about you, Perla? What are you taking other than biology? Maybe I can find a hot guy too."

I pull from the fake class schedule I'd tweaked with the help of that course catalog. "Oh, you know, the usual stuff. Writing, foreign language, all that."

"Which foreign language?" Casper asks. He plops gracelessly

down onto the beach towel and spills even more popcorn.

In my formulation of my fake class schedule, I had calculated the foreign language least likely for any of them to take. According to the student blogs, most first-years took Spanish and Mandarin, and the rest usually went with the notoriously lax French 101 professors.

"Italian."

To my horror, Casper leans in. "Me too! With who?"

Every drop of blood in my veins stills.

I shrug as casually as I can. "I honestly don't remember the name of the professor."

"Is it Donati? I heard she's tough."

I try to laugh off his earnestness, but in the face of this unexpected inquisition, I'm blanking on the details: the professor, the days and times of the class, even what building it'd be in. These feel like details any good Delmont student would know or be able to pull up on their phone in half a second. There's no way I can continue answering his questions with my nonexistent recollection of my nonexistent class schedule, so the most I can do is attempt to deflect. I nudge at his knee playfully with my shoe. "Wow, you really want the details. It's like talking to my parents!"

Tessa snorts and slaps a hand flat on the towel. "God, I know how that is. You all met my mom. I basically sent her home with a copy of everything we got at registration just so she'd stop bugging me about dorm security phone numbers and after-hours medical services."

"My mom made me FaceTime with her and take her for a 'tour'

of campus," Casper says. "Hey, let's FaceTime her so she knows I'm not doing keg stands."

We all break into doubled-over laughter because our parents must have all given us some form of warning about our newfound independence in the "adult" world. Yet even in the midst of the easy moment, worry worms through.

I've gotten lazy in adhering to my meticulous seven-part plan. Instead of my early night of face-down-in-the-pillow sleep and my day lounging in the grass by the Boulevard, I should have more thoroughly mapped out and memorized my fake Delmont life. I need a backstory that is concrete and ingrained enough that simple questions like these shouldn't flummox me. Otherwise, one stray question too many could make me unravel. Not everyone is going to be as easygoing and borderline socially clueless as Casper. I'll be found out, and Delmont will banish me home in shame, assuming my sure-to-be-enraged parents are even willing to take my disappointing self back. My stomach roils, and I don't think it's because I've ingested a pound of chocolate in under five minutes.

Perfect Perlie Perez would never have devolved into this kind of carelessness.

The title sequence music blares through the speakers, driving away those thoughts of my failures. The crowd around us erupt into cheers, and being surrounded in noise and happiness sends a thrill buzzing down my spine.

This feeling of newness, of possibility, is intoxicating. I give myself permission to enjoy this movie night. I've still got to scope out a few locations to stow my stuff before Samantha Simon arrives in three days, but it's best I not do that while everyone's wide awake. Also, it's not like I can excuse myself now, to run back to the dorms to do what—homework? No one seems to be taking the first day of class and all its accompanying assigned reading that seriously: a change from Monte Verde, for sure. And even if I had an alibi for leaving, I wouldn't want to. This time last year, as I faced another bland, anxiety-filled day at Monte Verde, I would have never looked ahead to imagine me sitting in the grass for a movie on a school night, surrounded by new friends.

Even though on paper I don't belong here yet, I can't help but hope that, deep down, I do. Now I just need to prove to the admissions committee that I'm just as perfect as everyone says I am.

On PicLine: kernels of popcorn on Erin's striped beach towel.
In the fringes, Casper's shoe, Tessa's left hand, my knee.
Caption: Movie night #studying #notreally
Nineteen likes.

ELEVEN

As if my PicLine post tempted fate, that feeling of belonging shatters when I return from my fake Italian class the next afternoon.

Someone plastered bright yellow flyers all over the Keith Hall bulletin boards. Clip art of a goofy inspector peering through a magnifying glass takes up the bottom half. The top half: *Dorm Health and Safety Checks tomorrow! Delmont Security and Resident Advisers will be conducting routine inspections to ensure all rooms are safe and habitable.*

I snatch it down from the board and flip it over. There's no further information on when exactly I can expect security and these RAs to barge through second-floor doors.

Still clutching the yellow flyer, I sprint back to my room: Samantha Simon's room. The logical part of my brain kicks into overdrive the second my spreadsheet flickers onto my laptop screen. I was planning on packing up and finding another space anyway. Tomorrow's Thursday, only a day earlier than Samantha

Simon's specially scheduled move-in. I can pack and sneak out first thing tomorrow morning. I've already had my eye on an uninhabited room on the first floor or a storage room in the basement level. Less climbing.

With my boiling anxiety down to a simmer, I shut my laptop and begin refolding the clothes Mom had helped me hang up a few days ago. They still smell of the laundry detergent back home.

Then I set my alarm for six a.m.

In the morning, it doesn't take me long to strip the ivory sheets off the bed and tuck my pajamas into my oversized suitcase. I cram everything else into the free duffel bag I'd gotten from the school's state-of-the-art athletic center, which has been tabling on the Boulevard all week. As quietly as I can, I roll my life out into the hallway before seven o'clock. The door clicks shut behind me.

For the second time in so many months, I'm alone, burdened with everything from my past and with few options ahead.

My throat tightens.

How can I really be Perfect Perlie Perez if I've done everything I'm supposed to and stuck to every plan laid out for my life, and here I am again? Perla's Academic Plan drew out a map for my life as a straight line. No curves, no detours, no speed bumps. So if I go off-road, it's my fault.

I've been at Delmont almost a week, and I'm not any closer to figuring out why everyone here got in and not me. Bio class has been just basics and no eye-opening reveal into what makes Delmont premed special, and the folks I've met don't go around blabbing about what made them stand out to the admissions committee. I seem to have taken the same classes as everyone, done the same extracurriculars, passed the same standardized tests. Maybe none of that is remarkable enough for any university to take a chance on a younger student with slightly-out-of-range grades and scores. It's unnerving to think I may never truly learn why none of my schools accepted me.

Standing in a hallway with everything I hold dear packed into a rolling bag, a duffel, and a backpack, I wonder what's the easiest way to get back on the right track. If there is an easy way, or a right track.

But there's no one awake for me to ask, no best friends to rouse with a text. And an empty hallway doesn't seem the right setting for soul searching.

I sling the duffel bag strap onto my shoulder and begin to walk. I take step after step but don't feel like I'm moving at all.

My tired legs naturally take me downhill, and I find myself in Lower Dell Village, the cutesy town of boutiques, bars, and ice cream parlors west of the school. I stroll past freshly washed crystal-clear windows, peering in at the outfitted mannequins and used textbooks. Once the stores open, I try on clothes I can't afford to pass the time and give my limbs a break from hauling my baggage all over the village. I need to stay away from the dorms until this evening, when inspections are over, hopefully without running into the few people I know at Delmont. The day is young, but I'm already too tired and hungry to recite spreadsheeted excuses with any sort of believability.

My phone buzzes.

Mom: *Ms. K says Camilla has already gotten an A on her first assignment.*

I grimace. Of course Camilla would call home to brag about that. She probably needed something, anything, to tell her moms other than "Classes are tough, food's good. Have I told you I'm dating a guy who doesn't go to Delmont?"

I don't consider calling Mom back yet. And even if I did have the energy to cobble together a solid enough lie right now, I know how this conversation would go: the same way it's gone dozens of times before.

That's great for Camilla.

But what about you? Mom would ask. *You should be doing well too.*

I haven't had any assignments yet.

Send me your class list, Mom would say, *so I can look up the professors and syllabi on my own.*

Then we'd stay on the line as I'd email her my fake but well-researched schedule, me waxing about how well I'm doing here and her asking what I've been eating lately. Even imagining this conversation is exhausting.

I tuck my phone away before my thumb slips and dials her. I crawl into the afternoon, ignoring the increasing grumble of my stomach. If I can wait until dinnertime, I can probably get someone to swipe me in for a meal.

But then the smell of baked goods and sugar winds into my nostrils at two o'clock, and my feet follow my stomach and my nose toward the source.

The Bubble and Bean, a mom-and-pop bubble tea and coffee shop, sits between a ramen restaurant and an electronics repair place. The storefront is painted green, with a big spotless window and a handwritten *Help Wanted* sign in the corner.

I tug the door open, and bells above the door chime. That heavenly smell is stronger in here, more distinct. Coffee beans and caramel and cinnamon. My mouth waters. With all the packing and lugging suitcases and wandering this morning, my appetite has grown to a level that a "later, I promise" can no longer appease.

I trudge up to the pastry case. Croissants, pineapple buns, sponge cakes, and . . . there they are, iced cinnamon buns with that sugary sheen that dreams are made of. My fingertips drift up to the case, as if I could reach through the glass and devour every-thing within arm's reach.

"How can I help you?"

I drop my hand and follow the sound of the voice. A teenage Black guy with a forest-green apron stares at me, dark brown fin-gers on either side of the cash register. A black plastic name tag pinned to his apron says his name is Jackson.

"The cinnamon buns are out of this world. My mom and grandparents bake the Chinese pastries, and the cinnamon buns, croissants, and a couple other items are from one of my dad's bud-dies, the oldest Black-owned bakery downtown. Forget farm to table: oven to mouth is where it's at."

I laugh, which of course means I now have to buy something. I order the cinnamon bun and fish my wallet out of my backpack, pushing past highlighters and pairs of clean socks that didn't fit into my duffel. It takes longer than I'd like due to my own haphazard packing. The guy drums his fingers on the countertop to a folksy song playing low over the shop speakers, so I fill up the silence. "Your dad manages this place?"

"He owns it. Bought it from the previous owner last year, so I've been working here after school."

With his closely cut black hair and trusting eyes, Jackson looks young, maybe as young as I am. Plus he said "school," and not "class."

"Are you in high school?"

"Yup, senior at Dell West. Go, Knights!" He does this corny lift of an invisible sword. "Half day today, which means I get to be here instead of at home beating the latest *GTA*."

"How long did it take you to beat the warehouse raid?"

He blinks, like he wasn't expecting me to dig into the specifics of the game so quickly. "Um, haven't gotten to it yet."

"Well, good luck," I say with a smile, remembering that blood-rushing sense of victory when I'd finally gotten through that mess of a mission. It was the kind of thrill that made me feel powerful and skilled and daring in a way that squeaking by on a pop quiz didn't.

I peer up at the menu board to choose a sugary, chewy-bubble drink, then decide against it once I see the prices. "Don't start that raid without super-heavy armor."

"Thanks. How 'bout you? You a Dell Eastie?"

I hand him one of the few five-dollar bills inhabiting my wallet.

"No, I go to Delmont."

With as many times as I've said variations of that phrase out loud the past few months, I somehow feel bad saying it to this kind-eyed stranger. He's probably starting off his senior year with the same hope I had last September. The words come out a little quieter, as if I'm already expecting a challenge and my voice is preparing for it.

Jackson's brown eyes widen. "Oh, I thought you were . . . Sorry, you just look kinda . . . One cinnamon bun, right?"

I nod. It could be because he's so clearly impressed or because I'm so loopy from low blood sugar, but I go on. "I skipped grades, so I'm younger than most first-years. I'll be seventeen in January though."

"Oh, nice, me too! I'm seventeen, I mean. Not hyper-smart and skipping grades." He shoves the cash register drawer closed with a ding and hands me my change. He grabs a set of tongs off the counter behind him and ambles back to the pastry case.

I wish he'd speed up. My stomach rumbles at the possibility of a cinnamon bun in the very near future. God knows I need the sustenance, but I also need something to keep my mouth busy so I'm not just spilling all the details of my life.

"So that makes you an Aquarius, then?" he asks, drawing open the glass door with excruciating slowness.

"No, a Capricorn."

"Ah, the cool and calculating Capricorn. Makes sense. Not often I run into a sixteen-year-old college student."

I snort. "Do you actually believe in that zodiac stuff?"

He shrugs and places my plate on the counter. "People leave their newspapers in here all the time. The horoscope column is usually the least depressing part."

The cinnamon bun nearly takes up half the dinner plate. It could be that my muscles are exhausted from hauling my belongings around, but it takes a surprising amount of effort to lift up the mass of baked good. "I cannot wait to eat this."

He smiles, and it brightens his already-easy face. "There's a water dispenser at the end of the counter. If you're trying to conquer this yourself, you might want to wash it down with something. Like those competitive hot dog eaters do."

I mumble some thanks, then almost sprint toward a high-backed green velvet armchair by the window. I dump my backpack and duffel onto the bench facing me: the perfect setup to being left alone.

I tug my MacBook out and open up my password-protected plan spreadsheet, my fingers drifting to my heart pendant as it loads. So far I've temporarily secured a room and have my eye on some backups (part two), found some friends (part three), dodged a parent visit (part four), and "enrolled" in at least one class (part five).

I'm pondering the next steps of part six of my plan, crafting a new personal statement, when a shiny metal fork-and-knife pair juts out in front of my face.

"Figured you'd need this," Jackson says.

I nearly slam my MacBook shut.

The horror of someone seeing my spreadsheet must be plain on my face because Jackson throws in an "Unless you were just going to smash your face into that cinnamon bun" and a forced chuckle.

Despite the hurtling of my heart against my ribs, I offer a low laugh to mask my panic. Judging by his polite smile, he hadn't seen a thing.

"Thanks." I snatch the fork and knife.

I stab the fork into the cinnamon bun like I'm planting a flag, listening to the sound of his footsteps fade back into the coffee shop din.

I take a bite, and it melts into a perfect mouthful of sugar and joy. I push my MacBook aside. I can get to the seven-part plan later. I have to do more important research on this oven-to-mouth concept.

TWELVE

Sophomore year of high school, Mom watched a wellness documentary and decided the whole family should go on Saturday-morning runs together. Saying no isn't an option when Mom makes it a big "family togetherness" deal. Mom and Dad would knock on my door at seven in the morning. They expected me to be in the car, water bottle filled and shoes tied tight without a complaint, in fifteen minutes. Then we headed for the track at Rancho College, the local community college, where we shared the cool morning air and dew-dusted lanes with the senior citizen walking group and a pair of exhausted-looking new moms pushing fancy jogging strollers.

I dreaded these runs. First of all, when I had to get up at six in the morning to make it to zero period at Monte Verde High, I held sleeping in on the weekends sacred. Second, I am not and never was a runner. Dad is the epitome of slow and steady, chugging around like a freight train, but Mom ran track in college and the speed never left her limbs. I'd push myself to match her pace but always ended up burning through my energy too quickly. I'd slow to a walk, but she'd keep on going, glancing at me every time she lapped me, like she just couldn't comprehend why her own flesh and blood—meticulously molded in her own image—couldn't keep up. It lasted all of one month before Mom stopped knocking on my door those Saturday mornings and started going out on her own. She never brought it up again.

I feel that same post-run exhaustion now as I drag my Delmont life back up to Keith Hall. I'd considered the end of those runs a win—I got to sleep in again!—but in the bright Southern California sunlight, I wonder if it was early proof that I wasn't as exceptional as we'd always assumed. I tried my hardest at something that would fit me better into the schema of our perfect family, and I fell short.

But maybe it matters that those morning runs weren't my idea to begin with. How could I be expected to throw myself whole-heartedly into something that I didn't love?

I wish I had a bite of that cinnamon bun left, for sugar to fuel these twists and turns of my brain and heart.

It's almost five o'clock. The security officers should be finishing up their dorm inspections by now. They and a few Keith Hall RAs mill around the first-floor lobby, near the massive wall of aluminum-faced student mailboxes. Voices scratch through their walkie-talkies. I slide into a worn purple armchair nearby to wait them out, tucking my suitcase, backpack, and duffel bag behind me. I grab a copy of the *Daily Dragon* from the messy stack on the coffee table to hide behind.

It's easy to fade into the background of a busy dorm lobby. Eavesdropping at home was much harder. Mom and Dad always seemed to know where I was in the house. The creaks and groans of our floorboards give me away nearly every time. The house held me to my word, whether I liked it or not.

But once in a while, when the TV blared a little too loud or if the neighbors partied too late into the night, I could sneak closer to their closed doors and hear them. The mundane of bill paying and scheduling aside, my parents would dream up our family's next moves: expansions, upgrades, always reaching up for the next bigger, better thing.

I never wanted to be the faulty cog that broke down the whole machine.

"Follow up with rooms 418 and 445 on the unpermitted micro-waves and that electric grill," one of the security officers says. He's a tall Latino man with a bushy black mustache and the same hint of a beer gut that my dad has. He dons a head-to-toe blue getup that could be mistaken for a police uniform, complete with a shiny golden *Campus Security* badge.

A girl in a blue polo shirt, the RA for that floor, jots something down on her clipboard.

"And room 803. They need to get rid of those candles."

The eighth-floor RA kicks at the linoleum and mumbles his agreement.

"And room 217."

My fingers clench around the newspaper edges at the mention of my room. I was so thorough this morning in my sweep of the place. I couldn't possibly have left something behind.

"You've confirmed that maintenance has already replaced that broken screen?" the security officer asks.

A girl a few years older than me tucks a red curl behind her pale pink ear. "I signed off on the completed job half an hour ago. That room's supposed to be empty for the rest of the semester anyway."

Relief flies at me from all sides. Not only did I not royally screw up and drop a bread crumb to tip them off to my existence, but Samantha Simon's room could be mine for a little longer?

This must sound too good to be true to the other RAs too, because one of them, a brawny blond guy with a hint of a mustache, shakes his head. "You sure? Did you confirm this with Residential Services?"

The second-floor RA's look turns as sharp as a dagger. "Yes, Raymond, I'm sure. We got a note from Admissions that the girl's visa is still held up, and the university allowed her to delay her start until spring. That enough, or did you want to call our director about this too?"

Her voice holds a hint of how-dare-you in it, like maybe the other RAs have been giving her grief about her responsibilities. If what Tessa told me is true, maybe our RA's turbulent long-distance relationship is burning up more of her time and attention than I thought.

My heart does a jig in my chest. I didn't realize how much my soul craved this bit of stability offered by a place to sleep. Everything about the last few hours, days, months has felt off-kilter, unpredictable despite my best efforts to plan and know and get it all right. Hearing that I could stay in Samantha Simon's room longer-term feels like a sip of ice-cold pink lemonade during a heat wave.

I remind myself to turn the newspaper page so it doesn't look like I'm grinning too long at an ad for rideshare and food delivery jobs.

The security officer proceeds with his endless-sounding list of violations, but I've heard all that I need. Angling my face away from them, I retrieve my bags and head for the elevator. The security officer's still rattling off to-dos when the doors close. I speed down the hall to Samantha's room. My room. I slide my keycard in the door's reader.

The reader blinks red.

No.

I try it again.

Another red blink, and no welcoming sound of the lock sliding open.

My mouth goes dry.

The maintenance-and-security staff must have deactivated my card after the screen replacement. No one's supposed to be in this room, after all. I try the handle again, as if the door will just swing open the more frantic I get.

Nothing.

I force a breath in and out slowly, but it does nothing for the fight-or-flight's havoc on my focus. I'll have to check the window, like when I'd beat Tessa on a race up to my own room. If I can pry it open and make my way back in, then voilà, Perla's own room.

I stash my bags in the empty study lounge, then backtrack to the elevator. My brain already whirs through the possible ways of explaining to my friends why I'm not entering my dorm room when we all part for the evening. I wonder how long I could possibly keep up this act. Lies multiply like weeds once they take even the most shallow root, and I've been feeling like such an amateur gardener lately.

The elevator doors open, and I step forward, nearly smacking into someone exiting.

"Sorry," we say reflexively at the same time.

The second-floor RA looks up from her phone and stares straight at me.

Her long curly red hair is swept back behind her shoulders, leaving her heart-shaped face in full view. The metal name badge on her chest glints in the fluorescent light of the landing. Her name is Genia. Her gray eyes narrow: she's doing the same rapid assessment of me, the person on her floor who she doesn't know.

My face heats under the intensity of her scrutiny.

A second ticks by, though it feels like a year in terms of open-elevator-door time, but she doesn't break eye contact.

"Excuse me," she says finally. "This is my floor."

My eyes dip down, as if she'd literally meant the floor was hers. I realize then that I am still planted right in front of the elevator doors.

She couldn't get around me.

"Oh. I'm so sorry. I was . . . I'm sorry." I can't stop mumbling apologies, so I will my legs to step to the side already. Nearly smashing foreheads with the RA was not a common Delmont occurrence I'd come across in student blogs or on social media. It dawns on me, at the worst time, that I can't anticipate and spreadsheet away every problem.

Once Genia is past me, I scrunch myself into the corner of the elevator, as if the mortification would decrease proportionately to the amount of space I take up.

I don't miss the second glance she throws over her shoulder at me before she brings the phone back to her ear and the elevator doors close.

My legs refuse to stop shaking until I'm sitting on the bare bed of my room. It had made scaling the tree more hazardous than it already is.

The brand-new, intact window screen sits against the wall, partially hidden by the hideous brown curtain. I'd managed to pull the whole thing out when I'd clambered up the tree. Ten minutes of jimmying open the rusty-framed glass with a broken branch and my now-raw fingers granted me access to the room. I don't need to give maintenance staff, or anyone else for that matter, reason to be snooping around here. Broken glass and another torn screen would likely have someone knocking on the door by the end of the day.

Once I've gathered enough energy and will to stand, I retrieve my bags from the study lounge and shove my suitcase and duffel bag into the closet. My fingers, dotted with bits of dirt and bark, tremble too much to attempt to unpack.

A knock at the door stops my heart mid-beat.

Did someone see me after all?

I don't know how much more of this I can take. Part of me wonders if getting caught would actually be a relief. Then I could stop—stop what? Stop lying? Stop being the person everyone thinks I am?

Then who would I be?

My crisis is interrupted by yet another knock.

"Perla? You up for dinner? I'm buying." A laugh. Tessa.

I suppress a flare of annoyance. I'd asked her at least twice in the last few days to text me instead of showing up at my door. It's risky enough for me to come in and out of this room, let alone have another person casually standing out front, banging on it so that they can hear her down at the elevators. My seven-part plan is perfect. The players, however, are not.

I wipe my hands off on my jeans and unlock the door to find Tessa shoving an envelope in my face. "This ended up in my mailbox. Looks like they got the room number wrong on the address."

I pluck it from her and almost cry with relief when I realize it's from First Cal-Am Bank. This must be my credit card. I didn't know until now how much I needed something good, some sign that I belong here.

"You okay?"

Tessa's question jars me back to reality. Her brow is tight, and she's gazing at me with concern, like she can't figure out why I'm looking at this envelope like it's a long-missing family member.

"Yeah, I just thought this had gotten lost. Glad it went to you and not some identity theft weirdo," I say, forcing my voice light. "I'll call the bank about it tomorrow and get the address fixed. Must've been my awful handwriting on the application. It's why I type all my notes."

Tessa's face relaxes. "My handwriting's pretty awful too. My mom threatened to send me to finishing school, whatever the hell that is."

I'm about to close the door behind me when I remember that my keycard doesn't work anymore. I wave the envelope in the air between us. "Let me stash this somewhere safe. I'll meet you downstairs?"

"You don't want me to know your hiding places? I'm a regular Sherlock Holmes, after flying through the BBC series this summer," she says with a wink. I laugh despite the prickle of a nerve that perhaps Tessa wasn't the right person to choose for part three of my plan.

Her phone chimes, and she tugs it out of her pocket and frowns. "Meet you in the lobby in five, then. Gotta call my mom first. But don't be late—I hear Godwin makes a mean chicken Alfredo, and it goes fast." She strolls down the hallway, already dialing, and I rush to my desk for anything to keep the door lock mechanism from engaging.

On my way to dinner, I tell myself over and over that I'm safe, that I handled today remarkably well, given the obstacles thrown at me. I need this little mental boost to keep my face from defaulting to a gloomy pout, the kind that will draw out "what's wrong?" questions from my new friends.

But even a credit card, a strategically placed piece of tape on my door to keep the latch from catching, and two bowls of chicken Alfredo don't totally banish the growing ache in my chest. And when I zone out at dinner and Tessa asks me if I'm okay, it's all I can do to nod instead of scream.

THIRTEEN

I stretch my fingers across my keyboard to give them a break after spending the past hour typing down Professor Desai's every word.

I've finished my third bio class, and to my surprise, this class I fake-enrolled in isn't wholly uninteresting: a completely different experience than the AP Chemistry class I took at Monte Verde, where I regularly pinched myself to stay awake. I've already decided to skip two of the other courses on my schedule. The calculus professor is too monotone, and Italian has too small of a class size for me to blend in. Part five of my seven-part plan requires me to sit in a couple classes, not every class thankfully. I use those freed-up middles of my days to beat some of the games I've got on my laptop for the second or third time, without Mom or Dad commenting about how other students are getting ahead while I'm lazing around doing nothing.

Independence has grown on me.

Next to me, Tessa powers down her laptop. "Don't forget. Free school spiritfest concert tonight and a free hot dog for each bit of Delmont gear! You know me: I'm going to wear every single piece of Delmont merch I've got."

"Delmont gearathon? You're on," I say, my competitive streak alive and well but friendlier this time. I don't have anything to prove to anyone—other than the free-hot-dog person. Then my mind drifts to my sad savings account. That's one part of this new-found independence I don't love. Funding this fake life is proving trickier than I'd imagined, and I hadn't budgeted for mounds of logo-slathered items from the student store.

I zip up my backpack, trying to avoid looking at the beat-up, thinning wallet in the interior pocket, but its metallic pink sheen catches my eye anyway. Auntie Trish gave me this designer wallet as a birthday gift a few years ago, with a hundred dollars' worth of Nintendo store credit tucked into one of the credit card flaps.

I wonder then whether Auntie Trish would float me some money but decide, no, that's not a good idea. Word would get back to Mom and Dad about it somehow. Our family may be pri-vate about our struggles and imperfections when it comes to the public, but inside our circle? Everyone knows everyone else's busi-ness. It's new not having my parents or even Auntie Trish around to bounce ideas off of, get some external validation that I'm doing the right thing, or, in this case, secure a little cash.

Every day here comes at this high price of self-imposed loneli-ness.

I remind myself that this is what I want. A big splurge on some Delmont gear for this spiritfest could be just what I need to solidify or start some new relationships here on campus.

The auditorium empties around us, with people rushing to their next classes or back to their rooms to study, sleep, or generally do whatever they want without someone checking if they've done their homework. Tessa and I rise to shimmy out of the narrow aisle in between seats.

"Psh, you really think you can outgear me, Perez? I haven't seen you wear a single thing with the Delmont seal other than your hoodie. The hot dog guy's going to know you don't have school spirit. Then that free hot dog of yours will be mine for the taking."

She fakes an evil-villain laugh, and I join in the fun by rolling my eyes, all the while unnerved that she's been watching me that closely. "Oh, I have school spirit." It's the money I don't have. "I'm going to wear so much Delmont gear you'll have to eat your words. And that'll be all you'll get, because your free hot dog? Mine."

We rib each other on the way out, throwing out awful hot dog puns and Tessa casually blaspheming by saying she's got more spirit than the Bible. At the doors, Tessa lays out a plan to meet up later, then heads to her next class, and I swivel around to orient myself to the student store.

"Did I hear you're going to the concert?"

I paint on a smile before turning to Brand. He's in a slightly wrinkled lavender V-neck, as if the shirt was stuffed into a gym bag just hours earlier. "Yeah, with some of the people from my floor."

"Me too. Got my blue-and-green gear ready to go."

"I'm going to go pick up a few more things." I choose not to let him in on this slightly ridiculous school-spirit-and-free-hot-dog competition I've got with Tessa. "I'm heading to the Dragon's Lair now if you want to . . ." That's as far as I can force my mouth to invite him.

I'm still an amateur at this socializing-with-someone-you-think-is-cute thing, as well as the whole idea of spontaneity. My four years at Monte Verde High were so rigorously planned out that I don't remember the last time I initiated something without at least twenty-four hours' advance notice. It didn't help that my parents had to drive me everywhere in public-transportationless Monte Verde and therefore held veto power over everything I did.

But that was Perfect Perlie Perez's problem. Delmont Perla has friends.

Delmont Perla has a little bit of a crush.

"Sorry, Perla, I'd love to, but I've got Spanish in ten. Opposite direction." He gives me one of those eyebrow-scrunched smiles that tells me he regrets having to say no. "Find me later at the concert, okay?"

I agree, and he strides off, backpack hanging over his sea-sculpted shoulder by one strap. He disappears into the crowd, but that fluttery warmth in my chest stays.

In contrast to what over-reasonable Perfect Perlie Perez would do, I let myself have this. I let myself live in this glowing, filtered world a little longer because I don't have homework to rush back for, extracurriculars to whisk myself off to, parents I have to answer. I deserve a good day, after all that it took me to get here.

I practically glide down to the Dragon's Lair. Crowds part for me. The sun shines brighter. Birds trill tunes high up in rhythmically swaying tree limbs. Even the club representatives and vendors sound like they're calling out in harmony as they wave their rainbow of flyers. The automatic doors of the Dragon's Lair slide open like palace gates.

I dance over to the women's section and surround myself in racks of clothes, all emblazoned with the Delmont seal. The shirts and sweaters sway as I pass. The gorgeous, diverse school-gear-clad models grin down at me from their wall-sized advertisements.

Try it on.

Buy it all.

You look stunning in blue and green.

I ferry a pile of shirts, a hoodie, and even knee-high socks to the cash register. The cashier croons a greeting. He floats my items across the scanner and drops them into a bag with the smoothness of a conductor.

"Your total is two hundred and sixty-nine dollars and thirty-eight cents."

A needle drags across a vinyl record.

"That . . . that seems high," I eke out. I barely have enough breath in my lungs to manage even that. I mentally count the cash in my wallet.

I can't go to the concert with only one measly Delmont hoodie. Well, more accurately, I can't score loads of free hot dogs and win this silly competition with my new friend.

"Well, the hoodie's sixty-five dollars . . ."

A real student wouldn't balk at the price of such a key item of Delmont life, would they?

"The T-shirts are forty-five dollars each . . ."

Tessa's expecting me to go in head-to-toe blue and green.

"These socks are limited edition. See the gold trim? The regular ones are fifteen dollars, but these are twenty dollars . . ."

And Brand's expecting me too.

"The long-sleeve shirt is . . ."

"It's fine," I blurt out. I fumble with the clasp on my wallet and pull out the credit card I'd activated only last night. It glows like magic in the bright white light of the store. I sign my name on the card-reader pad, and the music returns.

These are a one-time purchase, I tell myself, essential to my seven-part plan. I need my new friends to believe I'm a new student just like them, and what better way than to walk into this concert with them, all of us dripping in Delmont gear? The plan aside, this is my opportunity to make Delmont Perla who I want her to be: spontaneous, fun, answering to no one but herself. I'll pay this all off once my parents mail me that money through Tessa's dorm address.

The worries melt away when the cashier places the bag in my hands. I fly up the hill and up the tree to my second-floor dorm room to change.

On Pic-Line: seven-second video of Dragon Scales, the school's award-winning a cappella group, singing the Delmont fight song.

Caption: They are so good! #Delmont #Dragonscales #fightfightfight

Twenty-three likes.

Comment from Cam1llaKJ: How'd you get such good seats? I was up in the nosebleeds!

Notification:

Brand_DW started following you.

FOURTEEN

The next day, my phone vibrates with a text from Tessa. *Got some of your mail again!*

I put my ear to my door and listen for anyone walking by. Confident that th e hallway's empty, I sneak over to Tessa's room, throw on an innocent, practiced frown and knock.

She's already in her pajamas—a faded Olivia Rodrigo album cover shirt and black bike shorts—despite the fact that we'd returned from dinner less than twenty minutes ago. Dinner was the first time I'd seen her all day. The high from last night's concert brought us into the early morning, and I took every glorious, unstructured second of my Saturday to catch up on sleep.

I'd slept so soundly I even missed a couple texts from Camilla, asking if I'd be up for lunch or bubble tea. I doubt she simply wants the pleasure of my company: she could've said hi to me anytime we nearly bumped into each other in those Monte Verde halls. No, Camilla probably wants to explain away the boyfriend thing or at least make sure I'm keeping her secret.

Hanging out with Tessa instead doesn't require nearly as much emotional navigating.

"Sorry about that," I say to Tessa. "The bank made me fill out two different forms to change my address. I think it'll take a couple weeks for the correction to process." This lie took five minutes of scrolling through the bank's record of poor customer service on business rating sites. Doesn't hurt anyone, other than the bank maybe, whose reputation is already in the toilet.

Tessa gives a don't-bother wave, and some of the tension in my chest evaporates. I hadn't even realized my body was physically holding on to the stress of whether she'd believe me.

"It's not the bank. It's from your mom, I think. I'm beginning to think you gave my address out on purpose. You hiding from someone? The FBI?" She smiles, but there's a hint of something unreadable in her eyes.

I laugh to disguise the nerves as she crosses the tiny room in two steps to grab the envelope from her desk. I take it from her. "Honestly, I don't put it past myself to have given people the wrong address by accident. We've only lived here what, a week? I still get my own cell phone number wrong."

She doesn't know that Perfect Perlie Perez would never forget those details, and the more she doesn't know about me, the better. The Perla in front of her is fun, friendly, and endearingly absent-minded. Or at least that's what I'm hoping she thinks. I've worked hard to cultivate this image, and my credit card transaction history proves it.

Tessa doesn't return my laugh, and my shoulders instinctively tighten, but then she shrugs and seems to let it go. "Well, I'm off to use the one working shower before someone else snags it. If you get any baked goods in the mail, I'm taking a cut."

She strolls past me, and once the swinging doors to the bathroom close behind her, I speed back to my room, my pulse faster than my feet. Maybe I'm reading too much into Tessa's pauses. With one giant wall of tiny-doored mailboxes, mail mix-ups happen all the time here; just look at the growing, ever-present pile of "could this be your bill or local-business mailing?" envelopes in the lobby. But this envelope is specifically addressed to her room, as I'd requested. I'm not expecting any other mail, but I really hope Tessa doesn't read further into these continued supposed-to-be-accidental mix-ups.

Mom's envelope is thin, almost as ominously thin as my letter from Delmont Admissions. I push that sour note out of my mind.

One by one, I lay the crisp bills out on my bed. One, two, three, four, five twenty-dollar bills.

My expectations for some financial miracle float out of me with a long, disappointed sigh.

Until I get accepted to Delmont for real, I need something to offset my rising credit card bill, and this hundred dollars isn't going to help much.

A hundred dollars is twenty lattes.

A hundred dollars is ten sandwiches at the café across campus.

A hundred dollars is five pairs of limited-edition Delmont socks.

A hundred dollars is one textbook for a class I'm not enrolled in.

I reach for my phone.

Mom picks up on the third ring. "Perlie! I'm putting you on speaker." The sound over the phone suddenly expands to pick up the click of a turn signal.

"Hi. Is this a bad time?"

"No, no. We've got a few minutes," Dad says.

"We're heading downtown for dinner and a comedy show with the Kang-Jansens," Mom adds. "See? We can have just as much fun as you college kids." They both laugh.

I check my reflection in the black laptop screen. I'm not smiling. I am not having fun.

The thought of it actually rankles me. Here I am, struggling to stay afloat at Delmont, trying to fulfill some currently-out-of-reach dream that they planted in my head, and they're out on a double date?

"I got the money you sent, and I might need—"

"Perlie. Manners," Dad warns.

I gulp, instantly realizing my error. I need to sound appropriately thankful or we'll spend our entire conversation on me being ungrateful and immature instead of me needing more cash.

"I—"

"You know, your lola would've been furious you didn't start with a thank-you," Mom cuts in. "When I was your age, your grandparents didn't just hand Auntie Trish and I money like this for whatever we wanted. We had to work for it."

Mom's words resurrect the ghosts of conversations past in my mind.

When you're older, you'll understand the value of money.

When you're older, you'll see how hard it is, how much we sacrificed.

When you're older.

As if I'm not getting older every day.

I shake my head, as if a little toughness will force my brain to focus. "I'm so sorry, Mom and Dad. Thank you. I appreciate it. It's just so different than seeing you face-to-face, you know?" I throw in that last line to hopefully pull at any heartstrings in my reach, and it works.

Mom's voice softens. "You're welcome, Perlie."

"Were you able to put it to good use?" Dad asks.

"Remember, no drinking." Mom says it as routinely as she would a reminder to brush my teeth. I doubt they'd ever imagine me drinking. They probably wouldn't even dream of me having a purple-haired best friend with a state-school-attending sibling or me flirting with a cute boy. The realization stings. It suddenly feels like their version of Perfect Perlie Perez only exists in the pages of the red Academic Plan binder. There isn't room for anything else, and the thought feels constricting and uncomfortable in a way it hasn't before.

The neat line of bills on my bed shifts when I cross my legs. I need to redirect this conversation and get out of my own head so I can get money in my wallet. "Actually, it only covers a couple of my required readings. My English class alone has seven novels on the syllabus."

"Oh. Ernie, there's the parking structure." Some whispering that their microphone doesn't pick up.

"We can send you some more," Dad says. A distracted note in his voice tells me he's already adding this to his to-do list and is ready to move on. "You said you could get some of those at the library though, right?"

I slump. "A few. But there's already a wait list for some of the required books. And if I can't keep up with the reading . . ."

I let the impact of that sink in. I know them too well. They'd be mortified if I got anything less than an A because they were too cheap to buy a couple of books. So what if Mom has to forgo another Louis Vuitton bag? Her current collection isn't in any danger of withering away.

Dad takes the bait. "I'll send out some more first thing Monday morning. Okay?"

Relief floods through me. Another hundred dollars would at least put a dent into the debt that one concert outfit created. They don't know how much they're saving my hide, and I fight back the creeping guilt. I can't afford to feel anything when my survival and entire future is at stake. My parents, if anyone, would understand that sentiment.

"Thanks, Dad. Well, I don't want to keep you guys too long. Have a good time with Ms. Kang and Dr. Jansen."

"Will do," Mom replies. "And say hi to Camilla for us. You've seen her around, right?"

"Yeah, once. At the dining hall. And we're trying to meet up for lunch." True. Even though Camilla's the one doing all the inviting.

"Make sure you guys stay friends. You'll be carpooling for the holidays. It makes no sense for both families to do the six-hour drive."

I bite back a groan, not only at the continued discussion involving Camilla, someone I'm purposefully trying to avoid, but also at the fact that I'm not even thinking that far ahead to the holidays. I first need to get through the month.

We wrap up with a few more "I'll call you laters," and when the call ends, I gather the bills and lay them down one at a time again, as if they'd multiply.

I hadn't counted on my graduation money running out so quickly. Then again, with all my talk about fake scholarships, I doubt my relatives thought they'd be paying for more than lattes and a couple of textbooks.

My stomach growls, as if the mere thought of a latte is heaven.

I need to find a way to get more cash so I can eat, and I think there's a place I can do both.

FIFTEEN

Keith Hall is quiet and still in the weekend morning hours. It's easier to pretend that my life here is real if there's no one to question me.

What shatters the illusion is remembering why I'm up so early on a Sunday: I'm heading down to the Bubble and Bean to ask about the *Help Wanted* sign I'd spied earlier this week.

Hanging my towel over my shoulder, I grab my bathroom caddy and run my finger over the door latch to make sure the tape over it is holding. These rituals for keeping myself from getting locked out have become second nature. I don't want to have to trudge outside and climb up the tree to my room again. Especially not in my pajamas.

As expected for 7:30 a.m. on a Sunday morning, the bathroom's empty. From the one working shower stall, I hear the bathroom door creak open once or twice, but everyone on this floor seems to be sound asleep or at least lying in their beds scrolling through their phones.

The door swings open as I'm blow-drying my hair. My morning goes from serene to terrifying when I recognize the yawning figure behind me. Genia, the RA. I freeze my eyes onto the mirror, hoping she doesn't notice me.

She shuffles in in her red flip flops and places her bathroom caddy on the shelf above the far sink. Her red hair is smushed flat on one side like she slept funny, but the shadows under her eyes hint to her barely sleeping at all. Plastic bottles clunk against each other as she fishes for something. If I switch off the blow-dryer now, while she's distracted, I can be out of here in a few seconds.

I steel myself for the quick burst of activity. I kill the blow-dryer and yank the cord out of the wall in one swoop. I bunch the cord up, grab my caddy off the shelf, and reach for the door.

Then my traitorous bottle of shampoo thunks onto the floor, rolling straight for Genia's feet. I snatch it before it reaches her, but when I rise, Genia's looking right at me.

"Hey, are you on this floor? I think I've seen you around," she says. Her eyes may still be hooded with sleep, but her voice betrays her heightened alertness. And, unfortunately for me, her heightened suspicion.

I manage a weak smile, despite the flop of my stomach. She would know everyone on this floor: it's her job to. She created all those dragon-shaped door decorations with each resident's name. She would have lists upon lists somewhere in her room. She's probably PicLine-following most of her residents. On one of the student blogs I'd read, one person's RA had memorized everyone's birthdays. It might've been foolish to think that Genia, even distracted by some loser boyfriend hours away, wouldn't notice my strange presence on her floor, in her bathroom, for a whole semester.

"Yeah, I . . . I'm a friend of Tessa's."

"Oh, right, Tessa. With the pink hair."

"It's purple."

"Right."

I get the distinct feeling that I'd leaped over a trap Genia had set for me. Her eyes dip down to the caddy in my hand, then back to me. I resist the urge to swing my stuff behind me to shield it from her assessing gaze, like a toddler hiding stolen candy. I practically see her shuffling puzzle pieces into place. What temporary visitor would bring a fully stocked bathroom caddy around with her? Genia might not see the whole picture yet, but the fact that she's trying to jars me. I need to throw her off my scent.

"My roommate had someone over last night, and Tessa let me crash with her." I throw in a dramatic eye roll as I gripe about this fictional roommate.

Genia chuckles, the stranger-danger suspiciousness fading from her eyes a little. "Ah, gotcha. So you're in a double? Down in Godwin Village? Or Graycliff Hall?"

"Yup." My inner Perfect Perlie Perez realizes I didn't actually answer her question, but I refuse to offer any clarification that may damn me. There's something about Genia—the way she keeps her distance though she's pretending to be welcoming, the way she moves in this space like it belongs to her—that makes me think she's looking for any reason to challenge the mystery brown girl on her floor. Even if I'm able to dodge her this time, I begin to wonder how long I'll be able to keep this up before she starts asking questions that are impossible for me to answer.

"I'm Genia Mills, the RA for this floor," she says, completing her visual shift from Security Guard RA to Friendly Face RA. There's a forced hint of authority in her voice though, as if she needs to remind me that she has claim to Keith Hall first. Which she does, but I'm not about to let her figure out how and why.

I smile at her in the mirror and inch toward the door. I think about giving her a fake name, but no, I've already name-dropped Tessa as my reason for being here in Keith. If word got back to Tessa, a familiar name may at least keep her from asking too many questions. "I'm Perla."

She angles back to her bathroom caddy and starts to sort through it again. "Welcome to Keith Hall, Perla."

I take that as a dismissal and slip out into the hallway before she can look up. Back in the safety of my room, I move the door latch tape and close and bolt the door as quietly as possible.

My hands tremble as I hang up my towel.

Genia has seen my face twice. She now knows my name.

I shake my head, trying to clear it of the mess I've made. The only way I can fix this and hold on to this room is to stay out of Genia's way as much as possible. Then maybe she'll forget about these chance encounters. Dozens of visitors come and go from this floor. The fact that I've managed to avoid her this much so far already stands in my favor.

Confidence-withering doubt creeps in at the thought of avoiding her for the rest of the semester. It feels like we moved in only yesterday, and I'm already jeopardizing my stay. I have to keep believing this is possible, because what will I do if I get evicted? Even if I score this Bubble and Bean job, the wages and my dwindling savings account aren't nearly enough to pay for a cramped, shared-living situation around here.

I fly over to my MacBook and pull up my seven-part plan spreadsheet. Clicking on the icon helps to slow my racing pulse. I head to the tab for part two, find a place to stay, and add to my notes to make sure I'm keeping my growing tome of lies straight: avoid Genia Mills, RA, second floor, Keith Hall. Told her I'm a friend of Tessa's. I'm in Godwin or Graycliff in a double.

The whir of the laptop dies down when I lower the lid, but it takes another minute or so for my heartbeat to return anywhere near normal.

I lie back down on this Delmont bed that isn't mine, in this Delmont room that isn't mine either, thinking about the life that was supposed to give me both and wondering where it went wrong.

I tug down the hem of the one button-up shirt I brought with me. It's bright coral, not a color I'd choose for myself, but Mom insisted that I take at least one professional-looking shirt with me. "In case you go to lunches with professors," she'd said. Not that I had any intention of doing that this semester, but I'd grinned and shoved the shirt into my suitcase under her watchful eye anyway. Sometimes it's easier to go with what they want than to put up a fight. One extra shirt won't kill me, not when the far worse option is explaining I won't have professor lunches because I'm not technically a student.

I can't help but think then of when I got the date of my SAT practice test wrong a couple years ago and Mom practically exploded at me. She'd declined a speaking engagement to accompany me to an empty tutoring center. She barely spoke to me for days after, as if my mistake was some purposeful dig at her. As rational and smart as my parents are, they must think that I mess up as a subconscious—or, worse, intentional—way to undermine them.

The SAT practice test wasn't the first or last time I felt the ice of their disappointment. Over the years, to stay on their good sides, I learned to avoid letting them down. I learned to stop making mistakes. And on the off chance I made one anyway, I learned to cover them up.

When love seems conditioned on you being and doing exactly what someone wants, you do whatever it takes to keep them believing you're worthy.

But Mom was right then—I should've gotten the date right—the way she was when she dropped this shirt on my already-zipped suitcase. I'm thankful for it as I place my hand on the cold metal door handle of the Bubble and Bean. The bells above the door announce my arrival. At just before 9:00 a.m., the café is less populated than when I'd first come by—mostly people taking their orders and heading out for what Sunday has in store for them—but there's still a line at the register.

I stride over to the back of the line, and eight minutes later, I'm face-to-face with Jackson, the one who'd sold me on the cinnamon bun.

"How can I help you?" He lifts his eyes from the register and meets mine. A smile of recognition spreads, pushing away some of my anxiety.

"Hey, it's you! Back for another cinnamon bun? The baker gave us an extra tub of icing. I was just going to take a spoon to it in the back room later, but I can hook you up."

I shake my head. "Actually, I'm hoping I can talk to a manager. Is there one here this early?"

His smile slips a little. "I was joking about digging into the icing tub myself. I swear we're super sanitary here."

"No, this isn't about that. That sounds fantastic though." I draw in a steadying breath. "I need a job." I jut a thumb over at the front window, where the *Help Wanted* sign sits.

Jackson's eyes widen. "Oh. I'll go get my dad." He takes a step toward the back room, then pauses and backtracks to me. "Okay, Capricorn. He likes attention to detail and extreme cleanliness. Extreme."

He continues toward the back of the shop and disappears behind the swinging green door. When the door opens again, an older Black man in a black polo shirt trails behind him. Same black hair but speckled with the tiniest hints of gray, and brown eyes hidden behind metal-rimmed glasses. Jackson gestures toward me and whispers something to his father, who nods.

His father motions to two wooden chairs and small table in the corner. I ignore the wriggling self-doubt in my stomach.

Jackson jogs back to me at the register. "Take a seat. I'll bring you guys some water in a bit to see how it's going. Good luck." He angles to look behind me at the next customer. "Can I help you?"

The dozen steps to where the shop owner stands by the table, waiting for me, are long and uncomfortable. Am I swinging my hands too much? Too little? Who or what am I supposed to be looking at? Is it creepy for me to smile as I walk?

"Hi, I'm Perla." I reach out for his hand. Eye contact, one shake, two shake, drop. At least this part went well. I've been fortunate to have had the practice of introducing myself so often lately.

"Frank Simmons." He waves a hand toward the chairs. "Take a seat."

My chair scrapes against the polished concrete floor as I scoot myself into the table. I pull a folder out of my backpack and slide him the resume I'd printed at the copy shop down the street.

He picks it up with both hands and angles his head down to read it over his glasses. "So you're a student at Delmont?"

"Yes, sir. Just started."

"And you're already looking for a job? I guess you have to do what you can with those student loans, right?"

A light joke that I laugh at, hoping he doesn't catch the forced nature of it. I wouldn't know about student loans. I barely even know about being a student. Yet.

He lowers the résumé, and I glimpse the slightest downturn of his mouth. "This looks fine, but Perla, do you have any work experience?"

I spout out the answer I'd been practicing all morning. "I've had a series of volunteer positions. As you can see from my résumé, I've volunteered at the food bank in my hometown for the past three years. I helped revamp their website to make it more user-friendly. I've also—"

"Do you have any experience working in food service? In a shop like this?"

My confidence stumbles. I struggle to right myself. "No, but like I was saying about the food bank, I sorted donations." Frank leans back in his chair and sets the résumé down. I'm losing him. "And I had face-to-face contact with the food bank patrons who—"

A glass of water clinks onto the table between us, then another, pausing Frank's retreat.

"Need anything else?" Jackson throws an encouraging eyebrow raise at me before his father waves him off.

But that two-second distraction is enough for me to gather what's left of myself. I tamp down the panic and focus. Attention to detail, Jackson had said. Cleanliness.

As Jackson returns to the register, I try again. "I helped with inventory at the food bank. We had to count and log every single item that was donated, from the crates of tomato sauce to those individual serving boxes of cereal."

Frank gives the slightest of nods. His attention is back on me.

"And on Friday nights, we'd do a free dinner. I had to take a food safety course to make sure we were handling everything properly. Washing our hands, avoiding cross-contamination, and all that. I also managed cleanup after, like cleaning and disinfecting all the tables." I leave out the fact that by "manage" I also mean making sure the seventh graders didn't spend all evening smacking each other with broom swords.

Finally, a gift from the heavens: a smile. "Did you do dishes?"

"Dozens. Gigantic pots, pans, oversized serving utensils, you name it." A small exaggeration. I did dishes once. Mom swung by early to pick me up from my volunteer shift. She'd pursed her lips and pulled me out of the kitchen, declaring that she'd rather I spend my time studying than doing someone else's dirty dishes. I stopped volunteering there after that. I'd had enough community service hours to graduate anyway.

"Your class schedule. What are your mornings like?"

"Tuesday, Thursday, and Friday I've got an 8:30 a.m. biology class, but other than that, my schedule's very flexible. A new program Delmont's trying out, focused more on self-paced study time than class attendance," I lie through the smile on my purposefully cheery, honest-looking face.

"Are you eighteen?"

A twinge of anxiety, but I push through it. "No, but I can get written parental consent if needed." I should've never told Jackson I was sixteen. I blame that lapse of judgment on the fact that I was so hungry and light-headed the day I first wandered in here.

"You'll also need the school's consent."

Even though I curse internally, on the outside, my smile remains casual. "I can get that too." More specifically, my Digital Arts A-plus skills can get me that school consent. Official employment forms will require a whole lot of research and much more rule breaking. But I need this job, and if all goes well, these forms will get shoved into a file folder in a back room, the lies locked away for ages. It's victimless: I get a source of much-needed income, and Jackson and his dad get a new employee.

Frank pauses, eyeing me, then my résumé. I sit up taller, as if expanding my presence will make me look older, more imposing. Silly, I know. This might be something I learned on a Saturday-morning wildlife show about scaring off wildcats, but the threat is equally serious here. As cutesy as Lower Dell Village is, with its vintage-oil-lamp-looking streetlights complete with hanging flower baskets, major franchises and corporate names splay across many of the storefronts. The bigger the business, the more likely they'll have intense background checks that will expose me. If I don't get Frank to give me a job at this tiny, family-owned shop, I may not get another chance to earn some cash without putting myself at more risk.

A minute stretches by, punctuated only by the sounds of the espresso machine and bubble tea straws poking through plastic lids. I don't know what else to do with my hands, so I dig my thumbnail into my palm under the table.

Finally, Frank puts his hands on the armrests of the chair. "Starting pay's minimum wage. I've got forms in the back office for you to fill out. The school consent might take a couple days, but the sooner you can get these in, the sooner you can start opening shifts."

The next few minutes blur by with "thank yous" and paper-work. Frank looks eager to get back to whatever he was doing before my impromptu interview, and I want to let him, in case he suddenly thinks up a reason to rescind his offer.

On my way out, Jackson shouts a "Welcome to the team!"

Despite this win, the thought of adding the photoshopping of two employer forms to my to-do list casts a cloud of dread over me. I try to push the feeling away. I should be thrilled that I got a job. I'm getting what I wanted. I was just thrown a life preserver so I don't have to drown in debt while I crack my way into Delmont.

So why does it feel like I'm sinking faster?

Distracted, I almost collide with someone as I try to exit. I begin to blurt out an "Excuse me," but the words don't come because I recognize this someone.

"Oh, hi, Perlie!" Camilla says, far too cheerily on a Sunday morning.

That sinking feeling?

I've hit the ocean floor.

SIXTEEN

Camilla fills the Bubble and Bean doorway, and I take a defensive step back.

"Hi, Camilla," I manage, through the roar of panic in my ears.

Somehow, she must hear it too, because her eyes dip to the papers in my hand: my employment forms.

"You're working here?"

I'm about to deny everything when Frank appears next to me with another form. "You left the parental consent on the table. Can't forget that, right?"

I force on a grateful smile and take it from him before he heads behind the counter with Jackson. I hate that I don't even have a moment to celebrate this win—my first job!—because Camilla's staring at me, her forehead scrunched in that way that means she's thinking too hard. That can't be good.

I turn my smile on her. "Yup. Trying to build up my work experience. Good for the résumé."

It doesn't take that long for me to come up with believable

155

excuses like this anymore. The part of my brain that devises and manages my cover stories is a well-honed muscle. I've exercised it day after day, and now it's strong and ready to fire off as needed. I'd pat myself on the back for sticking to my plan this well, but this new moral flexibility isn't something I should be proud of, is it? A year ago, I wouldn't have thought to lie to Camilla or my parents or anyone, really. It had even shocked me to hear Camilla lying to her own parents about her beach cleanup day.

"A job? During the first year? Would your parents—"

"They know," I cut in. "And they're so mad. They think it'll get in the way of my studying. You know how that is." I'm banking on the idea that she must've gotten the same focus-on-school-and-literally-nothing-else lectures I did. I wave the parental consent form in front of her. "But they'll sign this when I push that work experience angle."

"Right." She tilts her head slightly, and I'm suddenly too aware of the fact that one of the smartest people at Monte Verde High is standing between me and escape.

"Well, I'll see you around," I say, trying to weave around her. I barely squeeze past, and to my horror, she follows me out.

I walk faster, pretending not to see her tailing me, but she catches up at the corner while I'm waiting for the Walk sign.

"Come on, Perlie, why are you really working?" she asks. All the nice-to-run-into-you friendliness she displayed a second ago has vanished. It's bright out, but she's got her sunglasses framing the top of her head like a headband. It's like she doesn't want a thin layer of glass and plastic to get in the way of her scrutiny of me.

Camilla doesn't pose her question in a hostile way, but she definitely knows something's off.

Of all the people for me to run into at the Bubble and Bean today, it had to be the one who grew up on a track parallel to mine, one who could spot every misstep because they'd be considered missteps in her own life as well.

My hand tightens around my papers—a mistake. They crumple slightly, and I immediately start trying to smooth them out. "I told you it's a résumé builder."

I repeat my lie because it buys me time. Ignoring the churn in my stomach, my brain shifts into overdrive. It's going to take every available cell to lose Camilla in this maze of my lies.

"BS, Perlie." She actually says the abbreviation aloud because our parents' reprimands against using curse words are that strong, "Since when is building your résumé more important than not flunking out? Your mom made you quit volunteering at the food bank because it took up too much time."

I'm knocked off balance at how close to home that hits, how recently I'd trotted out that example to Frank during my job interview. "You know about that?" I didn't tell her. We haven't truly spoken one-on-one in ages.

"Please. Our old house has paper-thin walls."

I swallow. I'm trying to dodge her bullets when I've been standing in a minefield this whole time. I try a different approach. "I don't have to talk to you about this."

"I'm walking back into that café in a few minutes to meet Rich, so either you and I can talk out here alone or I very loudly wonder about it with him in there."

The thought of my new employer getting any hint of this stokes my anger. "What's your problem? Why are you hassling me?"

Her brow scrunches in concern, as if genuinely taken aback that I would respond in a less-than-friendly way to her surprise interrogation. With those kinds of people skills, how was she that much more popular at Monte Verde High than I was?

"Hassling you? Perlie, we're friends, and—"

"We are not friends."

She purses her lips for a moment. "You know I've always thought of you like a little sister—"

"Wonderful."

"—and I can tell when something's up. And you, with your high-maintenance, high-income parents, have suddenly taken on a part-time barista gig during your first semester at your dream college? Not even an internship or some medical thing." She points at the paperwork I'm clutching like they're incriminating evidence.

"Whoa, high-maintenance?" I snap reflexively. "My parents look out for me, and they went through a lot to get me here. Just like yours did." Though as much as I believe what I'm saying, the words come out boilerplate and almost fake sounding. It makes me uneasy the way Mom's joke about me drinking did, like relying on routine is easier than deeper conversation. And why did my brain first go to defending them and not myself?

Camilla's voice goes gentle. "They can be and do all of that, Perlie. But that doesn't change the fact that you, and not them, seem to be hiding something."

In the face of what she's just said, the panic sets in. Camilla has managed to unravel months of planning in a matter of minutes.

This. This is why she got into Delmont.

And this is why I'm standing here, fumbling for excuses, trying not to ruin the forms that are my one key to funding my Delmont life for the next semester.

I have nothing to counter her with, and so she fills the silence herself.

"Perlie, did your parents cut you off or something?"

"No, no, nothing like that." I don't need her calling them up for some made-for-TV-movie-style family intervention. "I told you, they know." The words sound shakier this second time I spew out that lie.

Her brow wrinkles further. "Oh no, that full ride. My mom wouldn't shut up about it. Did you not get one?"

"No, it's not—"

"You know, it's not too late to go to the financial aid office and—"

"Camilla, stop." My voice cracks, against my will. "Please."

She tilts her head then, like she's solving a riddle and grabbing clues and truths out of the air around us. I take a step back, as if it'll save me from her.

"You lied. You lied about the scholarships," she whispers after a moment. Not a question. A statement, one with enough certainty in it that even my spreadsheet can't help me.

"I . . ." But nothing comes out. My mouth is bone dry. All the excuses evaporated off my tongue. I can't even defend myself.

She moves toward me, closing the distance that I'd tried to put between us. "Perlie, what else are you lying about?"

Something in me that had been stretched thin and wound tight and tighter since the day I opened that Delmont letter snaps. Tears start to dampen my eyes, despite all my willing them not to. I know how Camilla will see this. Tears mean I feel guilty. Tears mean I've done something wrong. And I haven't: Delmont's the one that made the mistake.

The sudden pity in Camilla's eyes starts the faintest fracture in that belief. Or maybe it widens one that had already been there.

"You can't tell anyone. Not a word." The desperation flows out of my mouth in a tone that sounds an awful lot like begging.

She shakes her head, like she's trying to rid her own brain of something distasteful she's learned. "Whatever's happening to you sounds like a big deal. Tell me what's going on. I can help you fix this."

I sigh, and it comes out a half sob. "This is exactly what I'm doing. I'm fixing this. You have to trust that I know what I'm doing. Keep it to yourself, okay?"

I try to keep it vague because, to be honest, I have no idea how much or how little she knows. Her sudden springing of secrets from my past on me earlier makes me not want to give her any more ammunition. She may act caring now, but I can't be certain there's not some sharp, competitive edge to all of this.

She lays a hand on my arm then. "I don't know. You're really worrying me."

Her words seem so sincere that I suddenly don't doubt at all that she's seen me like a little sister all these years. In the harsh, midmorning light, I get a good look at her. I'm eye level with the acne on her chin. Her yoga pants hug her thin legs. I remember Ms. Kang commenting about how her daughter sometimes forgets to eat when she's stressed. Her pink nail polish is chipping, and one nail's completely bare, as if she spent time nervously picking at it. She looks closer to my age. I'd forgotten we're only a year and a couple months apart.

Before I can stop it, the hideous Monte Verde competitive streak flares in me, a reflex like swatting around when you feel a fly buzzing by your ear. I twist my arm away from hers. "Don't worry about me. Worry about your Cal State Bartleby's boyfriend."

Camilla glances down at her hand I shrugged away. "Do you even hear yourself? I didn't peg you for being so narrow-minded to look down on someone like that, Perlie."

"I'm not—" I stop myself. Because to be honest, I did look down on him for it: for his silly uniform, for his not going to a top-tier school. Does that make me narrow-minded? I dig in my heels rather than poke at that uncomfortable new revelation that I, Perfect Perlie Perez, and this belief that my parents and I planned my whole future around, may be wrong. "Well, I bet your parents would love him. They have met him, right?"

I ask because I'm certain they haven't. Camilla's glower confirms that.

We call an unspoken cease-fire. She's not going to tell my parents that something seems off about my behavior, and I'm not going to tell hers that she's got a boyfriend.

Whether that means she's going to stop digging, I don't know for sure. I'll map this out via spreadsheet when I get to the dorms. It's the only way I can regain control of my spiraling life.

"Grow up, Perlie." Camilla turns to storm back to the Bubble and Bean, and I have nothing to say to her retreating form.

Ahead, the walk signal beckons me forward, and I take off, practically running, the employment forms in my hand flapping in the wind. However, as fast as I flee, as far as I get, I can't escape the storm cloud of concern over my head that Camilla Jansen-Kang, top 5 percent of the Monte Verde High School graduating class, daughter one of the most ruthless partners at Dad's firm, won't let this go that easily.

SEVENTEEN

The cursor blinks at the end of an unfinished line of words. How long had I been asleep in this bio lecture for?

I'm not the only one slogging through this morning's class. I glance down at the clock on my computer. Still fifteen minutes left. Unfortunately, I'm seated so far into the row that I wouldn't be able to escape without upending a handful of other sleepy students. I sink lower into my chair.

Tessa's already lost the battle against her late night. Her eyelids, dusted with a shimmery blue eyeshadow, lowered well before mine did and have stayed shut since. Her laptop's gone to sleep too, its black monitor reflecting her slumped-over image, hopefully blocking her from Professor Desai's line of sight.

Brand is still fighting. The pen in his hands dips as his chin does, and there's a pinch between his eyebrows like he's concentrating. His notes stop at the topic the professor discussed ten minutes ago.

Which reminds me to pretend to take notes, especially if

there's a chance he and Tessa are going to ask me later what they'd missed by snoozing. I clack at my keyboard, typing out what the professor says, word for word. I keep up with him as long as I can, but eventually, when my eyes refocus on my screen, a nonsensical cloud of words and punctuation fills the document. *Eukaryotic cells divide . . . Interphase? Three phases?*

Monte Verde High me would never take such poor notes. She'd probably revel in the fact that she took superior notes while others slacked off, thereby giving her the opportunity to get maybe one extra point above the others on a test graded on a curve.

"And a reminder that our first quiz is at the start of our next class," Professor Desai says, his voice a touch louder. "Ten multiple choice, two short answers. Ten percent of your grade."

The class collectively awakens. All eyes go to the TA now writing the quiz details on the whiteboard.

The professor smirks. "Don't look too surprised. It's on the syllabus. Now I know who hasn't read it."

A couple chuckles rumble throughout the auditorium but not enough to dispel the panic thickening like a fog around us.

Claws grip my left forearm. "What did he say? A quiz?"

Tessa's wide awake now. She scoots to the edge of her seat. I wriggle my arm out of her grip and point toward the whiteboard. I do my best to look as panicked as she is, to match the wide eyes and dropped jaw. We both type down the details from the whiteboard.

A tap on my right arm.

"Hey." A whisper like a wave. "My notes are a little . . . sparse."

Brand smirks and gestures down at his mostly blank notebook. "You free later? I could use some help piecing this together before I even attempt to study. Plus there's a gaming club meeting at seven tonight if you want to grab some free pizza and destroy folks at *Overwatch*."

I find myself nodding before he finishes speaking, as if my muscles are used to moving in a way that not only wants people to approve of me, but to gush over me. It's a good thing that the activities he suggested do sound interesting, especially the gaming club meeting. This could be my chance to get a larger view of Delmont life. It doesn't fit neatly into my part five "learn more about premed" goal because gaming is in no way related to my biological sciences major. But I've spent so much time simply trying to survive here that I haven't so much as written a sentence or two of my personal statement for my reapplication. I need to get moving on that, and this meeting could provide just the spark I'm hoping for.

"Yes to both," I say. "My notes could use some work too. Hopefully we were awake at different times. What about you, Tessa? You in?"

Tessa's eyebrow rises in a weird way. "No, thanks. You two go on without me. I have to touch up the color in my hair tonight."

Brand sets his pen on his notebook and inches it toward me. "Your number?"

He doesn't even hand me his phone like most people would. He wants me to write it down here, among his bio notes, like it's just as important. I scrawl down my phone number in the margins, concentrating on writing clear numbers instead of hearts and x's and o's.

"Ten percent of your grade," Professor Desai says, louder this time. He crosses his arms in punctuation. "No do-overs, no extra credit, no excuses short of a medical emergency."

More whispers sprout up around us as the anxiety ripples through the crowd. But me? I'm nervous for a different reason.

I have a gaming date with Brand tonight.

Tessa hops up and down so vigorously that I'd think she had the date, not me. Her gold hoop earrings swing from side to side, catching the sun. Her excitement's contagious, but I reach out a hand to stop her, in case someone, i.e., Brand, sees us. We'd barely made it outside before she broke out into her flailing, Muppet-like happy dance.

Tessa leans in. "I'm not even mad that you tried to invite me on your one-on-one study sesh. I'm more of lone wolf when it comes to studying anyway. You have to give me all the details afterward. And maybe whatever class notes I'm missing. Mostly the details of your little late-night study session though." She flicks her eyebrows up suggestively.

I roll my eyes, even though my ear-to-ear grin gives me away. "It's not going to be late-night. It's before dinner, at Molina Library. A very public place with lots of people around. Then it's at the student union for the gaming club general meeting. Also a very public place with lots of people around."

"Uh-huh, sure. Perfect cover."

The mention of "perfect" throws a shade of worry that darkens my mood. It isn't in my seven-part plan to find a boyfriend. With Tessa and the occasional dinner with Erin and Casper from down the hall, I've got enough friends to hit every task on my part three, "make a friend" tab. It's hard enough juggling lies between that many people and trying to balance the relief and guilt every time they buy one of my made-up stories. Getting close to yet another person is a bad idea, but Brand has insight into the gaming club and those classes for the Interactive Entertainment track that I might be able to sneak in as general education once Delmont accepts me. "Do you think I should cancel? My notes aren't that great."

Tessa's jaw drops almost as wide as it did when she heard about the quiz. "No way. You know this isn't about notes, right? Because he could've just asked you to email him. He wants to hang out with you."

I bring up a hand to shield my eyes from the sun, but really, it's to distract from the flush crawling up my cheeks. "You think so?"

It's Tessa's turn to roll her eyes. "I know so. It's obvious," Her face drops at the sight of my awkward half smile. "Oh, Perla. Oh no. Do you have those no-dating-till-you're-thirty kind of parents?"

"More like no-dating-till-you're-forty. I didn't even tell them there was a guy in my lunch group in high school. They would've been lurking in the bushes, with binoculars."

She snorts, then pauses, considering what I said. "You know, you don't ever really talk about your high school friends."

I shrug, a little sad that even though some of that is purposeful,

I don't have much to tell her about friends-wise. But above all of that is the slight terror at her noticing an omission in my back-story. "I didn't really keep in touch with any of them. I guess we weren't all that close."

To my surprise, Tessa nods, like she knows what I'm talking about. I would've pegged her for one of those people who keeps a close horde of friends everywhere she goes. "When I broke up with my ex, everyone I thought was my friend—well, turns out they were his friends instead."

"I'm sorry. I didn't—"

"Nah, don't worry about it, Perla. Timing worked out that I got to flee here to Delmont and leave them all in the dust. For me, this place is an opportunity." She throws an arm around my shoulders, as if physically taking me under her wing. "And, well, your parents aren't around here, and you're a card-carrying adult, damn it. You can do what you want. This place is opportunity for you too."

I laugh, even though she's completely wrong on that point. Being sixteen makes me a minor. And our views of Delmont as opportunity are very different. She sees this place as a door to a wide-open world full of possibilities. For me, it's a door to a narrow hallway, leading straight to doctordom.

But she's right on one thing: my parents aren't here, and I know I'm mature enough to manage my own social life. Thinking back on what I've accomplished in my short time here so far, I've made some good-hearted, non-cutthroat friends and even scored my first job. I can't imagine what Tessa or Brand would think if I pulled a "I have to ask my parents" for a study session.

Over the years, my parents have second-guessed or vetoed me on what careers I'm interested in, what outfits I wear to family parties, what size I should be. And usually, they won. But look where that's left me: on a campus of the dream school I'm not enrolled in. Maybe I should've been taking more control over my life all along. I've trusted them to steer me well so far, but now I'm ready to take the wheel.

My heartbeat accelerates, setting my course of action before my brain can catch up. I'm going to go on this study and gaming date, and I'm going to spend time with Brand. I'll find a way to work this into my seven-part plan.

Tessa and I make our way down the stone steps of building, weaving past the students streaming in. "You're heading to your English class next, right?"

Tessa groans, which I take as a yes. She swears her TA, a Henry David Thoreau–obsessed graduate student, is out to destroy her. I've encouraged the idea. It keeps the focus of our group dinners on something else other than me. "What about you?"

"Back to the dorms. I should fill in some of these notes so Brand and I actually have something to study."

Tessa slaps her hand on my shoulder. "Perla, a tip from someone more experienced: if all goes well, you won't be spending too much time studying."

On PicLine: my Introduction to Cellular and Molecular Biology textbook, open to the first page of chapter 3. Next to the textbook, a $5.25 iced coffee, with two pumps of sugar-free vanilla syrup.

Caption: All caffeinated and ready to go! #biology #premed #studying #coffee #Delmont

Twenty-four likes.

Comment from Brand_DW: Wait for me!

EIGHTEEN

B rand and I walk past the leather-bound series in the stacks, through the pillar-lined atrium, and under the high, painted dome on our way out of Molina Library. In the hour we spent going over our notes in one of the glass-walled study rooms in the basement, we covered the whole two weeks' worth of materials in impressive detail. If I was actually enrolled in bio, I wouldn't be worried about this first quiz at all.

I had plenty of group and partner projects back at Monte Verde High, but most of the guys I'd be thrown into academic dependency on weren't like Brand. He's teamwork, where they were sharp-edged rivalry. He's warmth and welcome, when they couldn't plow through these required team-ups fast enough so they could move on to the next assignment. I didn't mind most of the time—it's not like I wanted to spend any extra time with self-serving jerks—but being cozied up to academically, then ignored socially gets tiring.

Brand, on the other hand, didn't ditch me the second we

finished comparing notes. Then again, my social status at Delmont isn't as low on the ladder, and he has no clue how much younger I am.

As we studied, Brand spouted out information from the lecture that neither he nor I had written down. I'd kill for a memory as sharp as his.

His easy recall of facts and figures made me realize two things. First, this is why Delmont accepted him and maybe why they didn't accept me. He's the tree that belongs on top of the cliff, basking in the sun because he deserves it. Meanwhile, I, the side-of-the-cliff dweller, have to work harder for the chance at anything. Second, as Tessa had suspected, he probably never needed my notes at all. He can practically recite the professor's lectures for us.

It's this lingering mix of mortification and extreme flattery that flushes my cheeks when we finally step out of the library and into the warm evening air, where we can talk at a volume higher than whisper.

"Where to?" I ask as we descend the library steps.

Brand points across the expansive plaza, paved with bricks featuring alumni donor names. "Student union, right over there."

The student union is sleek glass and metal, a contrast from the stately brick buildings around it. It's like a futuristic portal to another world—one that can actually be *fun*, if I play my cards right with this gaming club.

As we near the student union and the possibility that I'll be able to figure out ways to keep this one joyful thing in my life, I find my pace quickening.

Not that I'm considering any careers other than medicine. Independence may be growing on me, but there still isn't room for huge revision or new pages in Perlie's Academic Plan. One night off won't hurt, nor will one or two Interactive Entertainment electives once I enroll here, or so I keep telling myself. Besides, if I ever needed an escape from the high-stress real world, it's right now, when I spend every other waking moment painstakingly crafting the "real" in Delmont Perla's world.

"So how are the rest of your bio sci classes going?" Brand asks, his thumbs tucked under his backpack straps.

My feet slow. I'd forgotten I told him my major, and I'd also been so engaged in scrambling to create bio outlines for the past few hours that this part of my cover story had been the furthest thing from my mind.

"They're okay. Interesting," I say, internally kicking myself. The evening had been going so well up until me having to fake my way through a conversation with someone who remembers every detail. I actually feel a little sorry that I have to lie to him. I'd been enjoying this new, friendly attention I've been getting, but I'd forgotten it was attention given to a facade. I want people to like me for me, but I can't even approach that yet, not with so much riding on the success of this Delmont Perla backstory. With a tinge of regret, I mentally reach for anything in my spreadsheet that can help me navigate this. "Fundamental Concepts of Chemistry!"

Brand side-glances at my outburst.

I drive the nervousness out of my voice. "I'm taking Fundamental Concepts of Chemistry. With Professor Lynch. No quizzes, but

I've heard horror stories about her midterm and final."

He nods, and I almost let out an audible sigh of relief that he bought that tidbit. "What about you?" I ask. "How's art?"

He opens the student union door. "Art is great. I just can't make any of it."

A wave of pizza smell hits me, and I enter the bright white student union open space. To our right is the Phoenix Tech Lounge, full of state-of-the-art computers, monitors, televisions, and beanbag chairs. According to a bronze plaque on the wall, it's all courtesy of an alumni donor, M. S. Phoenix, a name I instantly recognize as the person on the cover of one of the magazines in Mom's office: he turned his viral video Twitch fame into a multi-billion-dollar social media startup. Why did I think there wasn't any money in gaming again?

A guy in a Pac-Man shirt mans the check-in desk guarding the double doors to the Tech Lounge. "Welcome! Sign in. We'll put you on our mailing list so you can hear all about what our club's doing this year!"

Brand grabs a pen and scrawls down his name and, to my dismay, his school email address. I can't risk putting down my real name and the club getting a bounce-back when they find out Perla.Perez@delmont.edu does not exist. I decline the pen Brand offers to me next. "No, no, I'm just here to listen in."

Pac-Man takes the pen back and has the audacity to give me a smug "that figures" look, like I get from most boys when I say I game. They think I mean *Diner Dash* or *Candy Crush*, which are both extremely fun but somehow too lowbrow for the snootiest of gamers. I make it a point to join this club when I get into Delmont, then dash Pac-Man's gendered misconceptions to bits and crush his little ego.

The gameplay may be different, but I find the sensations the same. Whether a few minutes in between extracurriculars or a long evening while my parents schmooze at some professional gala, I've always loved the way I can immerse myself in a whole new world, with goals and skills vastly different than the ones I focus on in real life. I get the same joy from baking a wedding cake for a frazzled, hard-to-please couple that I do from solving the timed puzzle to enter the abandoned bunker before zombies descend on me. And in these venues, it's fine—maybe even expected—for the player to not get a perfect score on the first try.

"Go on in," Pac-Man says. "You can grab some pizza now but no eating or drinking at any of the machines."

As we stroll in, Brand's phone lets out a chime: a text message. He glances over to me, as if asking for permission. My parents always took their calls and texts, regardless of whether they were driving or in mid-conversation with me. Brand's thoughtfulness shoots an arrow into my heart. Death by crush attentiveness is something I'd be on board with.

"Go ahead," I say. "I'll check out the pizza offerings."

He focuses on his phone, and I head for the food. Two dozen people mill around a few tables piled high with pizza boxes and two-liters of soda. Nearby, a group chats about a summer coding camp, and a curvy white girl with blond pigtails and fashionably oversized pink glasses pours herself a soda. They move aside as I approach the table, making space for me.

"If you don't like bell peppers, stay away from the veggie," the girl warns with a wink. "It's like ninety percent bell peppers."

"Thanks." Not even a question about who I am or what I think I'm doing here. Just a helpful tip and a scoot a couple inches to the side so I can reach the stack of cheese pizzas.

"Hey, you want to go to a party?" Brand asks.

I peer behind me, straight into his eager eyes, then down to the open cheese pizza box. The pizza's so greasy I think I can almost see my reflection in it. My mouth waters. "When?"

"Right now. My friend Jimmy got a keg and a bunch of friends are coming over. I know him from high school; he'd be cool with me bringing you. His apartment's a block from campus. Want to go?"

Years of conditioning have me opening my mouth to say no, but I snap it shut. Perfect Perlie Perez would say no. Even if an extracurricular club meeting is in a field her parents frown upon, she would insist on staying. She'd probably raise her hand to ask about low-commitment opportunities to get involved and beef up her résumé.

That's not who I'm trying to be anymore, I tell myself, especially because Delmont didn't admit that Perfect Perlie Perez for some reason or another. Something in me still holds back anyway. I want to be the smart, easygoing girl that Brand thinks I am, but I've been looking forward to this gaming club meeting. Also, the main reason I'm here at Delmont is to learn about the premed track and get the inside scoop on how everyone got in, not how they plan on spending their nights once they get here. And I suspect secrecy and first-time alcohol consumption are a bad mix.

I must take a second too long to respond because Brand pockets his phone and makes the decision for me. "No pressure. Let's eat and stay for the meeting, then see how we're feeling."

He grabs a paper plate and introduces himself to a few people nearby as if we hadn't been interrupted by his friend's text at all. I don't know if I imagine disappointment in the more serious tone of his voice or the way his body seems to always face a little away from mine, but I get the distinct feeling that I came to a fork in the road of what kind of version of me I want to portray, and I took a wrong turn.

When the meeting starts, we grab seats on beanbags next to each other, and the girl with the pigtails pulls a short stool up to perch next to me.

"Was I right about the bell peppers, or was I right?" she whispers.

I laugh, keeping it quiet to avoid disrupting the gaming club president calling the meeting to order at the front of the room. "You called it. Thanks for the heads-up. I wasn't ready to become a resident of Bell Pepper Town."

She grins. "I'm Claire. It's my second year in this club, and I'm more than happy to see another feminine-presenting person in here. Welcome."

"Thanks. It's really packed in here," I say, motioning to the group milling by the door, looking for seats. "Is this normal?"

"For the first meeting of the year? Yeah. It'll taper off a little as the semester picks up, but there's still a lot of people." She angles forward then and waves at Brand. "Jimmy said you'd be here!"

He waves back.

"You coming over after the meeting, Brand?" Then she focuses on me. "You should totally come too, Perla! It's my boyfriend's party, and I finally convinced him to serve something other than chips at these gatherings."

It somehow feels worse having to decline both Claire and Brand, like the pressure to say yes—even when my gut tells me no—is doubled, but the gaming club president saves me from answering.

"Hey, all you in the back. There's a few seats up here, in the front," he practically yells from the front. "Don't be shy."

We let our attention drift to the president again as a couple more students squeeze past us. The president talks about what that the gaming club has in store for the year: tournaments, career nights, volunteer events. The room continues to fill up—no wonder Delmont saw the need for an Interactive Entertainment major—and some quick introductions reveal that the members are a mix of casual players to competitive trophy winners. Someone mentions a possible opening for a temporary quality-assurance gig, and he instantly becomes the most popular person in the room.

With every spurt of laughter, every friendly challenge, every bite of free pizza, I find myself feeling more comfortable in this beanbag chair. This may not be where my career is headed, but it's wonderful to find a space where, for once, I feel like I can belong. Where I can grow as Perla, and not be frozen in place, as Perfect

Perlie Perez.

No, my brain automatically corrects me, *Delmont Perla isn't even a real person yet. You have to get in first, Perlie.*

My muscles tense, my carefree mood spoiled. But this shadow on my evening renews my drive to open my personal statement document later tonight. I came here to this meeting for a spark, and now my goals are shining so bright I need sunglasses.

I see now what Tessa meant about this place representing opportunity. I'm almost giddy at the realization I can not only pursue the doctor dream my parents and I have been working so hard toward, but also join this fun gaming community. My parents won't have to know about the extracurriculars as long as I keep up with my bio sci degree.

I worry that, all this time, I've been trapped in a snow globe by other people's musts and shoulds, expected to be serene and beautiful even when upended. Each new challenge is a shake, throwing pieces of my world up in the air like little fake snowflakes: skip a grade, start high school early, find time or energy for another class or extracurricular. People like to marvel at the snow falling, forgetting that others' lives aren't there for them to gawk at, that sometimes pretty things break.

Sitting here, among so many intelligent, like-minded people, I realize that I don't have to be trapped. A world exists outside of my snow globe, and every action I take doesn't have to have a "point," as my parents have always emphasized. They've worked so hard to keep me on this path to being a doctor, at the expense of almost everything else that brings me joy or relaxation, and I stumbled off it anyway.

An hour later, we reach the end of the pizza and the meeting. Brand thanks me for my help studying earlier before heading out. One look around tells me Claire's left early.

I notice that Brand doesn't repeat the invitation to Jimmy's, but it doesn't bother me as much as I thought it would. If I thought I'd get my ultimate rebel-against-my-parents thrill from pursuing an older boy crush, I was wrong: turns out the defiant streak in my heart tends toward flashy graphics and bright-buttoned controllers.

NINETEEN

I grab a sugary energy drink from the vending machine outside of the bio auditorium. It's as hungry for my scarce quarters as I am for caffeine.

Energized from the gaming club meeting, I'd stayed up too late last night brainstorming ideas for my personal statement. Then I retooled my seven-part plan spreadsheet based on what I've learned about Delmont and the people here.

As I wait for the vending machine to deliver me my energy drink, I drum my fingers against my legs, the motion much like when I typed up Claire's info and the gaming club notes at one in the morning. Starting off yet another promising friendship on a lie grates me enough, but trying to explore an activity and join a community that I actually really like? It's starting to feel like some of the lying I'm doing is to myself. Without any answers to my post-midnight musings, I'd clicked to another tab and mulled over some of the unforeseen scenarios that have reared their heads instead.

One of the most concerning is my lack of money. To survive on campus—or anywhere, really—I'm going to need to eat, and I'd prefer not to rely on the fragile relationships I've started cultivating for this basic, recurring need. More lies mean more of this guilt that's been seeping into edges of my conscience during quiet moments lately. They also mean more opportunities to get caught.

That fear spurred me to then spend another hour perfecting my employment forms for the Bubble and Bean. The sooner I get these in, the sooner I can start work.

Mimicking my parents' signatures was the easy part. Coming up with a fake school contact was a little trickier: I set up a phone number on a free online service and route the calls to my cell phone. If Frank wanted to check up on my details, he'd reach me and not a school administrator, and I'd be ready for him.

I dropped off my paperwork on the way to bio this morning, and the long walk to class gave time for my frustration with my financial situation to teeter into more guilt. People have real hardships that prevent them from going to exorbitantly priced colleges like Delmont. My parents have not only saved enough for a private university education for me, but for medical school too. Unfortunately, there's no way for me to access any of it without making myself part of Delmont's next incoming class.

I sip at my newly purchased energy drink and let the bubblegum-flavored sugar rinse away the bitterness of my night.

Brand and Tessa are seated by the time I make my way down the auditorium aisle. We barely have time to exchange hellos before the professor starts talking.

"The TAs are passing out the quizzes now. You'll have fifteen minutes."

I cast a simulation of a nervous smile at Tessa. I know her test anxiety runs deep. A line of light peeked out from under her door at three in the morning, when I've scheduled my showers so I'm not running into the RA. She must've been up studying. With her carefree manner and penchant for sleeping in class, I wouldn't have pegged her as such a hard-core academic, but then again, I guess that's what it takes to get into this school without a legacy leg up. She and everyone else in this auditorium have something in them that I don't. I've barely managed to piece together what that extra something is, except for the suspicion that maybe I don't have it after all. The thought leaves a taste worse than warm energy drink in my mouth.

But I know I'm getting there. I'll be part of their Delmont ranks soon enough.

I take one quiz handout and pass the rest down. Pens scratch and click against paper all around me. I, the least worried person in this room, lean over my own quiz. There's an odd thrill to being in the middle of this quiet auditorium, like I've infiltrated some cult.

The questions don't seem too difficult. I try my hand at answering them—what do I have to lose? The fifteen minutes fly by.

"Okay, writing utensils down. Pass your papers to the middle."

All around, dozens of backs collectively unhunch, and pens drop onto desks like they're on fire.

"No talking please," a TA calls out. "Not until all the papers are in."

The stack's thick by the time Tessa passes it to me. I slide my nameless quiz into the middle and hand it to the next person. My quiz relays down to the end of the row and disappears into the larger stack in the TA's hands.

Tessa nudges me with her elbow. "What'd you think?"

I take in the bags under her eyes, the flat line of her lips. Part three of my plan, making a friend, flits through my mind. This is an opportunity to ingratiate myself more with Tessa by being a good shoulder to cry and commiserate on. At Monte Verde High, I would've blurted something along the lines of the quiz being a breeze if you'd studied. But here, when I'm trying to be a friend and not a competitor? "A couple curveballs in there, right?"

Her face softens like I've said just the right thing to soothe her anxious heart. I give myself a mental high five for a job well done: my friendship with Tessa solidifies more with each hangout, which is helpful under part three, and I've gotten my first quiz under my belt, a win under part five. My knowledge of Delmont—and my comfort here—has grown by the day. At this point, I'm almost excited to get back to the dorm to shoot out a personal statement draft.

It could be the high levels of sugar in my blood, but I'm near giddy as the professor begins his lecture.

At the side of the room, the TAs are splitting the quiz papers between themselves based on the *Discussion Section* line that I'd left blank. My paper is in there somewhere, and they'll simply think a frazzled student neglected to fill out their info, so stressed were they.

I pull out my laptop and settle into my chair, the thin cushioning molding around me like I belong in this seat. This is the first time I really, truly, don't care about a failing grade, and it's intoxicating.

The energy drink isn't enough to keep me awake the full hour, and I doze off, my face obscured from Professor Desai's view by the football players in front of me.

I'm back in fifth grade, in Mrs. Spencer's class. My shoes are brand-new, a size too big, and the girl next to me reeks of fruit punch, like she got into her sister's scented lotions stash. Mrs. Spencer hands me my graded math test from Tuesday.

"Remember, any grades D or lower must be signed by a parent and shown to me by the end of the week," she announces to the class as she walks by, "or I'll be calling home to discuss it with them directly."

Odd that she gives that reminder now. It's never applied to me before. She moves on to the fruit-punch girl and pulls another test out of her folder.

I have a bad feeling before I even turn the paper over to see my grade. The red ink that bleeds through the back doesn't form the familiar shapes of As or Bs.

I flip it to find red ink all over. We're learning the order of operations in math, and I'd gotten confused and started adding before multiplying. The tears come to my eyes almost immediately, but I manage to swipe them away with my sleeve before anyone sees me. That same red ink that formed so many "nice works" and "good jobs" looks so sinister in the shape of a D.

D as in division, which, with multiplication, is supposed to come before addition and subtraction.

D, as in Dad, who sighs when I show him and says I should show Mom too.

D as in disappointment, the look on Mom's face when she gets home after dinner, still in her gray shift dress and taking leftover pasta out of the fridge, and sees the test waiting for her signature.

Dad tells her he's already looked into math tutors and that I can start as soon as next week. I know for a fact that he hasn't, because we've spent every moment together since we got home, but I keep quiet. They float the idea of me dropping piano lessons to make time for the tutoring because piano doesn't seem to be my calling anyway. Mom puts her palms on her eyes, smudging her eyeliner, before grabbing a pen from her purse. Neither addresses me directly.

She signs the test hastily, then slides it to me across the cold island countertop. "Don't ever do this to me again."

I don't know what she means—it's not like I got the answers wrong on purpose—but I know better than to argue. I take my signed paper upstairs as she and Dad continue to murmur about me over cold fusilli.

"Don't ever do this to me again" burns into my brain.

So I don't ever do it again. I go to the tutoring. I do the extra work. I insist I drop piano so I can focus on other activities, not saying a word about how I thought I was actually getting better at it.

And I learn to forge their signatures.

TWENTY

My phone buzzes in my shorts pocket while my arms are full of laundry. I dump the load into my flimsy collapsible laundry basket, then simultaneously scramble to answer my phone and snatch up the underwear that landed on the lint-dusted floor.

"Hi, Mom." I tuck the phone between my ear and my shoulder and reach for the next wad of hot clothes from the dryer.

In my other shorts pocket clink the laundry quarters I've scavenged from everywhere: the floors of the dorms and dining halls, even unattended fountains across campus. Having clean clothes is going to be luxurious as much as it's necessary: Frank called to tell me my first Bubble and Bean shift is Monday.

Who would've thought I'd be this glad to be doing laundry on a Saturday afternoon?

"What's that noise, Perlie? Where are you?"

"Basement. Laundry room."

"Wow, my little girl, washing her own clothes." Mom laughs, and the sound makes me miss her. And not only because she and

Dad always took care of the laundry. Her words hold a hint of affection—she said "*my* little girl"—and pride, and I soak it up like a parched sponge. "Did you separate the light from the dark colors? Use cold water for the darker load?"

I tug out a handful of dark clothing and grayed whites, shaking my head at Mom's micromanaging from hundreds of miles away. "I do have access to the internet, Mom. Laundry isn't that hard."

I grimace at the red-spotted First Cal-Am Bank T-shirt, thankful she's not here to see the clear evidence against me. This mess-up isn't because I wasn't thorough. It's because I didn't want to waste the quarters for two loads.

"So what's up?"

"We just wanted to see how you're doing. You don't call us enough. How are your classes?"

Care, criticism, then straight on to business. I'm annoyed, but not surprised, at the speed through which she cycled through that first part.

"I had my first quiz. Bio."

"And how'd you feel about it?"

"Great." An honest answer.

"Good, good. Dr. Jansen said that Camilla's doing well. Loves her classes. She's joined some student government committee. Have you joined anything?"

I clench my jaw. "Nope. Concentrating on academics for now."

"Excellent. We're expecting all As on that report card."

I snort. "Parents don't get a copy of our grades in college." They especially won't get one from a college I'm not even enrolled in.

She is undeterred. "You can send us a copy or a screenshot, then. What are you doing next weekend? We want to visit!"

The blood drains from my face, and I'm paler than the free shirt in my hands. My hand goes nervously to my heart pendant, needing to expend some of this busy energy. "I . . . next weekend's not good."

"What about the weekend after? Your dad settled a matter that was supposed to go to trial, so we have some free time finally."

A dryer next to me buzzes. A girl who's been lounging in the corner with a magazine and oversized headphones strides over.

"Hold on, Mom." I set the phone down on the counter next to me.

I pile the rest of my clothes into my laundry basket and pull them out of the girl's way. I don't care that some of them are still damp against my fingertips. My mind shoots to my seven-part plan spreadsheet tab for part four: figure out excuses for parents so they won't show up at my door. Hiding my dorm squatting from Genia the RA has been hard enough. But hiding my parents from her and all my neighbors? I can't exactly ask them to climb up a tree to my second-floor room.

I pick up the phone again. "Sorry, someone else's laundry was finished. Had to move out of the way." The truth gives me time to piece together what I remember from my spreadsheet and pray it's a passable excuse. "The next couple weekends aren't good for me. I joined this college success mentorship program. I'm spending the next few Saturdays lunching with a fourth-year."

"You just said you didn't join anything." Mom's voice goes

steely.

"Not any social stuff like Camilla," I say, casting a silent apology into the world for throwing her under the bus with my excuse, "This is academic. I figured I should take advantage of whatever resources are available to me, being younger than everyone."

I prey on my parents' soft spot: my age. As much as they have pushed me to succeed and basked in my shared spotlight, they get fiercely protective any time someone hints I may have a disadvantage. This, of course, doesn't fit perfectly with the fact that they themselves seem to think I have the emotional maturity of a grade-schooler. But it must hit differently when someone outside the family criticizes me for something my parents are already raw about.

Suddenly, I wonder if this isn't so much about me as it is about them not wanting to be seen as wrong or as bad parents for letting their not-ready daughter skip a few grades ahead. Like the way they've shaped my school schedules and extracurriculars so far: How much of me has been based on what reflects well on them? The question stings, but I don't have an answer for it. No wonder this feeling of independence feels so fresh and new: I might've not ever had it before.

"What a smart idea, Perlie," Dad says, and Mom mm-hmms in agreement. "Seeking out help like that is very mature of you."

I know, even though this mentorship program doesn't exist. Great idea though. For a moment, I feel proud of myself: it was easier for me to take control of a conversation with my parents this time, even if it was through a lie. Dictating the terms of engagement with them isn't something Perfect Perlie Perez could ever do.

It's always been their way or the highway. Delmont Perla seems to be more independent and self-assured when it comes to them: my parents are just people, and the existence of Delmont Perla is proof that I can handle people. I'll pat myself on the back later when I'm folding laundry in my room.

The thought of the mundane tasks ahead, along with the unexpected grilling from Mom, drains me. Speaking to my parents right now feels like getting called on to give a progress report. I count my remaining laundry change as Mom tells me about some family party I'm missing out on.

"I've got to get going now, Mom. Say hi to everyone for me. I'm going to watch some YouTube videos on how to fold this stuff."

"Have fun."

"You do know I'm doing laundry, right?"

We both laugh, and then she goes and ruins it. "One last thing: you haven't sent me your class schedule yet. I've asked for it twice."

My jaw tightens again. I'd purposefully refrained from sending the schedule. Some part of me was hoping my parents would trust college me enough to let me chart my own academic course. The other part of me didn't want them to have more physical evidence of these lies I've concocted. "Sorry. I'll send it later."

"Send it now. I can show it to Auntie Silvie at the party and see if that Delmont graduate in her office has any tips."

"I have to go."

"But the class list—"

"I said I have to go."

The words come out brusque, which is rare for me, but I'm too disappointed in their doubts to cut back on the rudeness. For all they know, I haven't given them any reason to think I'm not doing exactly as we've planned.

A long pause follows. If I listen hard enough, I could probably hear a hairline crack start in their hearts at the way their little girl is pulling back from them. But part of me doesn't care. They're practically the reason I'm here in the first place.

Now that I think of it, if we lived in a world in which the Perfect Perezes weren't always on display, then maybe I wouldn't be in this mess. Maybe I could've talked to them about getting rejected from Delmont or listened when our high school counselor suggested applying to more safety schools, ones that don't headline some published list but would still be good for me.

"Fine," Mom says finally. "But you still owe us that class list."

Of course we'd end with a reminder of just how much I owe them.

Back in my room, I end up just shoving everything back in my suitcase. The energizing triumph of doing this adult thing for myself is gone, ground to ash by one conversation with my parents. Plus, folding is hard. Almost as hard as keeping my own lies straight in the middle of one simple phone call with my mom. I add details on the fake mentorship program into my spreadsheet, the one ultra-neat representation of my increasingly messy existence, then curl up for a nap on my warm but slightly damp bedsheets. The heart pendant digs into the skin of my chest from where I rest on it too heavily, but I'm too tired to move. I fall asleep and dream of the family party I'm not invited to, my parents telling everyone about their Perfect Premed Perlie.

TWENTY-ONE

"Brown sugar bubble tea, for Carlo," I call out into the shop as I set the plastic cup on the counter. "Carlo!"

"Perla, it's Carla, with an 'a,'" Jackson says from the register.

I blink at the chicken-scratch handwriting on the cup, and sure enough, there's a teensy mark that turns that "o" into an "a."

Rookie mistake. My cheeks redden. "Sorry. Carla? Carla, brown sugar bubble tea."

A girl in a Delmont hoodie and white earbuds strolls up and takes the drink. She focuses more on her phone than on me, and she doesn't even acknowledge my error or respond to my "Have a nice day!"

"I am so, so sorry," I say again, this time to Jackson, as the bells above the door chime at Carla's exit. "I'll do better."

At ten in the morning, the Bubble and Bean is less than at its busiest. The office-worker rush died down around nine thirty, and Jackson said more people are thinking about lunch than a second caffeine push right now, so luckily not too many people witnessed my flub. In fact, I'm pretty sure the curly-haired woman in the high-backed chair has been asleep behind her sunglasses for the past half hour. Still, I have no interest in getting fired a couple hours into my first shift for poor customer service.

Jackson flashes me a carefree smile that clashes with how on edge I am. "Take it easy. You'll get the hang of this, new girl."

I hadn't expected such quick kindness, and I loosen the shoulders that had subconsciously tensed. After checking in with Frank this morning and fudging my way through a couple more HR forms, I spent the first two hours cleaning, observing how the teacup sealing machine worked, and learning how to brew and pour plain drip coffee. Only after all the tables were wiped down and milk-and-sugar stations spotless was I promoted to sleeving, sealing, and announcing drink orders Jackson had made. And I'd already messed up.

I'll take all the kindness I can get. My presence at the Bubble and Bean and at Delmont depends on this kindness, or at least indifference, of those around me. The intense fear of discovery waned after these first couple of weeks here, though I worry it won't ever be completely gone, even after I get admitted for real.

It turns out people are more interested in themselves than in me. As long as I play nice and blend in—the art of which being Monte Verde High's Perfect Perlie Perez made me a master—everyone willingly accepts me into their lives and spaces. I developed a routine of going to my bio class with Brand and Tessa, occasionally dining with Tessa and whoever else she's gathered together from our dorm, chowing down on free pizza at gaming club gatherings, and avoiding Camilla and Genia the RA entirely. If I don't diverge too much from the Delmont Perla character I've carefully curated, they have no reason to ask any deeper questions.

Now I just have to keep this up for a few more months until I'm a student here for real. The tension in my shoulders ratchets up at the thought.

Jackson laces his hands in front of him and stretches out his back. "You want to try your hand at taking the next order? The cash register isn't complicated, and I could use a break from the insipid smiling."

The corner of my mouth quirks up. "'Insipid'? Are you taking the SATs or something?"

He moves aside as I take the spot in front of the register. "Har-har. I'll have you know that I have an extensive vocabulary. I just don't get to use it that much here. The only word over three syllables here is 'macchiato.'"

I peer up at the chalky, embellished menu above our heads. "There's also 'Americano.'"

He snorts. "You college kids think you know everything."

Jackson guides me through ringing up the next customer, then starts on her milk tea. There's no one else in line, so I grab a brown-spotted rag, remembering Frank's penchant for extreme cleanliness, and start mopping up a warm puddle of creamy whole milk.

"Big words sound out of place in most conversation." I smile, even as an unwelcome memory of behind-my-back whispering crowds my mind.

I learned the hard way my freshman year of high school that using big words did not in fact make me sound older. Instead, it reminded everyone how much younger I was than them. As if I thought being a dictionary would somehow distract them from the fact that I had only recently been allowed to watch PG-13 movies on my own.

"You could have said 'boring' or even 'tedious' instead. People on TV say 'tedious,' right?"

Jackson glances at me, his hands not slowing in their milk tea process. "You an English major or something?"

"No, biological sciences. Preparing for med school."

"Ah, very goatlike of you."

I still the swirl of my rag. "Excuse me?"

"Goat. Capricorn. You said you're a January birthday." He slides the plastic cup of tea to me to seal and announce.

Once the customer picks up their milk tea, Jackson continues. "Capricorns are very goal-oriented. That seems to describe you to a T."

A defensiveness flares in me. "Being goal-oriented isn't a bad thing."

I shut my mouth once I hear the unintended attitude that flowed out with those words. He's the boss's son, and I have to remind myself that he's not poking fun at Perfect Perlie Perez. He doesn't even know that version of me exists. He's talking to easygoing, laugh-it-off Delmont Perla. I relax my pinched face and finish wiping down the countertop. "And what about you? What symbol represents a Sagittarius? A jackass?"

He smirks. "An archer. We're more truth- and idea-seeking. Wanderers. Speaking of which, wander back over to the cash register. You've got a customer." He leans to his right, to peer over me at the customer. "She'll be with you in a moment, miss."

I set down the rag and wipe my hands off on my apron as I stroll up to cash register.

"Welcome to Bubble and Bean. How . . ."

The words wither on my lips. The customer is Camilla.

"Hey again." Her perfectly plucked eyebrows knit together as she takes in my green apron, my name tag.

"Hey."

A pointed cough from Jackson.

"How can I help you?" I finish.

Her eyes drift up to the menu. "I'll have a small nonfat latte. Please."

I dip my head to focus on the register and punching in her drink details, but mainly to avoid eye contact. I'm not, and haven't been, interested in further conversation with Camilla after our last disaster of a run-in where she picked apart my lies and I dug at her about her secret boyfriend. Unfortunately, my efforts to avoid her have worked possibly too well, if it's driven her to horn in on my newly earned Bubble and Bean turf. The sooner I can shoo her out of here, the better. "Got it. You can pick up your drink at the end of the counter."

For a moment, Camilla doesn't budge. She opens her mouth, as if she wants to say something, to talk more. I use every free wish I have left in the universe to will her away. Her jaw shuts, and she walks toward the drink pickup area. I don't miss the glance she throws back at me, the kind that tells me she wants to talk. This can't be good.

"What was her name?"

It takes me a second to notice Jackson's talking to me.

"Who?"

"The customer. The one who ordered this latte."

I shake my head to clear the fog. "Oh, Camilla. Camilla Kang-Jansen. We went to high school together. Our parents are friends."

Jackson rolls his eyes. "I don't need her life story, new girl. You didn't write it on the cup. You just need to tell her her drink's ready."

I force a chuckle, even though I'm still shaken by her unnerving gaze. "Sorry."

"Stop apologizing. You're learning. It's okay."

"Thanks." I take the cup from him, again grateful at the kindness and, to my surprise, a little guilty. It's been refreshing how he hasn't expected me to be perfect, to know everything from the second I walked in, to execute it all flawlessly. And I'm lying to him.

It's necessary, I tell myself, forcing that guilt down. Without this job, I can't hope to stick around Delmont long enough for my spring-semester application to gain me acceptance.

Keep it together, Perla.

I call out her name, and Camilla strides up to the counter and picks up her coffee. She lingers, her eyes intense on mine.

"You have a minute? I just wanted to check on you."

The "I'm fine" I give is more of a reflex than a truth. It's from years of answering my parents' "How are yous," for which "I'm fine" is the only acceptable, sufficiently grateful answer.

She lowers her voice. "I've been thinking more about your financial situation."

I knew she wouldn't let our earlier conversation go, but it's a relief to confirm that she only believes I didn't get scholarships. She hasn't yet suspected that I didn't get into Delmont at all, and I'd like to keep it that way.

"Thanks, but I'm all set. With this job, and, you know, loans."

"But are you sure you're not taking on too much?"

My legs weaken. Her words strike too close to a truth I've been ignoring. Because I know I'm taking on too much, between the seven-part plan and the trying to stay afloat, but painting a smile over it is all I know how to do. "Yeah," I say weakly, "I'm only here a couple days a week anyway."

"I'm just having trouble believing that your parents can't afford to send you here without you working. A partner at a law firm and a doctor with her own practice? That can't be all there is to the story."

The blood drains from my face, and I'm suddenly all too aware that Jackson, functionally my boss, is feet away, grinding more coffee beans.

"Not here, Camilla." The whisper comes out harsh, so I soften it with a "please."

She follows my gaze over to Jackson, then nods at me in understanding. "All right. I don't know what's going on, but call me if you need to. Okay? Even if it's only to get coffee and talk. I meant what I said about helping."

The genuineness in her voice cracks something in me. The last time we'd spoken, I'd essentially threatened to out her secret boyfriend to her parents, and she's still willing to help? Where was this sisterly sentiment when we were back at Monte Verde?

I start to wonder then if it was always there, and I was the one who chose not to see it.

It's all I can do to shove away the sudden, overwhelming feeling of loneliness. I can't go back in time to fix anything. And what would there even be to fix? I did everything right, didn't I?

"I'm good, Camilla. Thanks for coming in." There's a hurried gratitude in my words now because the coffee grinder has stopped.

Jackson's peering over with an "everything okay?" kind of look, and I think he's gearing up to get into manager mode and stomp over here to intervene.

"Talk to you soon, Perlie." Camilla takes a sip of her coffee and throws a ten-dollar bill into the tip jar.

The bells above the door ring hollow when she leaves.

TWENTY-TWO

I yawn on my way down the hallway to my room. It's almost midnight after my fourth closing shift at the Bubble and Bean, and from my month sneaking in and around the residence halls, I've calculated that getting spotted climbing up into my room is far riskier at this time of night than just speed-walking straight through Keith Hall. People may be awake, but they're distracted. Turned-up video games and movies echo. Muffled frustration floats out of Genia the RA's room as I tiptoe past. Tessa's lights are out.

My mind is already on what additions I need to make to my personal statement. I've dedicated almost every night this week to coming up with an impressive, or at least workable, draft. The first few drafts felt too vague and impersonal, even with the added knowledge from my bio class and classmates. I've been striving to weave in more specific, personal detail about myself, as Raj the application coach would've wanted, and connect why I am a perfect fit for Delmont's bio sci program and vice versa. Then, during tonight's shift, I had the extreme luck of having a few bio sci fourth-years come into the Bubble and Bean to commiserate about medical school and internship applications and tests, and I got to listen in on their conversation while I wiped down tables.

After I jot down my notes from eavesdropping, I'll pull up my spreadsheet and review what I've got left to accomplish on my plan, which I do every night, like some boring adult version of a bedtime story. I'll log whatever blurred truths I've told and to whom, as well as any notes on professors or classes I should take or avoid when I'm enrolled here for real, based on what I've gleaned from my new friends. Delmont Perla lives in this plan. It's what I'd be doing, who I should've been had I gotten an acceptance rather than a rejection months ago. My day doesn't feel complete unless I've opened and closed the spreadsheet. It sends me off to sleep with the growing confidence that Delmont Perla is and will be a reality.

Thinking of which tab to open first, I push at my door with my fingertips.

It doesn't budge.

I could've sworn I taped the latch so that the lock wouldn't engage.

My muscles preemptively ache at the thought of heading back outside and scaling that tree.

Finding an empty shower stall to stow my thousand-pound backpack in, I tug the hood of my blue-and-green Delmont University hoodie up and over my head to provide some cover. Yawning again, I head back outside to climb up to my room.

The crunch of leaves under my feet sounds louder at night, and I hold my breath—as if that's what would draw attention—as I slip past open windows. After a minute of struggle, I'm perched outside my second-floor window. I'd made a habit of purposely leaving the window a barely noticeable half inch ajar for this exact unreliable-tape scenario. I tug the lip of the window to slide it open.

It doesn't move either.

Oh no. Maybe I'd locked it in my hurry to make it to bio this morning.

I remember leaving it cracked open though. I'd worried about whether a squirrel could fit in through that sliver of space. I didn't want to come back to a tree-rodent-infested room.

I wonder if anyone would hear me if I broke the glass.

But one look with my face pressed up against the pane tells me that breaking in would be useless. Even in the dark, I can tell my room is not as I'd left it.

It's completely bare.

Someone has stripped the ivory sheets off my bed. They confiscated the economics textbook and my mug of free pens that I'd dared to leave on my desk. They ripped the schedules and syllabi that I'd tacked up to make the room feel more homey. My multicolor pushpins are gone too. I think I spy a lone pink one on the floor, the only evidence that this was my room at all.

A wave of dizziness washes over me so hard that I almost fall out of the tree. Someone found my room while I was on campus and at the Bubble and Bean today, and they cleared out almost everything Delmont Perla owns. Not that it was much, thanks to my purposefully spare packing, but everything that isn't on me or in my backpack is gone.

My fingers fly immediately to my neckline. At least I hadn't left this heart necklace in the room. I don't always wear it because it can look a little outdated and flashy, but Mom would never forgive me for losing a family heirloom.

My limbs trembling, I make my way down from the tree. I mentally take stock of what I'd left, ensuring nothing had a name or, God forbid, my parents' address written inside. However, I can't say, with certainty, that I hadn't left a trace of who I am. I can't even remember if my suitcase had an old luggage tag on it.

With my feet solidly on the ground, I peer up at the room that Perla Perez can no longer live in. Whoever cleared it may have my name and may be watching the door as we speak. I need to find somewhere else to stay.

I barely make it back to the shower stall before the tears spill out of my eyes. My Delmont hoodie sleeve rubs my cheeks raw as I try to dry them.

I grip the heart pendant hard. For a second, a childish part of me rears its head and almost wishes I had Mom and Dad here to tell me it's all right, that they'll fix this. But is the comfort worth their anger? After the tense way we left our last conversation, I don't know. The distance between us is too great and growing. They're home, being their perfect, successful selves, and I'm here, crying in a damp dorm bathroom. Loneliness might be a rare side effect of independence.

I can't believe I'd let myself get so comfortable in Keith Hall. I should have kept moving. I shouldn't have left my stuff lying around. But I made friends on this floor. How am I going to explain this sudden eviction to Tessa? More lies, I realize sadly, further complicating the messiness that our friendship sprouted from.

It's almost one o'clock now, and the sounds of night-owl activity outside have softened. I've cried so much I feel almost dehydrated, my mouth dry and sticky. I unlock the shower stall door and wash my face in the cold water of the faucet.

I can't let myself get overwhelmed. I need to come up with a plan to find a new room as soon as possible.

I have nowhere else to go.

I stare at myself in the mirror, willing my face to stop looking so damn sad.

Come on, Perla. You can do this. You hid for a whole month. You can do it for a few more.

Then, in spring, you'll be a real Delmont student and you'll never have to hide again.

The residence-hall front-desk attendants start at eight in the morning. I have time to burn until I can listen in for any room changes or building transfers.

I retreat back to the shower stall and lock the door behind me. The light of my laptop screen gleams like the gates of heaven. According to the housing tab of my seven-part plan spreadsheet, the closest alternative for the night is a storage room in the basement. I take the stairs, ignore the goose bumps on my arms as I trudge down into silence and dim light, weave past stacked bed frames and desks, and choose a dusty corner farthest from the door.

Something skitters nearby as I tug a mattress off a pile and drag it to my corner. I don't even want to think about what else has made residence in this room.

With my backpack as a makeshift pillow, I ball myself on the bare mattress. I fall into a fitful sleep.

Then, in the morning, before the maintenance people arrive, I grab my bag and walk out of Keith Hall without a destination.

TWENTY-THREE

Dad picks a heck of a time to call: 7:40 a.m., on a Saturday. As if he's testing me to make sure I wasn't out partying.

I answer. "You're up early."

"On my way to the office. Opposing counsel sent a demand after hours last night. Can you believe the sneakiness of that?"

"Ouch," I respond, mostly because it seems like the right response given the how-dare-they tone in his voice.

"Anyway, I just wanted to see how you're doing, Perlie."

I sigh, trying to put a positive, believable spin on anything. I'm on the benches by the library, clutching my one backpack of belongings. I have to keep my voice low so the few sleepy folks trudging between buildings don't hear me.

Ten minutes later, we've gone over my classes, and he's expressed disappointment, yet again, that they haven't gotten my schedule or visited me on campus.

"That's great to hear that you were able to find a used textbook after all," Dad says in response to the intricate story I'd just relayed about my bargain hunting for my fake math course materials. I get lauded on two fronts: academics and smart consumerism. "How are you on money?"

I readjust my hoodie as a breeze brushes through the leaves of the trees overhead. It's as if the world is determined to be serene when there's a storm thrashing around inside me.

I tell myself to refocus on the plan, but it feels more like begging than a command. The inescapable feeling of brokenness weighs down every part of me, leaning on my vocal cords and throwing uncharacteristic tremors of emotion through it. Perfect Perlie Perez is mature and driven, not like this desperate, messy girl on a bench.

I swallow to fight the tremble before I speak.

"To be honest, Dad, I could use a little more. I spend a lot of time in the library, and the cafés on that side of campus don't take dining hall swipes. But I'm more productive there."

I leave out the part that I'm racking up enough debt from fast food and emergency expenses—like all those replacement clothes I'll need after Delmont confiscated mine—that my credit card balance will have a comma in it. I don't have to speak it aloud to feel the threat of this financial debt, in addition to all the truth and success I owe people, pushing down on my chest. I struggle to inhale steadily without my breath hitching.

"Don't worry. We'll send some more."

A small ray in the darkness. "Thank you."

"You know Mom's going to want to see grades, right?"

My already-low mood crumbles further. I don't know what a

Delmont transcript looks like, but it should be easy enough to find one online and replicate it in Photoshop. Still, this is getting a little too complicated, especially when I'll be "repeating" classes when I begin the first-year curriculum for real.

"Dad, we talked about this. That's not how college works."

"Well, that's not how this family works. We want to make sure you're on the right track. Your mom will probably find a way to access your records."

"No, don't," I blurt out. I don't think my parents can touch any of my college-level records, but if they contact the school directly about anything even remotely related to me, it wouldn't take long for all of them to unravel the fact that I'm not enrolled.

"Why not? You are a minor, after all."

I obviously can't answer that truthfully, so I sidestep it. "Because I'm doing fine. Why can't you just trust me when I say so? Do you really need some piece of paper or an email from a teacher saying the same exact thing I'm telling you?" I try to needle an emotional response out of him to distract him from his earlier question, but this tactic fires back on me too. I hadn't truly recognized until now that my parents' Perlie isn't perfect unless someone tells them so. It stings, and the truth is hard to brush off once it comes from my own lips like that.

"Are you all right, Perlie? It's your first year at a very tough university. You can tell us if you're struggling."

"Really." I'm not sure I want to believe this offer, but despite myself, my hopes soar sky-high at the sound of him expressing any sort of concern. My pulse begins to flutter at the possibility.

"Because this feels like the first time you've acknowledged that my life may actually have its own challenges."

"That's not true. Your mom and I have helped you before. Remember when you failed that math test? We can always pay for—"

"No, no, it's not that," I cut him off, those foolish hopes plummeting like their wings melted. And that's why I was worried the offer was too good to be true.

I can't believe that I thought, for even a second, that Dad was going to see past the measurable marks of success and dig into how I felt. My heart had imagined concern where there was none. What I'd seen was problem solving: my apparent inability to excel, without complaint, during my first year at Delmont is a problem that he can and should solve.

But he can't solve this, not the real problem that's at the root of my panic. If my parents ever found out I'd lied about Delmont, they'd never treat me like an adult again. If they ever spoke to me again.

I shake my head, hoping the action will dislodge some of the gray that's darkened my mood. "Like I said, I'm doing fine in my classes, Dad. I'm stressed out with all these big papers due in the next couple of weeks."

"Why are you stressed? Do you feel unprepared?"

My jaw tightens at the continued interrogation and the assumption that I'm at fault for feeling this way, that it's something wrong with me. "No, I'm prepared. I've heard from folks in my weekend college-success mentorship program that some of my professors grade really hard."

The unexpected derision in his snort cuts like a knife. "Hard. You're really going to complain about things being hard?"

Somehow, the words I uttered seconds ago have warped as they transmitted through the air and his cell phone to his ears. I can probably thank that jerk opposing counsel who sent that late-night demand for Dad's sour attitude. He's acting like this is some courtroom argument, something that has a winner and loser, and isn't a simple catch-up between daughter and father. "I'm not complaining. You asked—"

"Your life isn't hard. Your mom and I spent all our time working and scheduling and driving so that you could focus on studying. Getting good grades. That's all we asked you to do."

I flinch at his sudden harshness. It hurts to hear him lay out the complicated give-and-take of our relationship like they're contract terms. But behind his words, I catch a hint of a familiar but unspoken sentiment that is so well hidden that I might've missed it if I wasn't actively grasping for an explanations on why he's acting this way: it's bitterness over his delayed career strides. Ernie Perez's hovering over his sixteen-year-old smarty-pants daughter required a lot of time and energy, at the sacrifice of all else.

I know some of his more old-school-thinking colleagues didn't take well to my dad's semi-stay-at-home parenting, but I liked him not spending sixty hours in the office each week. This time last year, he'd be at the kitchen table, his papers spread out across the worn wood, or in the living room with his feet kicked up onto the glass coffee table. I might've posted up near him with my own homework to pilfer some of his work snacks (the man is a gummy aficionado). At least until Mom would've come home and told us to clean up or to get our disgusting feet off the coffee table, you slobs.

But the snipes at his bring-your-family work gatherings always dragged the light out of his smile, put a barely noticeable slack in his posture. Watching his colleagues get praised and awarded for their time and dedication turned into me becoming the trophy that served as proof of his equal effort.

Add it to the balance of the already-colossal debt I owe him and Mom.

It doesn't automatically give him the right to be rude to me though. We may not always agree, but we're not on opposite sides of the table here. "I know, Dad. I just meant that—"

"So what do you want to do? You want to quit because this is hard?"

"I didn't say I wanted to quit. What's your problem?"

"My problem is that we've done so much for you, and you're going to complain about some tests?"

Tears start to prickle my eyes, and I know if I don't get off the phone now, I'm going to start ugly crying right in the open. The sacrifices are always theirs; the unquestioning thankfulness must always be mine.

"I am grateful, but why does that mean that I can't feel anything else? I know what you did, what my grandparents did, and how all of that led to my being able to walk onto the Delmont campus. I can be thankful and proud of where I am, and I can also be frustrated and nervous about everything too!" The words hurtle out so fast I'm out of breath. I haven't ever spoken to him like that, and his answering silence means he knows it too. But he's the one who started this downward spiral in our conversation.

The quiet drags on, but I know this isn't him listening. He's gathering his thoughts, his arguments. This is his calm before the storm.

"You can feel however you want to feel, Perlie. But at the end of the day, you run into an obstacle, you find a way to get over it." His voice is hard and almost impersonal, like he's talking to a client.

"I am finding a way to get over it. A—"

"We've talked about this, Perlie. We're from a family of immigrants: brown Asian ones. Some days, it feels like if we don't get ignored or minimized, we get excluded or actively hated on. We don't have the luxury of being ordinary here. Everything we do, everything we are—we have to be better." He sighs, and I can practically picture him rubbing his temples to fight off a migraine. "Growing up in diverse Monte Verde has shielded you from this, and that's not your fault. But the way this world works? We have to be exceptional. Because if we're not, we're no one. And we didn't sacrifice this much so that you could quit school and we'd have to make excuses to our friends as to why you're still living with us at forty."

I bite my lip to hold back the sob. He's right: he and Mom did shield me from the worst of this. Yet in shielding me from it, they also let me live in this fantasy world where merit is the only thing that counts, that degrees and rankings are what matter most. I've been on my own at Delmont only a little over a month, and I'm barely beginning to scratch the surface of how restrictive and flawed my way—my family's way—of thinking is. This is what Camilla snapped at me about, when she accused me of looking down on her boyfriend. It's what Tessa chose to ignore, when I couldn't comprehend why she found the professor's comments about other schools insulting.

Now that I'm beginning to recognize the cracks in the foundation, I can't just plaster over it and keep moving. I have to do the work to tear out the irreparable parts and build back up. First, I need to remind my own father that he doesn't have to be angry with me for struggling when my sky is falling.

"Dad, please. Calm down. I'm not going to quit."

"Are you sure? Because your mom was already worried you might not be emotionally mature enough to handle college yet."

Now it's my turn to be angry. "Yes, I'm sure. I'm staying. And I'm allowed to feel crappy once in a while. You don't have to make me feel worse by shaming me for it."

"Yes, well, it's no excuse for failing, Perlie."

He says this with all the serious finality of tone that declares that I, Father, am an adult, and I know far better than you do. His words slash so deep I glance down to make sure my heart isn't on the floor. I had been so proud at Delmont Perla's ability to hold her own against her parents. However, it took less than five minutes for him to make me feel like a petulant ten-year-old again, a child who is only allowed to feel and do things the way an adult wants them to.

I feel sick over the idea that I could've made a stand here if I was strong enough. I could have talked to my dad and made him acknowledge all the pressure that he and Mom have piled on over the years. But it's easier to flee than fight sometimes. What weapons do I have? I'm at a disadvantage, my arms lashed to my sides by the lies I've told.

I lock away the pain and continue our conversation subdued, almost emotionless. I choose the path that will lead Dad to think that this was a momentary blip on an otherwise-smooth trajectory. I choose not to challenge the vision of Perfect Perlie that resides in his head. She's such a large, imposing figure that there isn't room in there for someone like me.

As we speak, I hug my backpack tight like it's Delmont Perla, as if loosening my grip on her for even a moment will unravel everything. It might. This failed heart-to-heart talk with Dad confirms that I've done everything they wanted, leaped over the high bar they set for me. They're still not content. And today, miles from home, might be the first time I'm realizing that it's possible they never will be.

I may be fighting for a feeling that will never come.

When Dad finally hangs up when he reaches the office, I call the one person who will understand.

"Hello?" Her voice sounds sleepy when she answers. I'd forgotten it's not even nine o'clock.

"Hey, Camilla? Can I take you up on that offer of bubble tea?"

TWENTY-FOUR

We meet at one of the on-campus cafés. On a Saturday morning, a mere four other people inhabit the red lounge chairs or wooden bar stools at the counter. I didn't want to get anywhere near the Bubble and Bean, despite how delicious their drinks are. I don't need to arouse any suspicion from my bosses on top of everything.

A corner table next to a plastic potted plant affords Camilla and I some privacy.

In her oversized pink sweater and black joggers, weekend Camilla looks more put together than I have all week. She wraps both hands around a giant cup of hot green tea, like she's trying to draw warmth from it.

I stir at my mocha, destroying the swirl pattern the barista had drawn into the foam. It wasn't that pretty anyway. Jackson makes a much better foam design.

Between us on the slightly sticky wooden table sits a blueberry muffin and an almond croissant to split. Again, I'm certain the

Bubble and Bean has better.

To Camilla's credit, she doesn't seem annoyed at me for practically hauling her across campus to deal with me. She even paid. She hasn't pushed me to talk yet, though we both know that we're not here for a friendly catch-up session.

I take a sip of my mocha for strength. "Thanks for coming. I wanted to be around someone familiar."

She nods. "I get it. It's hard to be in a new place."

"It is. Especially when the old place calls and butts in." I brief her on my disastrous call with my dad earlier.

She listens, throwing in a few "uh-huhs" and "oh, I'm sorrys" where appropriate. While she sounds sympathetic, she doesn't sound shocked, as if she's heard the same thing, possibly from her parents, before.

Then it dawns on me that I'm the "old place" butting into her "new place" at Delmont. Guilt turns the sweet mocha bitter in my mouth. "I . . . I shouldn't have drawn you into all this. I'm sorry."

"No need to be sorry. I'm the one who offered to buy you coffee. I want to help." She leans forward over her green tea. "Though I wish you'd give me a chance by being truthful. Come on, Perla. We both know you didn't get into Delmont."

I almost drop my mocha.

Realistically, I shouldn't be so shocked that she, of all people, figured it out. Maybe part of me wanted her in on this crushing secret I can't bear to carry alone anymore. Maybe that's why I called her this morning. "How?"

She pauses a moment, and her words come out carefully, with

a hint of raw emotion I don't expect from how casual she's been acting since I texted her for this impromptu coffee meetup. "We were cultivated in the same petri dish. I felt terrible after I got wait-listed here when it's all my parents talked about for years. I took that feeling, magnified it times ten, and asked myself what I would do if I didn't get in."

My mouth opens instinctively, a denial ready on my tongue, but nothing comes out. It doesn't have to.

Because she's figured it all out, and she actually understands.

I think back to our last moments wandering the grounds of Monte Verde High then, when I caught her wavering as her friends tempted her to skip a beach cleanup for a boat day instead. Until that moment, it hadn't really clicked that I could spin the spur-of-the-moment lie into action. It's oddly comforting that Camilla and I could grow apart but still have our brains operate in similar ways.

But this isn't a few hours on a boat. This has been months of careful planning, restless sleep, and flexible language.

And instead of being horrified at Camilla's discovery about me, I feel a weight lifted from my shoulders for the first time since handing the faked admission letter to my dad. It's like a sudden change in altitude. The thick clouds are high above me now, not swimming around in my head, and the air feels richer, more nourishing. I don't have to gasp for breath here. The truth takes less oxygen.

"You don't know how much it means to me that you understand," I say. I set my mocha down to avoid another near drop.

"My parents would—"

Camilla holds up a single finger to shush me. "Not another word. Sorry, I want to help, but you shouldn't tell me anything that I can't deny later. I'm not as good a liar as you are. Um, I mean that as a compliment."

She smiles in a scrunched, awkward way, the way she used to when she was embarrassed as a kid. Like when she popped her water balloon, soaking her whole shirt even before the balloon toss started at our parents' firm's annual picnic. Before she became the polished, popular Camilla who never does anything wrong, who never has a hair out of place.

I nod, sniffling away a sentimental tear that had begun to escape. "You're not going to turn me in? Or say anything to my parents?" She may sympathize with what drove me to Delmont, but I still need to be sure I can trust her.

"No. This is your mess, Perlie. Your responsibility," she says. "But first, you've got somewhere to stay, right? Somewhere safe?"

I keep in mind what she said about details and denial and offer a simple "yes." The storage room will suffice until I find another empty dorm. I don't want to drag Camilla deeper into my mess than I need to.

"Good. How are you on money? I'd feel terrible if you were struggling to live and I'm cozy in my dorm room with my meal plan."

"My Bubble and Bean job's got me covered." I sniffle back another tear.

"You really thought of everything." She reaches into her

purse—I never considered bringing a purse to Delmont when I moved here—to hand me a tissue. As I dab at my eyes, she bites her lip, like she's trying to decide how much to get involved with me. I don't blame her for trying to minimize the damage I'd do to her life. Look at the destruction I'd already wrought on mine.

I'm running out of dry corners of this tissue, so Camilla offers the whole tissue pack.

Though I try, I can't seem to stop the tears. They flow out like my body's trying to rid itself of the toxic messages I've internalized over the years.

Grades and glamor are all that matter.

Sacrificing happiness and wellness isn't really sacrifice: it's a family obligation you should take on willingly. And with a smile.

Being unsuccessful means being unworthy of love and respect.

Poison, all of it.

A minute goes by while I empty her tissue stash. I feel lighter with each shed tear. I'm pretty sure I'm a puffy, red mess though.

Camilla tears off a piece of almond croissant, and crumbs flake all over the glossy blue plate. "Okay, my curiosity's getting the better of me. What's your plan? In the most general terms possible. I know you. You've got a binder or whole spreadsheet, right?"

I snort and point a thumb to the backpack hanging on my chair. Strangely, being off balance makes me want to cling to what's left of my plan more: it's the only thing that makes sense. It's comfort in the form of columns. I consider the least rule-breaking way to word everything. "I'm applying for the Delmont spring class. I just finished up a rough draft of my personal statement. It's not due for another month, but I at least like how this one's turning out. My previous versions weren't great. Inspiration's been tough to come by."

"Can I read it?" She wipes the butter and crumbs from the croissant onto her yoga pants.

The question catches me off guard. The only people who read my first personal statement were my parents and Raj the application coach. It wouldn't hurt to have another pair of eyes on this, especially when those eyes were recently admitted and not financially motivated to rubber-stamp an approval.

"Sure."

She slides her green tea aside as I pull out my laptop. I grab a fork and pick at the blueberry muffin while she reads. As suspected, it's a dry, crumbly mess. Frank and Jackson would never sell something like this at the Bubble and Bean.

We sit in silence until Camilla finally lifts her gaze from my screen.

"It looks good, Perlie." She swivels the laptop back to me.

The air returns to my lungs. I hadn't realized I was so starved for kind, simple words lately. Every other relationship I have right now seems like a complicated dance that hinges on me correctly anticipating the next step. I don't have to do that with Camilla anymore because she knows my secret and is still being nice to me. Having her see me as a little sister isn't that bad after all.

"Really?"

"Yeah. It's clear, well written. You drive home your passion for medicine and Delmont and paint how everything in your life led up to it."

In other words, I've reached expert level on lying.

"Thanks. I worked really hard on finding the right angle."

"You must have. You haven't wanted to be a doctor for years."

I nearly fall off my chair. Catching myself, I stand up to pretend to brush off muffin bits so that no one realizes how close I came to splatting on the floor. One of the only things I didn't blow out into a tissue earlier was this goal to become a doctor.

"Wait, what?" I'm still struggling with this massive personal upheaval, and somehow Camilla sees right through me in every way possible? And yet my parents don't.

"You can close your jaw, Perez. You're not the only one navigating someone else's dream for a while. You think I really want to be a lawyer like my mom?" She centers her green tea in front of her again and takes a sip. "Look, I don't agree with whatever it is you're doing at all. Seriously. I think it's risky, irresponsible, and most likely illegal in so many ways." Her gaze drops. "But I get it."

Before I know it, I've rounded the table and wrapped her in a hug. She pats my leg like you'd pet an overeager puppy, but she doesn't say anything further. She doesn't have to.

She gets it.

That tiniest brush of validation wipes away the mess of this morning.

I don't realize I'm still hugging her until she starts to wriggle away.

I drop my arms. "How do you deal with it? The constant pressure to be perfect? To stay on this whole life path that you're not sure about?"

"Perlie, I honestly don't think anyone knows for sure they're on the right life path. And come on, you're sixteen. You have plenty of time to figure it out. As for the pressure"—she shrugs—"you just have to find a balance. Our parents aren't going to love everything we do. At the end of the day, you're responsible for making your own path, your own perfect."

Her phone, on the table, buzzes with a text alert then. Rich's name pops up, and a faint smile flits across her face. Camilla's finding a way to create and protect her own happiness against all the forces pushing on her.

Balance wasn't even on my radar as a thing I could dream of having for myself, but now? It might be time for me to start thinking seriously about what makes me happy too. Through my puffiness and runny nose, I smile at the thought. Camilla's words are the ding that accompanies the fade of the Buckle Seat Belt light on an airplane after a harrowing takeoff.

Perla, you are free to move about the cabin.

She pats me on the leg again. "Just please don't make me regret helping you, okay?"

I return to my seat, giving her space. "What's there to regret? I've got a plan for this, remember? I'm Perfect Perlie Perez."

She smiles and slides her phone into her purse. "You sure are. Now, I've got to go meet Rich. Can I trust you to finish off this food on your own?"

"Trust me?" I grab my fork. "Of course you can."

TWENTY-FIVE

I rouse myself from the library armchair I'd napped in for the past twenty minutes. After this power nap and the subpar baked goods and mocha with Camilla, my energy levels are closer to resembling my normal. The soft sunlight streaming in through the stained-glass window above me boosts my mood after my late-night eviction and world-upending call with Dad this morning.

I'd planned to spend the afternoon scrounging around discount stores to replace my lost clothing—I literally have no other under-wear—but Brand's text offers a bright alternative, something to help me forget temporarily that my existence is a mess.

There's nowhere else for me to go right now anyway. I can't return to my new basement lodgings until the maintenance staff leaves for the day, I don't have a shift at the Bubble and Bean until tomorrow, and Camilla's off with Rich somewhere. Brand's offer makes the gloom of the Saturday disappear. And if I'm going to buy some new clothes, I might as well throw a swimsuit on the pile.

The online search results of "what do I wear surfing?" fail me. They yield mostly serious surfing champs or impractical strings fashion-taped to models, and I find neither helpful.

It's the first time that Brand has invited me out for a non-class-related activity since I turned down his friend's party. I'm not sure what to make of it, mostly because I'm woefully inexperienced in this crush department and Google isn't providing rapid, on-point results on this either, but I'm determined to put the best version of myself forward.

That Einstein quote above my desk at home floats through my mind: *Only those who attempt the absurd can achieve the impossible.* If I can attempt to bikini it up for the first time ever, maybe I can achieve what's always seemed impossible for me: get this cute boy to think I'm more than just a walking, ultra-competitive stack of textbooks, that I'm *fun*.

In my growing panic over my lack of swim apparel—and, well, any apparel—I knock on Tessa's door.

Her room is still dark when she opens the door. She's still in her pajamas, and I envy her being so at home here.

"Everything okay, Perla?"

"I'm going surfing!"

She rubs a palm against her eye. "Good for you?"

"And I have nothing to wear."

"So buy something?"

"And it's with Brand from bio."

The sleepiness drops from her face like someone ripped a curtain off it. "Get your credit card. We're going into the Village."

A couple hours later, I stand in the same spot I'd waved goodbye to my parents from a little over a month ago. That version of me was still unsure of herself, of her plan to fit in at Delmont. I'm trying, and I thought I was succeeding by making friends and branching out with the gaming club, but last night's room eviction feels like a physical "get out" from the university itself. Then with my butting heads with Dad this morning, nothing feels stable, like the cement beneath my feet my crack any time.

Forget it for right now, I tell myself. Enjoy the day.

Easier said than done. When you spend so much time trying to keep your head above water, it's hard to remember what it feels like to float.

My phone buzzes with a text from Brand: he's nearby. I resist the urge to tug the snug bikini top into place. This turquoise top cost me sixty dollars, the matching bottom another sixty, and the coral-and-black rash guard another forty—and this was for the cheaper XXL children's size. As Tessa had said as she looked me up and down approvingly, "That's the cost of looking hot."

These splurges plunged me even deeper into debt, but it's easier to justify when I've been so miserable all night and morning and these purchases pave the road to a happier me. There isn't anything about Brand or surfing that my parents can rail against from up in Monte Verde, no page in my red Perlie's Academic Plan binder that lays out a checklist for this. I'll ask Frank for an extra shift at Bubble and Bean to fight this debt-induced queasiness later, but if it costs $160 plus tax to feel in control of my life for once, I'll pay it.

A beat-up red Jeep speeds up the hill, and I notice, with dismay, two people in the front seats. The Jeep skids to a halt in front of me, and Brand leans out of the passenger side. A white guy with curly brown hair, and as muscly and tanned as Brand, leans forward from behind the steering wheel and offers me a quick wave.

"Hop in," Brand says. "This is Jimmy."

Jimmy, the friend whose party I'd skipped. Neither he nor Brand mention it as I scramble into the back seat, and we speed toward the beach, all speech drowned out by the wind and oldies rock music. I lean back in my seat, relishing the quiet and watching the scenery go from browns and concrete grays to more vibrant greens and blues.

Twenty minutes later, the engine switches off and the music dies away, replaced by the calls of seagulls and the crash of the cresting waves. Jimmy preps the surfboards, and Brand shows me how to go from lying down on the board to popping up to standing. As instructed, I bounce up and around the area of sand we've designated as my phantom surfboard. Suggestions don't sound like criticisms when they're set against the chorus of a sea.

Maybe I should only let my parents talk to me when we're at the beach.

Jimmy waves us over to get our boards. I'm using Claire's today; I apparently made a positive enough impression on her in gaming club that she's okay with lending her seven-hundred-dollar board to a beginner. As we near the water, Brand Velcros the surfboard leash around my ankle, his warm fingers brushing my cold skin.

"I'm a little nervous," I admit. I do want to try surfing, but it's nerve-racking attempting anything new, and there's no fading into the background or faking it when there's only three of us.

Brand flashes a smile at me, and I can't tell if the flutter in my stomach is from that look or from the waves. "We'll start small, okay?"

I nod and follow him in. The freezing Pacific Ocean stings my legs, but I fight through until I warm up. Or I numb. One of those. It doesn't matter.

But what had been so easy on land proves near impossible in the water. I'm unsteady, my icy limbs unruly and difficult to command. I watch a wave here and there but am barely able to pop up before the ocean sweeps my feet out from under me and drags me in, pounding against my nose and eardrums.

Brand moves farther into the deep. He seems restless with the easy waves that I can barely wrangle.

"Hey, wait up!" I call to him.

He turns. "You got this, Perla!"

I shake my head. "It's too far out."

"You'll be fine." He beckons me to join him, but I've already drifted out more than I'd intended to. I'm shorter than he is. My feet balance unsteadily on the shifting sand, and the pull of the receding water inches me into deeper territory.

I freeze. Perfect Perlie Perez would scramble back to dry land and call her parents. Then she'd probably spend the rest of the afternoon in her pink-everything room with an open textbook, regret, and a phone that no one's trying to reach.

That's not who I am anymore. And maybe I never was: maybe she was as much of a specter as Delmont Perla is, fashioned by people who only saw what they wanted to see. She may have always existed on a whole different plane, one I can't reach. I can't return to trying to be someone who isn't real.

I focus on what's in front of me. I tread forward a few inches, my toes barely grazing the floor, and I hoist myself up onto the board, as I'd seen Brand do. Not as gracefully, but I'm on top of it now, my stomach flat against the waxy board. Others farther out straddle their boards, but I'm afraid that any extra moves will send me straight back into the water.

A wave rolls toward me, hints of white mingling in the sun-streaked blue. I can get this one. I think. In the distance, another surfer is starting to turn her board, and I take heart from the fact that my instinct about this wave isn't wildly off.

My hands flail wildly in the water as I try to turn my board around too and paddle toward the shore.

I wonder if there are sharks in this part of the Pacific.

Probably.

Focus.

The power of the oncoming wave nudges my board, and I harness what's left of my energy to plant my frozen hands and shove myself up into a low crouch.

And I stay crouched.

One second.

Two seconds.

I'm doing it. I get bolder.

I try to straighten, to stand taller like the blond girl on a neon green board to my far right.

But gravity and my utter lack of strength training tell me I'm nowhere near ready. My legs betray me. They stiffen and falter at the wrong times. The surfboard pitches underneath my unpredictable weight, and then it escapes me entirely. I plunge into the frigid salt water. The surfboard smacks me hard on the shoulder, as if punishing me for daring to be what I'm not.

My head bobs up above the water finally, and the salt stings when I open my eyes. Brand and Jimmy are a few yards away, laughing and already paddling back out. I hadn't seen them come in, but I'm sure they caught the wave effortlessly, gliding over the water like they were gods of these seas. And here I am, probably looking like a soaked rat hanging on to a plank after a flood.

If I could sink to the bottom and disappear, I would. But Brand brings his hand up to shield his eyes from the sun, searching for me.

I paddle and drag myself and my board toward them.

"Not bad for a first try. Bit off more than you could chew though, eh?" Brand smiles, water dripping from his glistening hair.

"Yeah, you guys made it look so easy." I try to laugh off the embarrassment, but I worry he and everyone else on this beach can smell the fraud on me. He belongs here in the sea and sand like he belongs at Delmont. I don't.

"Maybe hang out on the beach for a while. Jimmy and I are going to go back out."

Jimmy and I. I am not included. It stings, even if he may not have intended it to.

"All right."

He shifts his hold on the board. "We'll get out of here in a bit and grab some burgers, okay?"

I nod, chalking up the roaring in my ears to the waves and not the sadness.

"I'll just . . . I'll just be over here."

Brand's eyes flit to my downturned mouth. "Hey, don't beat yourself up. So what if you wiped out? You literally just learned this today. Neither of us did any better when we were beginners."

"You're just saying that."

Jimmy snorts. "He's not. I've got some GoPro footage of when this guy first started."

Brand shakes his head at his friend, then turns back to me. "Look, no one's perfect. Give yourself a break. Soak in some sun and figure out what flavor milkshake you want. It's on me."

They swim away, the sun glinting off their tanned backs.

I roll out a beach towel next to my board and reach for more sunscreen. Between the fresh breeze and Brand's words, the sadness that had shrouded my shoulders as I emerged from the water begins to dry up. Safe on land, I feel lighter, with the sun warming my face and my toes in the sparkling sand and a gorgeous guy owing me a milkshake.

I pull my wet hair away from my face. It's been a long time since I haven't been good at something. It feels strange and uncomfortable to fail. This isn't something I can spreadsheet my way out of either.

It reminds me of my first day at the Bubble and Bean, with that name-callout flub, among other rookie mistakes. My life at Delmont has brought so many firsts, and I've tried so hard to excel at every little thing I do, like I did back home. But between Brand, Jackson, and Camilla, I'm starting to realize that people are willing to extend a little grace when something goes wrong because, sometimes, they expect it. Not everyone holds the yardstick as ridiculously high as my parents do. And the problem with measuring me up against a standard that high is that I'll always fall short.

I should've never expected that I was going to suddenly be some pro surfer after one lesson and some expensive swimwear.

Maybe I should've never expected that everything was going to magically fall into place so that I could get into Delmont that first time.

My heart aches for the time, energy, and tears I've spent struggling to mold myself into someone who others would be proud of. Anger simmers there too. I could have been cutting myself a little slack, making another friend or two, sleeping late, focusing on what makes me happy. But all of that opportunity is gone now, unreachable for me, like the water ebbing into the open sea.

I dig my toes farther into the sand.

I'll make it out into the water one day.

But for now, I'll have to live with being imperfect. And I think I'm okay with that.

On PicLine: my toes in the sand, with Claire's surfboard peeking into the upper left corner of the picture.

Caption: Tried catching some waves, but they caught me #wipeout #surfing #beginner

Twenty-six likes.

Comment from TessasaurusRex: SHOW US THE BIKINI

TWENTY-SIX

Perfect Perlie Perez would have thoroughly reapplied sunscreen instead of curating a PicLine post. Mom would have made sure of it.

The skin on my nose and forehead is raw and angry from my beach trip. I haven't had the fortitude to unscrunch my face from a frown since it first settled into that position this morning. I even left off the heart-pendant necklace I've worn nearly every day since I got it: the thought of it rubbing against the burned skin all shift made me tuck the necklace safely into my backpack instead.

Jackson's eyes widen at my sunburn when he unlocks the Bubble and Bean door to let me in. "Ouch," he says on my behalf.

It's six in the morning, way too early for any college students to be wandering into the Bubble and Bean on a Sunday. And way too early to concentrate on both conversation and my raging skin.

Saying that I'm grumpy would be an understatement. I had begged out of Tessa's invitation to the outdoor movie last night, not only because of my opening shift this morning, but because of my face's destruction from the sun. The horrific scurrying of rodent feet far too close to my basement mattress didn't help me get any real rest either. Then, as much as I slathered moisturizer samples from the twenty-four-hour drugstore on my skin this morning, nothing seemed to help, and I couldn't miss out on the pay of an eight-hour shift. My savings are a measly sixty-three dollars and my credit card balance has soared, thanks to the surfing gear and replacement clothes, and the tiniest emergency could obliterate that.

On the plus side, Dad texted me to say sorry for being so cranky yesterday. He blamed that work emergency—turns out his opposing counsel erroneously assumed that the new, white associate at the firm was in charge, and not my older, browner dad—and offered an apology in the form of overnighting me some cash. It eases but doesn't banish the short-fused monster that is my mood this morning.

"If you start the coffee brewing, I can load up the pastry case," Jackson says as I tie my apron strings behind my back.

As exhausted and fragile as a used coffee filter, I head for the industrial-sized bean grinder. I haul out a couple ten-pound bags of beans. With a grunt, I drop them on the counter.

"Whoa, careful there!"

I instantly feel guilty over my carelessness. Getting on the boss's son's bad side is a terrible idea.

I'm not sure Jackson has a bad side. Yes, he's to the point and his jokes sometimes don't land like he hopes. Yet from the times we've worked together, I haven't seen him get flustered at an obnoxious customer, even the one who insisted she ordered a pumpkin spice latte with almond milk though both Jackson and I distinctly remembered her saying soy milk. I find his relentless positivity both inspiring and annoying.

"Sorry. I haven't had any caffeine yet," I say.

"Why didn't you say so? My leftover iced milk tea stash is in the back, if you want it."

I light up like it's Christmas and dart to the refrigerator.

Ten minutes and twelve ounces of creamy tea later, I'm feeling friendlier. Even the sunburn isn't bothering me as much. I venture to relax my glower and the sting of movement dissipates after a moment.

I remember then that I'm guzzling down Jackson's private reserves.

"You want any? I might've drained more than half of your stash." I angle the glass toward him.

He shakes his head. "I had some before you got here. That's an extra, in case I need a midday pickup. I can't do coffee for some reason. Doesn't taste good to me. Probably because I'm around it all day."

I chuckle. "Well, wait until you get to college. Then you'll drink whatever will get you through the next couple of hours, ice cold or scalding or downright disgusting."

Jackson clutches his cleaning rag like he's drawing courage from it.

I lower my drink reluctantly. I'm used to that look from when people find out I'm the Perfect Perlie Perez, of Monte Verde local-paper and loudmouthed-parent fame. "What is it? Spit it out."

"It's pretty cool. Being so young and in college."

I scrutinize him, but, as usual for Jackson, he doesn't seem to have a single malicious thought behind his statement. People's compliments to me so often have a second, ugly layer that I have trouble accepting them from anyone. *That's such an accomplishment, for someone your age. You'll get into that school; they need more minorities. Your PicLine makes you seem so normal.*

Jackson hasn't said a single thing to suggest he's trying to jab at me or, worse, dig up dirt and expose me like a Monte Verdan would, so I let the compliment through.

"Yeah, it's cool," I say, tucking a strand of hair behind my ear. My fingers are icy from clutching the cold tea. "I skipped grades, spent my weekends and summers catching up or getting ahead, and here I am."

"Doesn't it suck being the youngest one there? I saw a TV movie about some eighteen-year-old prodigy in law school, and it honestly did not look like all that much fun."

I shrug. "Everyone's nice so far." I leave out the part about nosy RAs, overeager residence hall maintenance staff, and me telling everyone else very, very little about myself, especially not my age. If he had asked me about being the youngest in my Monte Verde class, my response would've been different. "You're a senior, right? Applying for college soon?"

"Yup, trying to figure out what to write in my personal statement."

You and me both, kid. I take another sip of tea to wash away the icky taste of that reminder.

"You thinking of staying close to home?"

He cocks his head to the side. "Not particularly. Dad's thinking of opening up a second shop in another town."

"Really? Where?"

"He isn't sure yet. He wants to scout out a couple more college towns. He says students have no problem spending all their loan money on fancy espresso drinks."

I snort. Frank isn't wrong.

Jackson leans back against the counter opposite me. "He's banking on my sister to run it, but if I get into a college near that location next year, then he might let me handle it."

I smile then at the determination in his voice. He has a confidence and adventurousness that I'm only barely scratching the surface of in myself.

I clutch my glass of tea. "What if your dad chooses some remote town for this second location?"

Jackson smirks. "Do you know anything about business? Why would he do that?"

I level a fake glare at him, which only makes him laugh. "But what if there's only a community college or something?"

"It's still got a whole lot of customers, and I'd still be able to take classes." He tilts his head. "Something wrong with a community college?"

The edge in his voice makes me pause. To Perfect Perlie, there would be. I smiled and nodded through years of my family's grim warnings of friends' children who attended community college, then dropped out or never transferred to their dream schools. They used these children as cautionary tales, not mentioning the ones who earned their degrees or ended up just fine and happy despite bucking their family's lofty standards.

To my parents, a successful student is one who goes straight to a prestigious university, like I should have, and routinely ends up with enough accolades or on honor rolls to keep their name golden.

Camilla accused this view of being incredibly narrow, but I assumed she was being overdefensive because we were talking about her boyfriend. However, with the way Jackson's looking at me now, his question forces me to justify myself and this deeply embedded view head-on, on my own, like I'm the one who came up with it. I obviously didn't, but it's hard to explain how that idea ended up in my head. Now that I think of it, I wonder what other bricks in my foundation were laid by someone other than me.

"I didn't mean there's something wrong with them, but . . ." But what? But that's what I've always been told from Monte Verdans and family and, surprise, I'm apparently part of that judgmental group too? The explanation I know I should spout out doesn't match what's growing in my heart. It feels wrong, but they're the only words I know. "Sorry. It's just that I spent my whole life vying with folks for this same goal, this same idea of getting into the best college, getting the best job. Some of them were vicious. Paying thousands of dollars for any college admissions edge, lying to other students about deadlines, trying anything to get ahead.

We don't do all that and then not go to a top-twenty school, you know?"

"Wow. Do you hear yourself?" Jackson's eyes widen almost imperceptibly then, like he's taking a second—or first—look at me. "Um, no offense, but you kinda need to grow up, Perla."

I'm suddenly furious. Every slight leveled at me by my parents' friends, every whisper of "She's so young," even Camilla's snipe at me when I threatened to out her dating to her parents—it all comes roaring back. Try growing up when someone else shapes nearly every facet of your life, from your "dream" job to the pattern of your dorm room bedspread.

"'Grow up'? That's harsh, Jackson."

"I'm not the one who casually insulted a whole slew of community colleges."

My frown deepens, and I ignore the pain that flares as my face crinkles. "I'm trying to explain where I'm coming from!"

"Fine." He shrugs, like he's not convinced. "But you know, at some point, you should own up to your actions and beliefs and not blame it on your family or your old school or whoever. Take responsibility."

It's the other side of the coin of what Camilla said, when my doctor dream had started to fray over candid conversation and a subpar mocha. It's up to me to make my own version of perfect, but that also means I'm on the hook for everything bad that may come with it. My mess, my responsibility.

How I hate that word right now.

I fold my arms across my chest. "Most people would crumble

from the responsibilities I juggle all the time."

Everything I've done since opening that Delmont letter has been about fulfilling a responsibility: a responsibility to my parents and to myself and to that damn red binder academic plan to be the best, the most successful, the Perfect Perlie Perez. And honestly, it's that sole, narrow focus that made those warped beliefs easier to swallow and made dissent so much harder.

"I bet. But I still need you to understand that, unlike where you come from, grades and all that don't matter in here. At the risk of sounding like my dad, what matters is your word: whether or not my family can rely on you."

His words douse my anger.

To Jackson, my word still means something, and as misguided as that notion is, I have no desire to change that. He looks at me like he sees a better version of me, like the Perla I want to be. Not in terms of grades or looks or money, but in character.

But Jackson doesn't know me as well as he thinks he does, and that must be that Sagittarius spirit he blabs on about. Always the optimist, confident and hopeful about the future. It must be easy to be confident and hopeful when you don't realize people are lying to you. It's endearing, if not a little heartbreaking too, especially when I'm the one doing the lying.

I take another sip of tea. "You just don't know what it's like in Monte Verde."

"You're right, I don't," he says, shaking his head. "Your hometown sounds way too intense."

Something splinters in me because, for once, I'm hearing my

views, my upbringing, my whole life talked about like it's a *bad* thing. And I'm beginning to agree.

But when you believe something for so long, it's hard to simply let it go. I find myself defending this view, though my heart's not completely in it. "Prestige is a big deal to a lot of people there. We prided ourselves in being like this, being the best of the best, trying to be even better."

"Being the best at what?"

"At what my parents want." The warped answer comes so quickly and clearly it almost knocks the breath out of me. Where had that come from? And how had the "I" in that statement dropped?

My parents want me to come to Delmont, then go off to medical school and become a doctor.

I'm not sure that I want all of that anymore.

Jackson freezes. "Seriously?"

"I . . . I don't know what made me say that." The Bubble and Bean feels too quiet, too empty then, and these new thoughts too loud. "I guess it's hard to parse out how much of the Delmont doctor dream is mine versus theirs, you know? Now I know why: I've never had to dissect it like this before. I never had a reason to. No one back home would bat an eye at anything I've said."

Jackson's eyebrows knit. "I'm being a jerk. I shouldn't have pushed you to—"

"It's fine," I say, though it's clearly not. My heart still belongs at Delmont, but the edges of my dream feel fuzzier now. What I thought were small moments like sitting in on gaming club meetings or flipping through the course catalog actually pried my eyes open to the possibilities, bit by bit.

My pulse starts to pick up. I grip the empty glass harder and force a breath, but it doesn't help. I'm almost dizzy. Is it from being out in the sun so long yesterday? The fact that I've only ingested milk tea, milkshakes, and pastries in the past twenty-four hours? Or is it because my whole being is resisting this revelation that everything I've been basing my life on may be flawed?

I blink, and when I open my eyes, Jackson has hopped back.

The glass is in shards on the floor. I didn't even realize it had fallen.

"I'm so sorry," I say, springing into action. My face redder—somehow—than it was earlier, I sidestep the glass and grab the broom and dustpan from their spot in the corner.

Jackson's already squatting over the wreckage, a rag in one hand, a trash can in the other. "It's okay, Perla. It happens all the time."

The shards clink together like discordant music as I sweep. Jackson points out pieces I've missed and mops up stray dots of milk tea. Together, Jackson and I make quick work of the disaster I'd created.

When he rises, I gulp and offer the answer I'd been retooling. I almost owe it to him, after he helped clean up my mess. "The best."

He raises an eyebrow.

"I've revising my answer. You asked earlier what I and all the other Monte Verdans have been trying so hard to be the best at.

And that's what it is: being the best at being the best. It's not a great answer, I know. Seems I have work to do finding out the answer to that question myself."

Jackson wipes his hand off on his apron. "I don't want to be rude," he starts, which of course means he's going to say something a teensy bit rude. "You know that makes no sense. Like that literally means nothing because there's no standard definition of 'best.'"

"Yeah, I'm kind of seeing that now," I say, but it comes out as a half sob. I take a deep inhale and release it slowly. "This sunburn, this conversation: it's just a lot."

His mouth curves into a kind smile. "I know. All these Delmont kids come in here thinking the same way as you. And I know you're so sorry for it that you'll give me the whole cinnamon bun icing tub."

I laugh and instantly feel a little lighter. He might be tough on me, but it's the kind of toughness that folks reserve for their friends, the "I don't want to see you make a mistake" kind. It softens the blow of such an unexpected brain and heart workout so early in the morning.

A buzz pierces the silence of the shop. Jackson tugs out his phone.

"Speaking of cinnamon buns, Dad's dropping them off in ten. We should've been done with this by now."

I leap toward the coffee grinder. I'm nearing livable levels of energy now that tea courses through my veins.

"You meet your dad," I call to him over my shoulder. "I'll start the pastries once I get the coffee brewing."

Jackson shoots me a thanks and heads for the back room. He's his normally cheery self again, while I'm standing by the empty pastry case, my dreams and plans crumbling in my hands.

As I cut open the bag of beans, a question simmers at the back of my mind: Did I really drop that glass? Or did I throw it just to see something break?

Perfect Perlie Perez would've never broken something on purpose. But maybe that's not who I am anymore.

Like that milk tea glass, there's no way to piece together what has shattered into so many pieces. I'm not sure I want to either, and frankly, I don't even feel all that guilty that everything's broken. I know it's going to take a lot of work, navigating the sharp shards around me, making sure I don't fall backward and slice myself open, but I feel like it's time to lift my gaze to the distance and see for myself what I can build on my own.

I roll up my sleeves and get ready to work.

TWENTY-SEVEN

The study lounges throughout the residence halls have become my second homes the past few weeks. When I'm too lazy to lug my meager amount of stuff around between class and Bubble and Bean shifts during maintenance staff hours, I cozy up on a couch in a quiet lounge and play. A student napping next to a thick textbook isn't an unusual sight. My bright white earbuds keep people from trying to talk to me. And, best of all, there's no pressure to buy anything in order to stay.

I tend to avoid my former home of Keith Hall second floor, but Tessa had another much-needed envelope from my parents, so we made plans to study after dinner with Erin and Casper, which she swiped me in for. She's started calling her never-endingly flirty friends Casprin, which rhymes with "aspirin," which she says she pops two of every time she's around them too long.

I haven't told her I don't live in Samantha Simon's room anymore—I have an easy work excuse for when I'm not around to answer her knocks—and her energy drink habit keeps her out of the Bubble and Bean. It's better that we minimize our hangouts. After spilling my guts to Camilla and Jackson, it's hard to reconcile these growing parts of my conscience with the fact that I'm still lying to everyone.

My back against the wall, I kick my socked feet up onto the lime-green sofa. My laptop balances on my lap. Wedged between my hip and the sofa is a water bottle I refilled with Sprite at the dining hall.

At her table, Tessa bobs her head silently as she types, her earbuds thumping a beat I can't hear. As far as she knows, we're both working on our English composition essays. I faked a different professor than she has, and it wasn't hard to convince her that my essay prompt isn't an analysis on a classic like hers is but is a personal one instead.

Behind the document on my screen sits my seven-part plan spreadsheet. Since Camilla thumbs-upped my draft a couple of weeks ago, I've been making tweaks based on extra knowledge I've gathered. I have notes on Tessa, Brand, and even random folks I've been stuck at the dining hall tables with only a handful of times, speculating the reasons for their admission: have an exceptional memory, volunteer abroad, win two national high-school writing awards, community organize for a heartstring-pulling cause, and have family member as alumni and, more importantly, as big donors.

Erin, for example, volunteered at an eviction prevention nonprofit and is convinced this altruistic bent is what caught the Admissions folks' eyes. So I stretch a little story about a medical mission to a needier part of the city (i.e., when I helped Mom pass out brochures at a farmers market across Monte Verde) to add that specificity and personality for part six: reapply for the next incoming class at Delmont.

If this were a video game, this would be the big battle against the zombie horde, the final race for the gold cup, the castle on the mountain guarded by a dragon. This is where I prove I'm worthy and come out victorious, like how I soundly beat Brand and two other gaming club members at *Mario Kart* after last week's meeting. This time, I've got some experience with the lay of the land and the possible pitfalls. Crossing the finish line should be easier.

Tessa groans and plucks out an earbud. "I don't know why I'm having such a hard time with this essay."

I smile in sympathy. "Same. It'd be great if the words just wrote themselves."

"That'd be the dream." She takes a swig from her energy drink. "I wish I'd started this sooner. When's yours due?"

"Next Monday, but I've got a couple other papers and labs to finish up too." The application window opened earlier this month, and I have two more weeks to hone an amazing, socks-knocking-off personal statement to convince the admissions committee to overlook my forced gap semester and realize I should have been at Delmont all along.

But like Tessa with her English essay, the words that should have flowed easily from my fingertips stay stuck in my brain. It's only been a couple of weeks since my conversations with Camilla and Jackson began ripping at the seams of my dream—my parents' dream, if we're being truthful.

It wouldn't take much to ignore them and buy back into the goals and mindset I grew up with. I know all the reasons why I should care about positioning myself for future dollar-based, aunties-approved success. Yet I can't bring myself to type out "medical school" or "doctor" in this personal statement without my chest tightening anymore, even though it's in this document a dozen times.

And it's gotten worse than that. I've found a sense of guilt crawling in around the edges, as if fracturing the image of Perfect Perlie Perez reawakened my sense of ethics. I don't have the same excuses to fall back on, the same reasons for overlooking the people I step around or on, the same reasons to not take a more active role in shaping my own life whether or not my parents agree. I'm constantly reminded that Delmont Perla is a lie, and I have a lot of work to do to essentially make an honest girl out of her come spring semester.

I click from my spreadsheet to my personal statement, glaring at the blinking cursor halfway down the screen. It hasn't moved for six minutes.

This personal statement is so far from that trustworthy, reliable ideal I'm reaching for, but Delmont is still at the root of what I want. Getting admitted for real will unlock more of my dreams, if not being a doctor, then something else (or something else in addition to being a doctor, if that's what it takes). I have to distinguish myself from the pack, the way my Delmont friends have, but I don't know how. I can make up for that trustworthiness part later, when my ability to eat and sleep in peace doesn't hinge on my pretending to be a student.

Tessa obviously got into Delmont. I should just ask her to break my writer's block.

I sit up. "How would you describe the Delmont student population? In one word."

Tessa sets down her drink next to her dog-eared library copy of *The Picture of Dorian Gray*. "'Pretentious.'"

"I can't write that in my essay." The admissions officials would toss my application in the proverbial online burn pile immediately. "The professor would dock points for sure."

"Ugh, I don't know." Tessa shifts on her chair, and it squeaks under her weight. "'Smart'? 'Diverse'? 'Ugly'? What do you want me to say?"

I snort out a wholly ungraceful sound. "Something useful maybe?" I turn back to my laptop screen, a smile on my face. "I can't use any of that, but thanks anyway."

"How about 'nerdy'? Or 'entitled'? Or . . ."

She's still throwing out negative descriptors when the study lounge door creaks open. Genia the RA shuffles in in her on-duty polo shirt, with messy stacks of the *Daily Dragon* crinkling in her arms. My limbs tense as she strolls over to the recycling bin.

"Hi, friends," Genia says, dusting her hands off on her pants after she dumps the papers. "Working? Or just refreshing PicLine?"

I force a laugh to match Tessa's genuine one.

Tessa raises her book, her thumb wedged between the pages to hold her place. "Essay for English. Thirty percent of the grade."

"Ah, have fun with that." Genia's eyes drift to me. "Welcome back."

I smile close-lipped to match Genia's and ignore Tessa's furrowed brow. If Genia expects something self-incriminating, I don't give it to her.

She returns her attention to Tessa. "By the way, we're doing a pre-Halloween candyfest next week for all the residents of our floor. If you want to help decorate and get first dibs on the good candy, the sign-up sheet's on my door." She glances at me. "You're welcome to join too."

Genia rattles off some more details on her way out. Tessa mumbles something noncommittal, running her fingers absentmindedly over the spine of her library book. I keep my mouth shut and pray that the memory of Genia's odd "welcome back" phrasing dissolves into the cosmos.

Tessa waits until the study lounge door clicks behind Genia before she turns to me, her eyes narrowed. "Perla, what was that about?"

I struggle to force my face mildly amused, like this is some hilarious joke we're all in on. I unwedge my water bottle and twist open the top. "She thinks I don't live here."

"And why would she think that?"

"I don't know. Something wrong with her resident lists probably."

"So where does she think you live, then?"

"In Godwin. I ran into her in the elevator, and she somehow came to that conclusion herself." I take a sip to buy myself sometime, but the intensity in Tessa's gaze stays constant. "I'm not going to correct her. Not my job to make her better at hers, right?"

"But that's dishonest."

The atmosphere shifts. With that one statement, the easy, laid-back Tessa, who trusts me and laughs off my frequent ID-forgetting morphs into something darker, her stern-mom voice out in full force. And where I should've felt victorious after dodging Genia's questions, I feel rattled and guilty instead. I can tell Tessa's gearing up to ask me questions that I can't answer truthfully without ruining everything, and, for a moment, I genuinely wonder how I'm going to keep this up.

"Did you know Casper and Erin are dating now?" Tessa adds out of nowhere.

I lock my doubts away. No, I didn't know about her friends. I don't know them outside of that one outdoor movie and the occasional meal Tessa herds us together for. They live down the hall from where Samantha Simon's room was, and getting on bestie level with people not key in the big plan isn't on my spreadsheet.

I shake my head, and she continues.

"Yeah, Casper was still with his girlfriend, well, his ex. It's kinda messed up, all the lying, don't you think?"

Who other people are with is literally at the bottom of my list of worries. This Tessa, the one who very clearly dislikes the idea of dishonesty, unnerves me. This Tessa might turn her Delmont-accepted intellect toward unraveling my story, and I'm already feeling icky at having to mislead her this far.

I clutch my water bottle like it's a talisman that will ward off her negative attention. "Come on, this isn't that. It's a misunder-standing. Probably some weird clerical error. It's not my fault." I can't help the hint of desperation that works its way into my words. I need her, my first friend here, to understand, to believe me.

"I guess," she says, an odd thread of emotion in her words. "I just don't like that kind of stuff: not telling people what's up."

The emotion in her voice doesn't match this relatively benign wrong I just committed, so there must be something else driving her anger right now. But because asking her what's really wrong may open myself up to the same demand for answers, I let this moment's opportunity to be a good friend float by with regret.

"This isn't a big deal," I say. "I'm on the official dorm roster; I'm just not on hers, I guess. Otherwise, how would I be getting into the building?"

Please accept this one line and let the matter go, I plead silently. *Don't make me dig myself deeper with you.*

"Fine, whatever. I don't want to talk about this anymore. I've got a ton of work to do." She scoots her chair in closer to the table.

Despite Tessa dropping it, the low feeling lingers. I don't like the bad note that rings between Tessa and me, so I force a smile at her. "You know, the less involvement I have in floor-wide can-dyfests, the better. I hoard anything with peanut butter. I'd ruin Halloween."

Tessa's eyes stay dark for another moment before she flips to the next Post-it bookmarking *Dorian Gray*. "Well, more candy for me, I guess."

A joke, but the light is missing from it. The conversation moves on, but I don't feel any less scrutinized or any less guilty. I don't have room on this paper-thin line of survival I'm straddling to try to be a good friend without jeopardizing my presence here on campus. The frustration makes me want to scream.

But the sooner I get accepted into Delmont, the sooner I can stop lying to everyone, and the sooner I can stop feeling this guilty.

Tessa suddenly starts to pack up. "I have a FaceTime with a friend from high school. Totally forgot about it."

"I'll be here if you want to keep working on our essays together."

She only offers a small smile in response, then heads back to her room.

I eat the last half of a stale, surplus pineapple bun from the Bubble and Bean alone, wondering how I'm still managing to alienate everyone when I'm not even Perfect Perlie anymore.

The next day, Jackson's sister stays home sick, so I miss bio to pick up her Bubble and Bean shift and that extra cash.

Tessa's not in her usual seat when I show up on Friday. I keep having to stop myself from scanning the auditorium for her.

She doesn't answer her door on Friday night. I run into Erin and Casper in the cul-de-sac as they're loading up Casper's car for a weekend trip together. Erin says she thinks Tessa went home for the weekend.

Flitting between the Phoenix Tech Lounge, study lounges, occasional swipe-ins from Camilla, and the long tables in Molina Library, I keep polishing my rough draft of my Delmont personal statement, beat the zombie video game for the third time, and dodge Mom's calls.

I don't go near Keith Hall again until my phone chimes with a text from Tessa, a week later.

TWENTY-EIGHT

*A*t *library, will come over in a few,* I respond, even though I'm in an empty Graycliff Hall study lounge across the cul-de-sac.

I wriggle my laptop back into my backpack, pausing to tighten the rolls of extra clothing I've jammed into the second pocket. My rotation of T-shirts (usually hidden under my Delmont hoodie), leggings, jeans, and multi-packs of underwear, ankle socks, and sports bras take up too much space, but I've only got this one backpack to ferry my life around in. I returned my surfing gear for store credit and bought boxes of fancy protein bars instead. Jackson lets me keep those in the Bubble and Bean back room for my lunch breaks.

After Delmont staff cleared out Samantha Simon's room and threw away my stuff, I've been too afraid to store these latest belongings anywhere else.

With a zip, I haul it all back to Keith Hall to see if I can patch things up with Delmont Perla's closest friend. It's hard for me to even think *my* friend, not when Tessa doesn't really know who I am.

Crews of students mill around the second-floor hallways, paper decorations and fake cobwebs in their hands. I don't recognize any of them, and, thankfully, they don't seem to recognize me.

I weave past two students taping up cardboard witches and bats and slip into the bathroom to make sure it's not obvious that I slept on a basement corner mattress. Fake spiders cling to the lime-spotted mirrors. I shudder. I don't know why they decorate in here. The bacteria level itself is horrifying.

Tessa answers her door after two knocks, one hand on the door handle and the other scrolling through her phone. Her lips purse in an almost-carved-from-stone way that makes me think they've been like that all morning. I haven't seen her since the night in the study lounge, and for a moment, I think I'm hallucinating that she messaged me asking me to drop by.

I stay outside. What do you say to someone who went from everyday hangouts to ditching you for almost a week? "Hey."

Tessa peers up from her phone. "Come on in."

No hints as to what she wants to talk about or if she's been as off-kilter as I am about the sudden drop-off in our friendship. Has she figured out I don't belong here? If she did, would she even talk to me, or would she go straight to the administration? How many more lies am I going to have to tell to keep this life going?

I ignore the fierce twisting in my stomach and follow her into the room.

Tessa heads for the desk chair. It feels awkward to stand there, so I plop down at the foot of her bed and set my backpack at my feet. A wind blows in from her open window, and I'm hit with a wave of jealousy that she gets the ease of a locked door and fresh air.

My life would have been so different right now if I had just been accepted into this school like I was supposed to.

I could've had a cozy, secure room of my own. I could've had a clean, honest past that I'd laugh with Tessa over during a dining hall dinner I swiped myself into. I seem to only be drifting further from that reality, and my chest tightens at the thought.

Tessa pauses to wrangle a charging cord and plug in her phone. Another squirm of my stomach because I truly can't read her. Goal-focused Perfect Perlie thinks that if Tessa's going to out me, she should get it over with already. Then I can argue back, try to convince her otherwise. I can't argue with silence.

But the me who is sitting at the foot of her bed, trying to take up as little space as possible, wishes there was some sort of friendship do-over button we could push, one that would have us laughing again without me having to explain the truth of why I'm here.

"What did you want to talk about?" I ask.

She leans to the side so she can slide an envelope out from the back pocket of her jeans.

"Oh, shoot, sorry you keep getting my mail." I peek down at the return address. My parents sent more much-needed cash. "I told Dad my room number twice. I don't know why they keep . . ."

"It's fine. That's not what I wanted to talk to you about."

My heart stops altogether.

"I wanted to apologize for ghosting," she says. "That thing about Genia and your rooming situation bothered me more than I thought it would. I really, really don't like when people lie."

Instinctively, I open my mouth to tell her I didn't lie, but even I, with my increasingly flexible ethics, know that's too far. I cross my ankles, not sure how to sit right now without looking guilty.

She drags a hand through her purple hair, the color that practically served as a welcome beacon my first day here. I can judge my time at Delmont by the fade of the purple. It's a shade duller now and more grown out, as if the color was left behind in Tessa's hometown with her old friends and high school self. I wonder if we'll still be hanging out when she picks her next hue.

"I know you didn't lie to me specifically," she says, "so I feel like I have to explain."

"You don't." Selfishly, the relief that this conversation seems to be leading away from me and my deception is all I need. I'm in the wrong here. I did lie, and the last few days alone seem only a fraction of the punishment I deserve from someone as trusting as her. But I can't even admit it or properly apologize without exposing myself as a fraud, so all I can hope for is a Tessa-led way back to being dinner pals again. That unfortunately means continuing to keep my distance, as much as my heart responds to the sadness emanating from hers.

"No, I want to. It's not cool that I'm letting something that happened to me get in the way of our hanging out. Besides, I might need some bio notes." She flashes a tentative smile at me, which I return. "I had a terrible boyfriend in high school. We dated two years. I thought we were going to do the long-distance thing when we got to college, but he broke up with me a week before I left for Delmont. It didn't take too much online stalking for me to figure out that he'd been cheating on me. For a while."

The smile drops from my face. "That really sucks, Tessa." The truth, for once, and it's a relief to tell it.

She sniffles and drags her forearm against her nose. "After a pretty bad anxiety attack, I just shut that whole mess out. Thought I'd left it all behind when I came to Delmont. Not dealing with it is starting to screw me up though. I hate being around Erin and Casper now. I didn't like the thought that I'd be completely friendless if I ditched you without a word too. So this is me saying sorry and hoping you'll let me swipe you in for dinner."

I rise from the bed and wrap an arm around her shoulders. I give her arm a squeeze, a move I'd seen on TV enough to replicate. I don't have too much firsthand experience with being comforted myself. My parents usually countered my disappointing days with a "Try harder," which even I know isn't appropriate for this situation. It was meant for slow mile runs and spotty memorizations of historic dates: things they and others could measure and analyze. Sadness didn't fall in the category, so I'm genuinely unsure how to handle this, and the realization makes me feel like a massive letdown in a way that a low standardized test score never did. And despite the fact that some distance from Tessa and the increasingly complicated lies around her right now is smart, I do want to be a good friend to her. I want her to like me.

"Apology and dinner not needed, but accepted."

Tessa's hand goes up to catch a tear slipping down her cheek, and I reach for a box of tissues nearby. That feeling of guilt surges again over her apologizing when I'm the one who's lying. Tessa proves she's the type of person who will choose truth time and time again, and I do the opposite. This imbalance between us will only grow.

Could I fix this by telling her about why I'm at Delmont? I lower myself back onto the bed corner, and my leg nudges my overstuffed backpack.

The contact jolts me. My whole life right now is in that backpack, all because I've been careless. Leaving myself vulnerable in any other way is a terrible idea when I have so much riding on the persona and backstory I've built up. I've been at Delmont well over a month. It's not only my and my family's pride at stake now. The hyperlogical part of me shrieks that I've probably broken all sorts of laws that the university and law enforcement officials would be more than happy to prosecute. It only reaffirms for my brain that coming clean to Tessa is a terrible idea, even if my conscience begs otherwise.

As my Delmont personal statement began to shine this past week, an unnerving side of the story wove itself together before my eyes. This lying is only temporary, I'd been telling myself, and it's wholly justified. Delmont should have admitted me in the first place, after all. I'm just fixing their mistake.

But seeing Tessa's free thinking, Camilla's annoying sharpness, Brand's impeccable memory? It all made me wonder whether

Delmont had made a mistake at all. Maybe I'm not the kind of perfect this university was looking for. Maybe I didn't truly belong here this semester. Maybe the biggest lies are the ones I've been telling myself.

My quiet contemplation doesn't go unnoticed, and Tessa peers at me over a balled-up tissue dabbing at her nose.

I force a smile. "Hey, how about we hit up that Halloween candyfest after dinner? I was going to hide out in my room, but for you, I'll go."

"Aren't you worried about Genia spotting you?"

I have to play this right. I can't give Tessa any more reasons to doubt me or ask questions I can't respond honestly to. The guilt on my soul is too heavy, and I need to find a way to lighten the load or I may collapse from it all. Just a few more white lies to wrap up this cover story and move forward, I tell myself.

"No. I'll fill Genia in the next time I catch her alone." Which will hopefully be never. "But bogging her down with all that administrative stuff would probably ruin her Halloween, and she was so excited about this event. So let's print out some masks online. Get into the Halloween spirit and hide from the RA for a night."

Tessa breaks out into her usual full-throated laugh, and the last of the uneasiness disappears. "I won't shove you at Genia, but I do get to pick your mask as part of this dinner offer. Deal?"

A free dinner and candy? "Deal."

We spend our dinner at Godwin Dining Hall looking at possible printout masks on our phones. Diet Coke almost shoots out of my nose twice.

Tessa ends up being a green-faced witch.

I am a bunny.

TWENTY-NINE

My eyes fly open. Something's off. I fumble for my phone in the darkness, accidentally touch something furry, stifle a scream, and plant my bare feet on the cold basement floor.

I blink once, twice. Fluorescent light darkens the far corner of the storage room.

The maintenance staff is already starting to arrive.

What time is it?

My eyes take a second to focus on my phone screen.

I stifle another scream.

I'm late for my shift at the Bubble and Bean.

"Come on, open the door, Jackson!" I bang on the locked glass, the bells above swaying, but not ringing. They don't want to let me in either.

Jackson stands on the other side, a rag in one hand, his arms crossed. "I should let you stay out there until my dad comes to drop off the pastries. He can let you in."

"I'm only half an hour late!" There it is again, the whining in my voice that makes me sound like a petulant child. Maybe it'll stir some sympathy in his stale-scone-hard heart. I don't exactly want to add that I had to virtually creep out of the storage area spy-style, weaving around beds and ducking behind bookcases as staff showed up. Good thing I've got excellent timing and sneaking skills from all those video games.

"Well, I got here on time, and I spent that half hour doing your work in addition to mine."

So the whining didn't work. I'm going to have to bargain if I want to get paid today. Or ever again.

"Please? I'll stay an extra half hour to make up for it."

He shifts his weight to his other foot. His arms don't uncross.

"I'll clean the bathroom."

An eyebrow raises. "More."

The bastard is enjoying this.

"Fine. You get an hour head start on the extra icing tub."

He grins, and his hand moves toward the locks. "It's technically my extra icing tub anyway and I'm being benevolent by sharing."

In a minute, I've got my hair swept up into a ponytail, my apron hanging from my neck.

Jackson plants the rag in his hands on the counter. "So what's the story?"

The guilt already starts to curdle in my gut as a lie about late-night fire alarms or sidewalk closures forms on my tongue. I swallow those words down. I found a way to lighten that crushing weight on my soul by pledging to be more honest with Tessa, so I try the truth this time too.

"Our dorm had this Halloween candyfest thing last night, and my friend wouldn't let me leave until she'd eaten all my Twix."

He turns his attention on the machines in front of him. "A candyfest? You're going to have to do better than that with my dad." He pushes a button, and the coffee grinder starts, churning as loud and abrasive as the panic in my skull.

Here I was, thinking we were friends, and he's still going to turn me in? I guess I shouldn't have expected special treatment for being truthful this time: he doesn't realize I've been lying about everything else.

The reminder of the sheer dishonesty around me—standing here in the Bubble and Bean—sits chalky in my mouth like those Smarties I couldn't off-load last night. I can't shake the guilt entirely, but it's easier to set aside when fear hits so much stronger. I can't lose this job. Next semester, when I start at Delmont for real, I'll have loans to take care of my meals and lodging. But now, even with the money my parents sent, I'm already down to two non-protein-bar meals a day, with at least one a prepackaged, high-sodium mess. Desperation always seems to win.

I plant my hands on my hips, like an exhausted athlete. Which I am, after that sprint all the way here from the dorms. "You cannot tell him I was late, Jackson. I need this."

He pauses the coffee grinder. "And you think we don't need reliable employees?"

"I was late this one time! What happened to that benevolence of yours?"

He sighs then. "This isn't some big corporation, Perla. It's literally just my dad, my sister, me, and a couple of part-timers." He shakes his head. "You know I'm trying to get my dad to agree to let me manage that second Bubble and Bean, whenever it happens. What's it going to look like if I let employees walk all over me?"

My shoulders slump. I see this as being late to a shift. He sees this as something much more consequential. He sees his life riding on it.

"I really want this second shop," he says. "What would you do if something threw a bunch of green shells and banana peels between you and your finish line?"

I smile at the *Mario Kart* reference. If only he knew that someone basically dumped a truckload of banana peels on my route to Delmont.

"I'm sorry, Jackson. I swear it won't happen again. You'll be great at running whatever business you have your heart set on."

"Not just any business: the Bubble and Bean. I can't imagine myself in a cubicle for the rest of my life. Can you?"

"I don't know. I'm supposed to go to medical school."

"But?"

I blink. "But what?"

"Listen to yourself. 'Supposed to' and 'want to' aren't the same thing. I thought you were looking at this whole mine and their doctor dream thing."

I shake my head and drop my eyes to the clean tile floor. It's too early in the morning for this kind of talk. "Yeah, I know, but it's the plan. I go to Delmont, I go to med school, I become a doctor, I join my mom's cosmetic dermatology practice, we start a business empire, we get a reality show." Much of the latter part is not, in fact, in the plan, but that increasingly judgy look on Jackson's face makes me uneasy.

Jackson raises an eyebrow. "Huh. You know you said 'the plan,' right? Not 'my plan.' And you're the one who picked on me first about word usage."

He smiles, a small peace offering. His face still shines with earnestness and hope that I stopped seeing in the mirror ages ago. Jackson doesn't live by some red binder that sits high on a bookcase shelf like it's a trophy. Even though he's gunning for that Bubble and Bean 2 position, he doesn't try to live up to the gleaming perfect-child image his parents have spent a lifetime cultivating for him. To him, the proof of his worth is in the hard work and execution, not in the pieces of paper. I envy him.

My own confidence wavers again, like a pillar beneath my foundation was shaken. "You know, I think I've always pictured my future in a medical examination room or at a surgical table. I can't honestly say that that's what I want to be at Delmont for now."

My parents won't be happy, but how they feel matters to me a little less these days.

The world around me suddenly brightens, like an old-time movie going Technicolor. There it is, that growing feeling of possibility leaking into what I thought was an airtight future, and I'm thrilled and terrified at the same time. A lifetime of being told what to do led me nowhere. My own ingenuity, my own actions brought me to Delmont. I'm ready to think bigger, to figure out my own definition of perfection.

"So what's next?" Jackson asks. "You'd be a pretty good English teacher. All that word-usage stuff reminds me of mine."

I laugh. "Sorry about picking at your word usage. I really am a jerk to you, aren't I?"

His question—"what's next?"—presses on me, begging for an answer. I realize then that talking story lines and gameplay during gaming club meetings feels like home more than any thought of biological sciences did. I've learned firsthand that enough people succeed in that industry that Delmont made a whole major for it, and maybe there's room for me in there too. The thought invigorates me more than a large milk tea and half a tub of cream cheese icing.

"I don't know what's next, but I think I have an idea." It's as bold a pronouncement as I can make this early in the morning. "Anyway, we're good, right? You're not going to tell Frank I was late?"

"If you think I'm just going to let this go because you're nice and smart and funny—" He scowls then, cutting himself off. "Don't let that all get to your head. Stay that extra half hour today, polish up that bathroom, and I won't tell my dad this time. But if you're late again, I can't cover for you. Got it?"

My insides untwist at the thought that my job is safe for another day, that honesty—though a little painful—did pay off. "Thanks." I shoo him away from the coffee grinder. "I'll finish this. Go get started with the extra icing tub. You only have a fifty-minute head start."

He sighs, part amused and still part frustrated, and heads for the back room.

I don't know if it's the close call at almost losing my financial lifeline, the decreasing importance of Perlie's Academic Plan like it's a flag being lowered, or the fact that someone called me nice and smart and funny, but my blood is buzzing.

I don't realize my cheeks are pink until I see my reflection in the shiny metal of the soy milk carafe.

THIRTY

My month-long residency in the storage room is over.

Long after the gaming club meeting ends and the maintenance staff heads home, I leave the Student Union with a belly full of greasy pizza and sneak down to the Keith Hall basement. I immediately notice that the bed frames are stacked differently. New bookcases line the wall, and someone leaned my mattress up against a shelving unit. Above the door is a hole in the drywall, and loose wires dangle from it, like someone was halfway through a security camera installation when their shift ended.

I don't stay long enough to figure out if there's another corner I can inhabit.

I leap up the stairs and into the cul de sac, where the sun dipped below the horizon hours ago. Staking a spot at a well-lit planter, I pull out my laptop and open my spreadsheet.

My breath comes too rapidly, like I can't get enough air, and I close my eyes and focus on inhaling.

How did I get to this point? Delmont has thrown me out, yet

again, and I have no one to blame this time but myself. Living on a borrowed basement mattress wasn't going to be long-term, but I'm running out of options.

I shiver against a chilly breeze that ripples a café umbrella nearby. In the darkness, it's hard to miss the lack of housing alternatives through the too-bright glare of my screen. Samantha Simon's room and the storage area are off-limits. The two other rooms I've been keeping an eye on are now occupied, as residents shifted around and international student visas came through in the last few weeks.

I have nowhere to sleep tonight, and this Delmont hoodie is too bright to blend in at the library stacks past closing and not nearly thick enough for me to rough it outside. My head starting to throb, I pull out my phone and text my last lifeline.

The yellow of the towel wrapped around Camilla's wet hair is the same shade as the one I'd lost when Delmont staff cleared out Samantha Simon's room. Our moms must shop at the same place.

"Hurry up," Camilla says, yanking me into her dorm.

Godwin Village rooms are just as small as the ones in Keith Hall, but the lighting is a warmer orange and the furnishings aren't as worse for wear. Godwin Hall is newer than Keith Hall, and everything is that welcoming shade of beige that was so in style a decade ago.

Camilla's class schedules and an art print of a palm tree partially cover up an off-white discoloration on one wall. A dozen pairs of shoes and two suitcases peek out from underneath her twin bed, which is covered in a navy-blue down comforter and fluffy, oversized pillows. The floor, where I'll be sleeping, is thankfully uncluttered.

The door clicks shut behind me, and the room suddenly feels far too tiny for both of us to stand here together. When Camilla offered to help me weeks ago, I'm certain she wasn't expecting me to ask her to house me. But I've kept good—mostly—on my pledge to stop lying to Tessa, and she's not going to let me bunk with her without asking questions I can't answer, and Frank and Jackson won't hand over a key to the Bubble and Bean to let the new girl close up (and sleep in the storeroom) for the night.

The adrenaline lingers, as if my body's expecting me to be kicked out of this place too. I spent the whole walk here peeking over my shoulder for some unknown pursuer. But the logical part of me tells me that no one's out to catch Delmont Perla in the act. They don't even know she exists.

But with a deep breath of citrus-scented air here in Camilla's room, the horror sets in. I try to curve my mouth into what I hope comes off as a sincere smile. "Thanks. It'll be temporary, I swear. Until I find a new place."

Camilla moves toward her closet. "I've got an extra blanket in here. Put your stuff away when you leave in the mornings so it's not too obvious someone else is staying here."

I blink. "Mornings? Plural? I just said—"

"I heard you, but if it keeps you from doing something that'll get you killed, sleep on my floor as long as you need to. I'm over at Rich's most nights anyway. He has a full-sized bed in his apartment, not this measly twin." She reaches for her backpack then. "You hungry? I didn't eat the pretzels that came with my sandwich."

She tugs out a bag of pretzels, and my stomach grumbles my response for me.

Still standing, I start to inhale the bag while she turns back to the mirror on her nightstand. Having something in my stomach helps steady my nerves, but not by much. I feel like the slightest wind could rip up my fragile roots at any moment.

Camilla lays a few more ground rules—avoiding her neighbors, keeping the noise to a minimum, not touching her stuff—all while dabbing and smearing various concoctions on her face. In between salty bites, I "yup" and "got it" after each rule.

"I appreciate this, Camilla, but I really am going to try to find another place to stay so I'm not in your hair."

She sighs and angles to look at me over her shoulder. "Perlie, it's okay to ask for help."

I don't have anything to say to that. It feels like a lesson I should've learned ages ago, but I was too busy planning out extracurriculars and test prep to pay attention.

A wrinkle forms on her forehead at my silence. "Are you sure you know what you're doing? This is getting messy, and I hate to say it, but . . ." She lets out a breath. ". . . I don't think this is going to end the way you want it to. You should consider coming clean."

Suddenly, the pretzels go chalky in my mouth. "Do I know what I'm doing? I . . ." I start to assure her that yes, I do know— I have a whole seven-part plan on it—but something stops me.

What comes out instead is "No. I don't think I actually do. I wouldn't be here eating your leftover pretzels if I did, would I?"

The unmistakable misery in my words fills every corner of the room, like fog sweeping in from the sea.

A rustling grabs my attention, and it takes me a moment to realize that my pretzel-bag-clutching hands are shaking.

Camilla's eyes go wide, and she clutches my arm just as my legs falter. I let her lead me to her desk chair as the tears start to flow, hot and messy. I try to wipe them away, still clutching the pretzel bag, and crumbs spill onto her desk.

I can't even cry without wrecking everything around me.

Camilla gently takes the bag. "Hey, hey, I know it'll be all right."

I almost laugh then, because whether or not she means to, now she's the one lying. How does she know it'll be all right? She can say that as we sit in her very own dorm room, filled with her very own textbooks preparing her for pursuing a career she loves, only an easy phone call away from her proud parents.

I have none of that, and the lack is like a hole in my chest.

"I need to fix this, but how?" I ask her as much as I ask myself. "Sometimes it feels so overwhelming, like it's impossible to keep all this up, but what will happen to me?"

"I don't know," Camilla responds quietly, but we both see the outlines of the possible repercussions.

For what feels like the hundredth time, I rerun the scenario in my head. Admitting I didn't get into Delmont will only lead to more loss, more anger. If I felt lacking earlier, outing myself for my deception will leave me with nothing. I'll never get the dorm room, the career in anything, the parental support, if I don't keep on this path.

As much as I want to be honest, as much as I want to break free from this tight, life-draining web I've spun around myself, I can't. I'm not strong enough. And realizing that is painful in its own way.

I'll have to learn to live with this hole in my chest.

It takes a minute for the tears to stop. Camilla sits back on her heels and watches as I reach for my backpack.

"What are you going to do?" she asks.

I pull out my laptop and set it on the floor between us. "I'm going to submit my application for Delmont's spring semester."

She bites her lip then but says nothing. I see the uncertainty, the hint of disappointment in her eyes anyway. She's not going to stop me though, just like she didn't out me to my parents when she discovered my deception. And it's not only because I have a secret on her too. It's because she does understand, deep down, what I'm doing and why. In addition to our shining boast-worthy sides, we share a hideous underbelly.

I navigate to the Delmont admissions portal and pull up my materials. I blow out a breath to steady myself. "'The best way out is always through.'"

"Robert Frost," she recites automatically. Then she offers me a gentle smile. "From that whole poetry project junior year. I can't believe you remember that by heart. Nerd."

I laugh, if only to keep the horror at bay. "If I get into Delmont, then all of this gets wiped clean. I know this isn't the 'coming clean' you'd meant earlier, but it's the only real option for me. It's what I've been working so hard toward."

She reaches for my hand and squeezes it.

With my other hand, I tap my touch pad, and then all my work, all my hopes for redemption, transmit with a click. It's almost anticlimactic to see the simple *Your application has been successfully submitted. Keep this confirmation number for your reference* message again.

Camilla draws her hand away from mine.

It's done, and in some ways, it suddenly feels like the worst lie I've ever told. It's a story to some faceless admissions committee about a doctor dream that isn't mine, but more than that, it's part of a larger story I've been struggling to convince myself of: that I belong here at Delmont.

"When are you supposed to hear back?" Camilla asks.

I close my laptop. "I'll get my official acceptance letter in a month. Until then, I need to keep up the appearance that I go here."

Camilla's phone buzzes with a text, but she makes no move to get it. Instead, she keeps gazing at me with that forehead-wrinkled look, the one full of the same kind of worry someone extends to stray puppies. "Let's go celebrate your acceptance early then. Give me a second to get dressed, and we'll go hit up the late-night café for cheese fries. I've got swipes to burn."

I smile, thankful for the offer, but am in no mood to celebrate. I've never been one to turn down cheese fries though.

Camilla pulls on her Delmont hoodie, matching mine, and we head out into the night together.

THIRTY-ONE

Tessa

Where are you? Been knocking at your door. We were supposed to do dinner then movie night. Asked Genia but she still has no clue about where you live!

Sent 6:21 pm

Perla

Switched rooms. In Godwin now. Turns out I wasn't on Genia's list for good reason

Read 6:22 pm

Tessa

LOL and your room card still worked? Super unsafe. We should sue the school. I'm coming down there for dinner

Sent 6:23 pm

THIRTY-TWO

The pace of Delmont life slows as Thanksgiving approaches. Some people leave campus early to beat the traffic and airport rushes, but most of the first-years I know are staying. Finals and winter break are only a few weeks away, and so is the date I'm supposed to hear from the Delmont admissions committee.

I should be excited. Soon, I'll get my actual admittance into Delmont. It'll make all this heartache and stomach acid worth it. It'll erase the grime from the awful things I've said and done to people. But I find myself trying to ignore that response date altogether, as if part of me questions how much of a victory this really would be.

Mom and Dad had actually sounded upset when I'd told them I wasn't coming home for Thanksgiving. I couldn't get around this holiday without spinning a few more white lies, so I said I couldn't lose twelve hours of studying to sitting in a car. I threw in mention of an optional Sunday meetup for my fake college-success mentorship program, focusing entirely on strategies for acing finals. My parents relented, not without some grumbling and "the family will want to see you" guilt trips, and I'd wondered if they had the same twinge in their chests when they'd hung up the phone too.

In reality, I couldn't bear to be wrapped in any hugs, to be forced to lie again and again every time anyone asked about Delmont. I couldn't listen to everyone back home spout those same crushing platitudes about what constitutes success and how and why to achieve it. I'm not strong enough to weather a visit back when I'm still trying to build my own image of the world around me. That doesn't mean I don't miss the comfort of home though.

I perch on the side of the staircase into the Student Union this afternoon, waiting for Brand. I pull up my text messages, leaving unread the one I'd gotten from Tessa last night. I'd sworn to back off my friendships a little now that my personal statement is in, to stop shoveling more of that muck on my soul and, selfishly, to make it easier to last the rest of the semester uninterrogated. But Brand is my key into the gaming club. Having him around lends credibility to my being there as well.

Tessa, on the other hand, is too close. She kept knocking on Samantha Simon's door, for heaven's sake. She keeps tabs on me and, even with Casprin drawing some of her attention, she seems intent on spending all her free time with me, which could prove dangerous. I can't continue to dodge questions about my hour-to-hour whereabouts, about classes I don't have, about the finals I won't be taking.

Lucky for Brand, he wouldn't pop up at someone's dorm room

door unexpected like Tessa would, and he doesn't know my schedule well enough to know where I'm supposed to be and when.

Plus he's the one who showed me there's a whole big, reputable gaming industry out there, not only job-hopping people in their families' basements. Who knows what other dreams will unlock if I stick with him and peek in on his course list now and then?

I spot Brand coming down the Boulevard, earbuds in, sporting a fresh haircut. I hop down from the fountain, nearly keeling over when my one used, thousand-pound bio book shifts around in my backpack.

Off in the distance, behind him, I catch a glimpse of what I think is Tessa's purple hair. I swallow my guilt at seeing her to force on a light smile as Brand approaches.

Brand plucks out the earbuds before pinning me with a wide smile. We make our way into gaming club meeting together, lingering at the entrance of the Phoenix Tech Lounge before spotting a row of empty seats.

I squeeze through the aisle between computer tables and plop into my chair first. I hang my backpack on the chair behind me as Brand pulls out his phone.

He angles the screen at me. "Jimmy's hosting a get-together tonight for a few folks sticking around for Turkey Day. You in? He's got that new PS5 fighting game, the one with the aliens."

The table shakes as another person rolls up a chair next to me. It's Claire, my other favorite gaming club face.

"Yes, please come," Claire says to me. "It gets so boring beating all these guys' butts."

Brand laughs but doesn't counter her. From what I've seen on the few meetings I've stayed to watch people play, Claire can pick up the basics of a game very quickly and somehow reach expert level even faster.

An opportunity to hang out with other gaming folks and check out the latest big release? Since I turned in my application, I've felt aimless, adrift, like I'm in some sort of purgatory waiting for my true acceptance. I've forced myself to sit in the back of a couple more lecture halls to see if any other fields pique my interest, but nothing sticks. The highlight of my weeks has been these club meetings and events. Gushing over graphics and gameplay with other Delmont students may be just what I need to make me feel like I belong.

"Sure. When and where?"

"His place is on Commonwealth. I'll swing by at nine. We can walk over together. You're in the dorms, right?"

I nod. I wouldn't want to show up the party without him, my social shield, there. It'd be like going up against a big boss on my last life, without armor. It will be good for my full-fledged-Delmont-student cover to have someone else able to independently verify that I came out of a lived-in dorm room too. If Brand can vouch that he physically saw my supposed home, it's an extra line of defense in case anyone asks why I'm lurking around Godwin Village. Besides, I've already told Tessa what building I'm in, and Camilla's going to be at Rich's tonight. "Godwin, room 115."

His smile nearly makes me forget the earlier Tessa guilt altogether. "Perfect. See you at nine."

The table shakes again as Claire dumps a massive textbook in front of her. The title catches my eye.

I read the spine aloud. *"Information Systems Principles?"*

Claire flashes me a pink-lip-glossed smile. "It's rough, but it's required for my business administration degree. I've got a summer internship with HR for Ubisoft in their Saint-Mandé office, so I'll take any extra info about the industry I can get. I don't want to make a total fool of myself."

My jaw drops, not only because her French pronunciation is spot-on but because she's already got an internship with a top gaming company lined up. I'm sure it's a combination of what my parents have been saying and my own eyes-on-the-doctor-prize way of thinking so far, but even with my doctor dream slipping away, I've all but convinced myself there wasn't really a career path for me in gaming. Claire's coveted internship abroad at an internationally known company is a door that I didn't know existed.

"That's amazing. What will you be doing there?" I force myself not to scoot to the edge of my chair in my sudden enthusiasm.

"A lot of the job will be working on recruitment and communication campaigns. I'm a whiz at spreadsheets, so the project management part of this is right up my alley."

A puzzle piece clicks inside of me, filling an empty space that I'd long overlooked. A trajectory like Claire's would be a chance to truly be a part of a community I feel at home with, creating games that will give others that thrill of the win that I craved ever since I pressed my first start button. Auntie Trish lightheartedly termed games my "self-care," but they were more of a lifeline through those hard, lonely years at Monte Verde. And I can help bring this joy to others. This could be a way for me to combine everything that I love into a career.

It doesn't escape my attention that "everything I love" doesn't include medicine. The thought simultaneously feels freeing but sad, not unlike seeing my parents drive away from Delmont months ago. Finally, I'm letting go of a long-held dream that wasn't entirely mine to begin with, so this moment of grief, this corresponding heaviness in my chest isn't surprising.

But the feeling of something new sparkles before me, begging to be seen. I roll my chair closer to Claire's.

"So," I say, "what other classes do you need for that business administration degree?"

THIRTY-THREE

On PicLine: a picture of myself in the mirror, my phone covering most of my face. I'm in fitted jeans, a black retro Metroid tank top that I thrifted for the price of a bubble tea and a pineapple bun, and a borrowed swipe of Camilla's burgundy lipstick. My heart pendant necklace doesn't go with the look, so I leave it off.

Caption: Ready for a night out #party

Thirty-three likes.

Tessa

Nice PicLine post! Looking hot! Going out without me? RUDE!

Sent 8:21 pm

Camilla zips up her backpack and shoves her phone in her back pocket. "You promise you won't give anyone else my room number?"

When I'd told Camilla about the party tonight, she'd scolded me for being "sloppy," and I've spent the last hour apologizing profusely. Our minds work so alike that I thought she'd see it my way—with folks becoming accustomed to seeing me in the dorms—but she disagreed. Because Camilla is the only thing standing between me and another hidden-housing search, I'd asked Brand to meet me outside instead of coming to Camilla's room after all. Then I offered to do her laundry for a month. Jeopardizing my one honest friendship right now is the last thing I want to do.

"I promise," I say.

"You'll call me if you need anything, right? Rich's is only three blocks away, and I can be here in—"

I make a sweeping motion with both hands to usher her out the door. "I'll be fine, Camilla. Say hi to Rich for me."

She hoists her backpack up and slides the straps over her shoulders. "And make sure the door doesn't slam when you close it, okay? My neighbor already passive-aggressively mentioned the noise and the residence hall quiet hours to me twice this week."

I dramatically roll my eyes. "You know, you're starting to sound like our parents, with all your rules."

She sticks her tongue out at me, a twinkle in her eye, before she waves and heads out.

It's almost time for me to meet Brand, so I grab the gray clutch I'd borrowed from Camilla—she brought, no joke, eleven different purses to campus—and double-check the tape on the latch before leaving too.

Brand is already in the building lobby when I step out of the elevator.

"Nice Samus shirt! Ready?"

I smile at his instant recognition of my new top. He gets me. "Let's go."

We hike toward Jimmy's, and when we arrive at a blocky apartment complex, we can hear the music even from downstairs. The bass thumps into the open, palm-tree-dotted courtyard, and I'm surprised someone hasn't already banged a fist on the door to shut them up. Judging by the fact that every other window facing the courtyard sports Delmont flags or *Go, Dragons!* team gear, no one's going to call in a noise complaint.

"I thought you and Claire said this was going to be a small get-together," I say carefully, trying not to sound too Perfect Perlie Perez.

I'd been pumping myself up for a casual hangout around a PlayStation, something to help me ease into the Delmont social scene. I'd been hoping this low-pressure, friend-making expedition will prove I belong here among these Delmont folks. Fading into the background isn't the same as fitting in, and the latter is my next side mission while I hurtle toward the final "you're in!" win.

My doubts have grown since I submitted my application. I've questioned whether I was doing the right thing with my whole plan and reapplying, whether I'm as smart, capable, and socially competent as any Delmont student, despite whatever the admissions committee says. I could use some external sign from the heavens on all this, like a new friend or a lead on a safe place to stay.

But my vision of close conversations with a few helpful faces crumbles as we near Jimmy's. This raging party is a whole other beast entirely.

Brand shrugs. "I thought so too. Looks like his roommates probably invited a couple more people. I already called dibs on a controller though, so you and I are good."

We head up to the second floor, and when Brand knocks, a drunk, red-faced Jimmy swings the door open. I didn't think it possible, but the music is even louder inside. Brand ushers me into the too-crowded apartment and points to a tiny empty spot between a foosball table and the couch.

I follow, futilely attempting to "excuse me" my way through the dozens of people here. Four people cram together on the fake leather couch, button-mashing their way through a *Super Smash Bros.* match.

Once I've staked out a seat on the couch arm, Brand leans close. "You want a drink?"

Claire, at the far side of the couch, screeches as her character gets knocked off-screen, and the other players and everyone around us laugh. I don't drink. But my mouth is dry, the excitement contagious, and my voice not my own. "Sure."

"Save my spot," he says as he heads for the kitchen.

Jimmy's playlist music thumps inside my chest, the beat drumming in my veins. Jimmy joins us in front of the TV, and he and Claire shuffle around and end up closest to me on the couch, his arm around her shoulders. I squeeze into a smaller ball to make a pathway for a newly arrived group of guests swarming the kitchen, angling for booze or pizza. Each attempt to introduce myself to someone near me falls flat, and I don't push it: it's hard to split concentration between a game and a conversation. So I settle on cheering folks along, trying but failing not to take their disinterest personally. I had come here looking for a sign that I could fit into the Delmont student body, and this feels like a Magic 8 Ball flashing me a *Don't count on it.*

Brand returns with two sticky red cups. "I'm not a great bartender, but hopefully all this ice will melt and disguise the disgustingness."

I take a sip and whatever cheap drugstore rum he used slams onto my tongue.

"It's fine!" I shout despite the fact that I'm sure the scrunch of my face gives me away.

I sip again, and the rum burns my mouth, then my throat, then my core. It spreads warmth into my limbs, loosening my muscles, making them more susceptible to this music's heavy beat. My parents would be livid. Perlie, at a party, drinking alcohol, with a boy? But they're half a state away, and I have never been so thankful for it.

I shake off the earlier failed "Hi, I'm Perlas." I am determined to have fun tonight. All the heartache of years spent squeezing into the unyielding mold of Perfect Perlie, of breaking off parts of myself so I'd fit—it falls away. I don't know who I am yet, but tonight, with the music and energy crackling in my blood, feels as good as time as any to find out.

After this *Super Smash Bros.* match ends, Claire plants the controller in my hand. "Here. Show these boys what's what," she says before snatching the drink out of my hand. "Don't drink this sludge. I'll get you something better."

As she flits to the kitchen, Brand pats me on the shoulder. "You've got this, Perla."

And just like that, I feel welcomed, at home. I've got a game controller, a seat in front of the screen, and people cheering me on. I choose a character—Samus, of course—and wait for the other players to settle on theirs. Claire returns with a cocktail, one with fruit juice and vodka, and it's a thousand times better than Brand's. When I tell him so, he gives me a mock-hurt look, and Claire shuts him up by making him one too.

The match begins, and I finish my sugary drink faster than I'd intended to. In between lives—I can't believe I got cornered and knocked out by a hammer—I toss the empty cup into the trash can a few feet away. I'm immensely proud it goes in, rather than bouncing against the rim and falling out. Perlie would have missed. Perla's a great shot. And of course I win the match.

I hand the controller to Brand next and settle in my spot on the couch arm, alternating between watching the TV and the crowd. I'm at a party, and I'm enjoying myself. I don't remember the last time this happened. Maybe Chuck E. Cheese when I was eight?

I hear an electronica version of a song I like, and even to my surprise, I rise from the couch arm and start dancing. Me, the girl who managed to skip homecoming, prom, and any other school-sanctioned occasion involving music and socializing. Me, who sits at the edge of family weddings, watching everyone else get "a little bit louder now" on the dance floor to "Shout."

But I remind myself that that person, the bookworm built on grades and prestige and some false sense of pride, is gone. Strip away the pressure of perfect academic marks and those people I endlessly stress about making happy, and this is me, this is who I can be. Night-embracing, music-swaying, free. Maybe this was the sign that I was looking for: that I have the capacity to be happy just because, that it's enough that I'm proud of myself for making it so far. Claire joins me mid-song, and we laugh and dance together as if we've been doing this for years.

THIRTY-FOUR

I don't know how long I'm at the party when the lights start to swirl together. The music, once rhythmic and immersive, begins to feel off-key. It throws me around, the beats hitting all wrong, the notes discordant. My stomach, though full of things sweet and bubbly, feels sour and stone-heavy.

After I lose a match, I practically shove the controller at Claire, then scan the apartment for the bathroom and stumble toward it.

Claire grabs my elbow before I get too far. "You all right? You look—"

"Fine. Bathroom." Full sentences aren't a possibility right now.

Someone nearby tells a joke about some sociology professor, and everyone but me laughs. I feel too off to pretend I understand the punch line.

I stagger out of Claire's grip. The lights above the mirror shine too bright on me and all the grossness that is a guys' bathroom.

I plant my hands on the cold granite counter and drag in stuffy air scented of stale beer and hypermasculine body wash. My vision refuses to cooperate. My eyes drift from spot to spot, focusing on nothing. Sweat beads on my forehead and temples. I drag my clammy fingers through my hair. I close my eyes, ignoring the swirl of my surroundings, and concentrate on getting enough air.

My first time drinking and I've overdone it.

I feel sick.

I want to go home.

And this Delmont place that I thought was home? This doesn't feel like it anymore. The brief joy earlier wasn't a sign: it was a mirage. And here I am, blinking, dehydrated and alone in the desert.

A fist bangs on the other side of the door. "Hurry up in there."

I become acutely aware of how far I am from my actual home right now, from my comfy pink bed and the familiar fuzzy faces of Bip and Bop. I'm six hours away, alone in the dingy bathroom of an older student from a school I don't go to.

The sudden shame over submitting my spring semester application hits me like a tidal wave. What do I think I'm doing here? One stolen semester, one carefully crafted personal statement, one loud party won't make me a Delmont student. As of this second, I'm not sure I ever can be.

I run my hands through the icy water of the faucet and dry them on the already-damp brown hand towels hanging from a ring next to the sink. I steel myself for the onslaught on my senses and pull open the door.

The beat of the music sings a hard "go, go, go."

So I stumble and elbow my way through the throng of laughing strangers toward the exit. The fresh night air outside beckons me, promises me salvation. The world tells me I can't stay in this muck of an apartment for another second.

"Perla? You leaving?"

Except I came here with Brand.

I angle my head over my shoulder but keep moving toward the door. "Yeah, don't feel well. Heading back."

He lowers his controller, and his eyebrows furrow. I brace to argue with a "You want me to walk you home?" But when he opens his mouth, he says, "You're good, right? I'm going to stay. They're loading up the alien game, and I've got next."

The disappointment adds another thick, suffocating layer to the atmosphere. Be cool, I tell myself. You feel and probably look awful, and you don't want him to see you at your worst, in the bright lights of the residence hall you don't live in. "Sure. That's fine."

"Text me to let me know you got back safe, okay?"

I manage a smile, then plow my way to the door. I just need to get to Camilla's room. I can smooth over this quick, awkward exit in the morning, when my stomach isn't trying to destroy me.

I barrel down the stairs, missing the second step from the bottom of the flight. I land with a twist of my ankle that sends a bolt of pain through my leg. My jaw clenches as I try to forge ahead.

Weak streetlight bathes a bench on the main road. A car zooms by, pumping the same music I heard at Jimmy's. The desire to sit overwhelms me. I can rest for a few minutes, then head back to Godwin.

The second I sit, that plan melts away. A warm wind wraps around me, and I breathe in deep for what seems like the first time in hours. My eyelids lower, and I soak in the feeling.

New plan: close my eyes, let these swirling colors die away, get up energized in a few minutes, then make it back to Godwin.

A car door slams nearby, and my survival instincts force my eyelids open. A familiar silhouette casts shadows in the streetlight.

"Perla?"

A familiar voice too. Even the gait of the approaching steps is familiar. I squint into the darkness, struggling to keep my eyes open and focused.

Someone crouches in front of me, his hands planted on his thighs. Jackson.

"Hey, are you okay?"

My lips feel heavy, messy. "I need to go home."

He frowns as I speak, but I'm too tired to enunciate or explain further.

"Come on. I'll give you a ride."

He springs back up and opens the car door.

I shake my head, and it sends the world in a spin. "No, I can walk."

Jackson glances behind him at the cars whirring by on the main street. "I don't think it's a good idea. Crosswalk's kind of hard to see down there. I can drop you off in front of your building. I won't even take it out of your paycheck or tell my dad."

A giggle bubbles up out of me. I will all of my energy into my legs and hoist myself up.

"Were you at the party?" I ask. "I didn't see you."

He shakes his head. "Closed up at the Bubble and Bean for the night."

Of course a high schooler like him wouldn't have been invited. I'm apparently also too exhausted to be embarrassed about my nonsensical question.

The sheer thought of a bed propels me into the car, and my fingers feel thick and clumsy as I try to buckle my seat belt.

"Here, I got it." Jackson brushes my hands away, and a second later, the seat belt clicks together.

"Which building?" he asks, starting the car.

"Godwin. East."

I don't know if he says anything else. I fall asleep, comfortable in this worn front seat, air streaming in from the sliver of the open window.

THIRTY-FIVE

Someone bangs on the door, and for a second, I think I've dreamed everything up. But another two bangs has me peeling my sweat-beaded face off Camilla's pillowcase. She's going to be furious I used her bed.

The makeup I'd carefully applied earlier tonight smears against the blue cotton. All the lights are on, and I'm cradling a half-empty bottle of water I don't remember buying.

It must've been Jackson.

Somewhere from behind the blossoming headache comes the memory of him opening my car door for me in the driveway outside Camilla's building. I'd argued with him about walking me to my room. I at least had the wherewithal to know that he'd think something was off if I'd taped open the lock of my own dorm room.

Three more too-loud knocks.

"Hold on, I'm coming," I call toward the door. Could Jackson have followed me? If so, he'd better have brought something to settle the acid in my stomach. Only then could I hope for enough brainpower to talk my way out of this.

I take a sip of water to swish around in my dry, sour mouth and pause a second at the edge of the bed to let the hurricane in my head calm.

What time is it?

I glance around for my phone, but it's not on Camilla's bed or plugged into the charging cord. I can't have been asleep that long though. That low-grade rum still runs like poison in my veins.

I wobble toward the door.

"Jackson, I don't need you to take care . . ."

The words die on my lips.

Brand's forearm is perched on the doorframe, his free hand dangling a cell phone. My cell phone.

"Looking for this?"

In my rush to leave, I must have left everything behind. I grab my cell phone back and mumble a thanks, fully aware of my rat nest of hair and the raccoon smudges of my eyeliner and mascara.

"I was waiting for your text. When I didn't see it, I found your purse on the coffee table." He pulls Camilla's gray clutch out of his back pocket. "I was going to keep it, but it didn't match my outfit." Judging by the sleepy eyes and thick words, he must have come straight from the party.

I offer up my gratitude to the universe for the fact that I am back in a dorm room and not hanging out on that bench. He would have walked right past me and banged on Camilla's unlocked door until it gave way and swung open.

Brand lolls his head to the side. "Sorry, I had to open it up to make sure it was yours. How'd you get into your room without your room key?" He waves Samantha Simon's old room key—the one I purposely fumble with as I walk through the lobby or wait in the elevator—in front of me like a piece of candy.

The alarm bells instantly cut through the fog in my head. "I . . . front desk. Temporary key."

He accepts this lie like every other one I've slung at him. "I'm starving. Jimmy's pizza was cardboard. You wanna go grab something to eat? I know a 24/7 diner down in the village."

The thought of the fifteen-minute hike into town renews the fizzing of my stomach acid. "No, I should really be getting to . . ."

Voices drift around the corner. To my horror, they do not sound like the cheery type of voices of partiers stumbling home after a late night. They reek of authority. The static of a walkie-talkie drains every bit of blood from my face. Whoever's coming will round the corner in a matter of seconds, and they stand between this room and the main entrance to the building.

I could shut the door, but Brand's still outside.

"Get in here," I whisper to him, not bothering to hide the urgency in my voice.

His eyes fog over with confusion. "But the diner . . ."

"Not now!" I grab his shirt and try to drag him in, but he's heavier than I'd imagined and those rum drinks slow his movements.

"Excuse me, young man. Young man!" a voice bellows down the hall.

Panic bolts through me. "Hurry!"

But Brand wrenches out of my grasp and peeks back outside, a damn grin on his beautiful face. This boy must have never gotten in trouble in his life. "Yes, Officer?"

Boots thunder toward the room, and suddenly I'm penned in by Brand and two campus safety officers. Not sworn-in police officers but still not the kind of people I want asking me questions in the middle of the night. Shining brass badges sit above one pocket of their blue button-down shirts, black plastic name tags above the other. Officer Walton and Officer Khan.

"We've gotten a noise complaint," Officer Khan, her piercing green eyes the same shade as her geometric-patterned hijab. "Someone banging on a door or walls."

The mustached Officer Walton eyes us both, and I get the feeling that my lies will bounce off of both of them. I summon the most forlorn, apologetic look I can manage.

I don't even get a chance to speak because perfect Brand straightens and says, "Yes, sir. That was me. I'm just returning my friend's purse. It took me a while to wake her up."

Officer Khan peers at the clutch under my arm and frowns. "We still have to write this up. I'll need your student IDs."

Brand goes to fish his out, and my fingers drift to my clutch as I scramble for an excuse. I paint on my best feigned surprise. All that guilt over lying to my friends and family doesn't even make an appearance. I'm purely in survival mode now. "Oh no, my ID's not in here. It must have fallen out. Brand, did you see it in here earlier?"

Brand casts me a dejected look. "Sorry, Perla, I don't think so. But wouldn't you have used it to get a new room key? They might have it at the front desk, right?"

I cast him as strong of a "shut up" look as I can manage, but the message doesn't seem to reach him.

Officer Walton takes Brand's ID and scribbles his name down on a form on his clipboard. He glances at me. "And he said your name is Perla?"

I nod. I can't even pretend I'm Camilla now.

"And your last name?" Officer Khan asks, a hint of impatience in her voice.

It's been years since someone I'm not related to used that "you're in trouble, missy" tone with me. I already feel my throat tightening. The slightest rise of volume in someone's voice immediately sends me back to elementary school, getting scolded by the teacher for spilling water on a keyboard in the computer lab. But what I could get scolded for here is much, much worse.

My "Perez. Perla Perez" comes out as a whisper.

"Louder, please."

I repeat it, hating the waver in my voice, and Officer Walton scrawls it down too.

I want to throw up.

"Birthday?"

I tell him and realize, belatedly, I'd given them my real birthday, not the one I'd written out in my detailed seven-part plan backstory tab, the one that would make me a legal adult.

Calculation flashes in Officer Khan's eyes. "You're only

sixteen?"

No one accidentally misstates the year of their own birthday.

"I turn seventeen soon," I correct her, ignoring the deepening of the officers' grimaces and the drop of Brand's jaw.

Officer Khan glances at my room number and reminds Officer Walton to add it to the form.

I shove down the terror at what this means for Camilla, who saved me from creeping and sleeping around the library stacks, and the dread at the fact that I'm back where I started, having to find yet another place to stay.

The rest of Officer Walton's questions center around Brand, like what time he arrived, whether he lives on campus. Officer Khan occasionally glances at me, as if assessing my responses to Brand's answers. Her gaze is unnerving, but there's nowhere I can hide from them. I just want them gone as soon as possible.

Officer Walton tucks his pen into his shirt pocket. "Someone will follow up with you in the morning about the complaint. You keep it down now, got it?"

We nod and "Yes, Officer" dutifully. Once they disappear around the corner, Brand turns to me, his brown eyes devoid of the warmth they'd glowed with a mere ten minutes ago. "Sorry for getting you in trouble with all that noise. I'm going to go."

My throat tightens again. Not that I'd wanted to drag myself out to that 24/7 diner, but it's clear that the invitation from him for any kind of get-together is closed, nailed shut, and buried underground. "Yeah, of course. I'll see you in class?"

His brow tightens. "I don't think we should hang out anymore."

My stomach dives. I think I know where this is going. "What? Why not?" I ask anyway.

"You're sixteen." He lowers his head and drags in a breath. When he meets my eyes again, the cold distance in his gaze makes my chest tighten. "I'm nineteen. I got you a drink, and you're just a kid! I could get in serious trouble for that. My dad would kill me if I got kicked out of Delmont. You're too young, Perla. Sorry."

I don't have the words or the strength to argue with him or beg him to stay, so we force lackluster goodbyes and I watch him walk down the hallway before I close the door.

I fight the urge to sob, scream, throw something at a wall to watch it shatter. Everything is broken anyway. What's one more object? But nothing within arm's reach is mine: it's all Camilla's, another reminder of the fleeting nature of my time here.

The idea of earning another noise complaint compels me to text Camilla rather than call: *I messed up. Noise complaint. Leaving your room now. I am so so sorry. Tell security whatever you want, I'll back up your story.*

I check to see if she's read my text while I drag my backpack out of her closet, but she must be asleep and won't see this until morning.

Sleeping with a free and clear conscience? I've forgotten what that feels like.

I start to pack through the film of tears blurring my vision.

THIRTY-SIX

My eyes red and dry now, I peer around at Camilla's room. I don't have any tears left, and if I did, I don't think I could spare the energy to wipe them away if they fell. Exhaustion—and let's be real, the generic-brand rum—overtook me last night. With all the alternate housing locations on my seven-part plan unavailable, I was supposed to leave early and hunt for a new place on campus. Instead I sat down for a minute, then woke up four hours later, my mouth sticky and bitter. I forced myself to my feet and began to gather my things.

In the growing light of morning, I realize how tired I am of looking over my shoulder, juggling my lies, continuing to compare myself to everyone around me to see where I've fallen short. My brain and my bones are screaming to me that I can't keep fighting a losing battle.

Delmont doesn't want me, in any form. It's made that abundantly clear. And to my surprise, the realization doesn't gut me. They rejected me, and now I'm rejecting them too. Even as my experience here has started to open my eyes to all the cracks in my foundations, this place brings out the worst in me. It's made me someone neither I nor anyone else would be proud of.

I have to face the truth: it's time for me to find somewhere, anywhere, that will at least let me exist as the imperfect person that I am. I can no longer be Perfect Perlie Perez or Delmont Perla or whatever other dream my parents and I have concocted.

Officer Walton had said someone would reach out to me this morning to address the noise complaint. I don't plan on being here the next time someone knocks. I pat for the wallet in the pocket of my jeans. There's a hostel two miles away that might take my credit card until I can figure out my next steps. The long walk will give me time to clear my head and drum up the immense amount of courage required to finally call my parents and ask for the help and support I've needed all along.

My phone rings, and I instinctively jump. I reach across Camilla's nightstand of skin care goo and unplug my phone from the charger.

Camilla is breathless. "Perlie! Are you all right? Are you some-where safe?"

"I'm still in your room. I . . . I fell asleep. But I'm leaving now."

"I was worried you were in a police van or something."

Her concern threatens to kick-start my tear ducts again. "I'm really sorry, Camilla. I didn't want to get you in trouble."

"I'll say the officers got the room number wrong or that I was out and didn't know someone was in my room. You know my mom would flip out on them—lawsuits, press, the whole thing—if I even hinted to her that Delmont housing isn't secure. So don't worry about me. I thought this all through when I first got your text about needing somewhere to sleep. Get yourself somewhere safe, Perlie. That's what's most important."

I sniffle back a tear. "I'm sorry I said before that we weren't friends. You're probably the best one I've ever had. Which is kind of sad, considering we didn't speak at Monte Verde High at all."

I can practically hear the smile in her voice when she responds. "I told you, it's more of a big-and-little-sister family thing. We can fight and have off days and still look out for each other. Kind of like us and our parents, am I right?"

That brings a choke of a laugh out of me. My world is collapsing, and she's trying to hold up a sliver of sky so I can escape. I'm hit with an overwhelming sense of regret that I didn't see the glimmer of this friendship earlier, that I'd focused on all the wrong things that I missed the gold in front of me. Before I can apologize again, my phone buzzes. I glance down at my screen, and that's when I see that I have three other missed calls. It's not even eight in the morning. My blood stills in my veins.

The calls are from Mom.

And she's calling again.

"I have to go. It's my mom," I tell Camilla.

"Oh." That one word carries all the dread I'm feeling. "Good luck, Perlie."

I bite my lip, then answer Mom's line.

"Perlie! Where have you been?"

"Sorry, I had my phone on silent for the night. I needed the sleep."

I should have known something was wrong when Mom didn't pounce on my lack of sleep to snipe that I'm not taking care of myself properly. "I have been trying to reach you all morning. I got a message from someone saying they're a school officer or something at Delmont."

The phone nearly slips out of my hands. I force my voice calm. "What did they say?"

"They said they found you in the dorms last night as part of some noise complaint, and when they ran the records as part of their report, they didn't have you in the student database. They did some sleuthing and found our home phone number. They said they wanted to talk to an adult or guardian before approaching you again because you're a minor."

As I listen, I slide on my backpack straps. If those campus security officers have found out I don't belong here, I need to leave Camilla's room right now.

"Perlie? Are you listening to me?"

I swallow hard. My heart screams at me to come clean, that this is my chance to admit what I've done and ask for their help. But my brain defaults into save-myself-at-all-costs mode because of all of the training I've put it through the past few months, and my cowardly self lets it. "Don't worry, I'll sort this out. They probably typed my name in wrong or something."

A month ago, I thought my easy lying was an asset. Yet all it's doing is making it harder for me to extricate me from this mess. I could kick myself for taking the wimpy way out if it wasn't so important that I get myself to safety first.

"That doesn't make sense, Perlie. They were able to find our phone number. They couldn't have gotten your name wrong."

The veneer of politeness drops. "I don't know, then, Mom. They're wrong." I wriggle my feet into my shoes as I speak.

"Well, good. That's what I thought too. When I couldn't reach you, I emailed the registrar and the residence hall staff to get this cleared up. I don't want them bothering you when you should be focusing on academics."

I would have collapsed if the need to escape wasn't energizing my legs. The thought of actual written evidence of my deception existing makes this all too real. My private, password-protected spreadsheet is one thing: I can delete that. But emails to and from school officials mean that now the world can piece together what I've done and hold it to my face.

Yes, I was going to try to find a way to tell my parents at some point. No, I'm not prepared to have that long, messy conversation this very second, while trying to pack up my life and escape campus security.

"What's gotten into you?" Mom's words drag me out of my own head. "You're not even talking and the few words you do say sound upset. Is everything all right? Do you need us to come down there?"

I glance back around the room to make sure I've gotten everything. No mistakes this time. I can't afford to leave a single trace of my existence in here, for Camilla's sake. "Everything's fine, Mom. Look, I've got to go."

"Where do you have to go this early in the morning?"

Frustrating builds in my clenched jaw. Carrying on a civil conversation is on a rung far lower than survival. "I'll call you later."

I tuck the phone between my ear and my shoulder and reach for the door. My backpack strap catches on the handle, and I twist to free myself.

"Perlie, what's going on? This isn't like you."

"I told you, everything's fine. I have a few things to . . ."

The flash of bright blue down the hall jams the lies back down my throat. The RA closes in, and behind him stalk the two campus safety officers from last night.

"That's her," Officer Khan says. Her voice shoots down the hallway, authoritative and too loud.

Mom's still talking when I press the button to end the call. I don't bother to say goodbye. A chain of panic wraps so tightly around my chest that uttering a word is impossible.

Before I can flee back inside the room, the officers loom on either side of me.

The RA, a broad-shouldered, thin-lipped guy with brown-and-red stubble, frowns at me. "Perla Perez? We're going to need you to come to the director's office."

With the smiley family pictures and limited-edition comics on the bookshelves, Resident Director Le's office is homey enough to make me feel comfortable, which is precisely why being in here sends prickles of unease through my skin. A tall, lush plant towers in the corner. On his desk sits an inspirational quote-a-day calendar. Yesterday's quote was about ambition. He hasn't torn the sheet off to reveal today's quote yet. Then again, I'm sure he wasn't expecting to be called in before the start of his workday, on the day before Thanksgiving.

"Do you want a glass of water?" he asks after showing me to the seat across from his.

I shake my head. If I ingest anything, I'm likely to throw it up. I can barely keep my own stomach acid down at the mere thought of what might happen to me. Every fear I've suppressed with an internal pep talk or retooling of my seven-part plan emerges from the darkest corners of my brain. I have no plan for guiding this conversation or trying to talk my way out. I'd only made the decision to come clean mere hours ago, and that was before the campus security officer clamped a hand on my forearm and led me here.

"No coffee, right? Stunts your growth?" He smiles as if he's told a joke, but nothing about this is amusing. He coughs and thumbs through the copy of the incident report Officer Walton brought in. "So, Perla. Care to explain why you were in Godwin Village?"

"No, not really." The first true thing I've said all hour. As much as the truth is practically trying to claw its way out of my throat, I've watched enough legal dramas with my dad to know that laying out the "here's everything I might have done wrong" to someone with their own team of lawyers is a bad idea. My survival instinct overpowers my conscience, and denial is the only tool I've got left.

Mr. Le frowns. "I'm not your enemy here, Perla. I want to help you."

Isn't that what everyone older than me says? They all think

they're helping. And they all want to help so much that it's suffocating and as growth-stunting as Mr. Le assumes coffee to be.

"I didn't do anything wrong." The lying doesn't feel like a reflex anymore. Every word grits out like sandpaper.

Perfect Perlie Perez would've dug in her heels and said that with her application in review, she was going to be a Delmont student anyway. She just moved in a few months early, and it's Delmont's fault for being a semester late with that acceptance letter.

But I know now that isn't the truth. Perfect Perlie Perez believed so many things that didn't hold up to the scrutiny of the real world, and I find myself sad for the person I used to be. There isn't a world that exists in which she would've thrived and been content. The thought breaks my heart because Perfect Perlie Perez wasn't some dark-hearted villain: she was a sixteen-year-old, cornered, desperate. There's a reason only children believe in fairy tales though. I should've known there was never going to be a happily ever after here.

Mr. Le glances over the report again and takes a deep drink of coffee out of his *#1 Dad* mug. "At a minimum, you impersonated a Delmont student and stayed overnight on university property, in a dorm room not assigned to you."

I stay completely still. The slightest rumble could bring down the whole tower of lies I'd carefully stacked and cemented piece by piece. I may have been in ruins long before I sat in this chair, but I'm not about to help the university staff build a case against me.

"For how long?" he asks.

I'm not answering that.

He sets down his mug. "The safety officers spent the last few hours going over recent security camera footage, and they have you in and around Keith Hall last month too, well outside of our visitor policies. I have to tell you that, if the university wants to, it could press charges. From what I see here, you're on the hook for trespassing, fraud, theft of services . . ." His eyes drift back down to that damn report. "You could face jail time."

Jail. The word sends my self-preservation instincts into overdrive. I jump out of my chair, smacking my hands flat onto the desk between us. "I told you, I didn't do anything wrong." A last attempt to somehow get him to let me go, my weak version of fight before flight. If he stood and opened the door for me, I'd grab my backpack and hike as far away from campus as my legs would take me.

Mr. Le doesn't even flinch. Not even a strand of his neatly combed black hair moves. As if he'd been expecting this outburst, was purposely trying to needle it out of me.

"But you did do something illegal, Perla. We believe you've been living on campus unauthorized. Our safety staff is combing more common area footage now. It's only a matter of time before they string together how you've been managing to stay here."

My shoulders slacken, and I lower my head, staring at the shoes my mom bought me months ago, my new pair for the start of my first year at Delmont. Unbidden, Camilla's and Jackson's lectures about responsibility come to mind. I wonder what they'd think of me now, knowing that they were right, that I was about to take their advice but time ran out.

This is when I grow up, as Camilla had snapped at me to do months ago. This is when I take responsibility, as Jackson had encouraged. This is when I start to deal with what's really happening, not what I think should have happened.

Mr. Le continues. "The one grace is that because you're a minor, the school might be willing to be more lenient. Maybe just a restraining order, if you agree to attend therapy and sign a nondisclosure agreement, among other things."

I barely register his words through the rush of blood in my ears now. Jail time. Restraining order. It's no use wondering if I could have gotten away with this if I'd been smarter, more dedicated. Or if my parents were wealthy enough to donate a library and buy me in. A tear slips off my face and drops onto his desk.

"I don't want to talk," I say, my voice shaky. For someone who's used to winning, I recognize defeat when I feel it. "Call my dad. He's a lawyer. He needs to be here for this."

Mr. Le nods. "All right. We already notified your parents, and they're coming to pick you up. That holiday traffic is going to make that drive a nightmare. You can stay in my office in the meantime. I've asked Officer Khan to keep an eye on you until they arrive."

I crumple back into the chair and bury my head in my hands. I shut my eyes tight, trying to stem the free flow of tears. Some of it is horror. They'll know I lied. Everyone—my family, Tessa, Brand, Jackson, everyone in Monte Verde—they will all know. And they will hate me.

But a larger part of it is relief, and the realization shakes me. I could feel everything unraveling weeks ago. I could feel my heart slipping out of my mission, the lies growing too heavy for me to shoulder.

Me sitting in this chair, facing Mr. Le: this was my greatest fear for the past few months. It's almost unreal that the concept of this man, surrounded by comics and plants, inspired so much awe and dread in me. But if I've fallen off my cliff and have been hurtling to the ground all this time, I've finally hit it. This is the bottom. I can only hope that I'll be able to recover and move on one day. That line I quoted to Camilla comes back to me: *The best way out is always through.* If this doesn't count as going through, I don't know what is.

"Do you have anything to say for yourself, Perla? Anything that could work in your favor so I can help smooth this over?" Mr. Le's voice has softened, like someone talking to a wayward child who's been put in the corner.

I lift my head a couple of inches, just enough to meet his eyes. I don't feel the need to lie anymore. That's all done now.

"No, Mr. Le. I'm through."

THIRTY-SEVEN

Officer Khan marches inches away from me. I can tell she wants to grab my arm and usher me to the driveway like police do with murderers in crime shows, but Mr. Le gave her specific directions to minimize the spectacle.

I'm not in handcuffs, but I might as well be, with all the attention we're getting. Officer Walton totes my backpack behind us, like a glorified bellboy. No one would ever mistake this for gold-star service though. Everything about my stiff gait, the campus safety officers at my side, and the grim set of their faces advertises my wrongdoing to everyone we come across.

I'd considered myself lucky that Delmont was so far away from my parents' house. The distance cut down drastically on the possibility that they'd just show up uninvited. Now, however, the downside is becoming apparent. Because in the five hours it took for them to speed here, students have gone to their morning classes, and many are returning to the dining halls for lunch. And Officer Khan, Officer Walton, and I cut straight through the throngs.

A couple too-loud murmurs float in my direction. A few people point their spindly, witch-hunting fingers at me. I try my best to ignore these faceless students who are not and never were my peers, despite my efforts to blend in.

"Perla!" A voice slices through the quad, and my heart twists at Tessa's voice.

I don't turn to her, but I hear her shoes slap against the pavement as she dashes toward me. The hood of her gray sweater flounces behind her.

Officer Khan puts up a hand. "Stay where you are, miss."

Tessa halts at the gruff order. She'd dyed her hair from purple to electric blue. Had it been so long since I'd seen her? That seven-part plan of mine really did work: it'd be almost amusing if the truth of it didn't make me so miserable. I had columns and rows and links on how to make a real friend like her, but I hadn't planned for how the emotions would stick after I'd forced myself away to preserve my cover. My throat goes scratchy with long-overdue tears and apologies as confusion shadows Tessa's face.

"Perla? What's going on?"

Where do I begin to explain to her that nearly everything she knows about me is false? Tessa has been nothing but kind to me in my time here, and I'd taken advantage of it. The second she learns the truth, I'll be no better than her cheater ex-boyfriend, than Casprin, in her eyes. The deception will cloud every other good thing in our friendship. But I owe her this and more.

"Tessa, I'm so sorry."

She shakes her head, as if she's rejecting my apology. "I don't understand, for what? What did you do?"

One hand still up, Officer Khan puts the other on my shoulder and tries to steer me around Tessa. I swivel to face her. "Just thirty seconds. Please."

Officer Khan exchanges glances with Officer Walton, and though she drops her hand from me, she doesn't move away.

I force the words out past the boulder-sized lump in my throat. "I lied about being a student. I don't go here."

More confusion clouds her eyes. "But you—you lived down the hall. You went to class with me. You even gave me notes."

As much as I want to look anywhere but straight into her hurt eyes, I hold my gaze steady. She deserves it. "I made it all up."

The truth spills out ugly and jagged, ripping to shreds any real friendship that we may have built over the past months. Her lips bunch, like she's holding back a scream. Tessa drags a rough hand through her blue hair before she lets out a strangled sob.

"What? Is this some sick joke to you? Messing with people like this?" she yells.

"No! Hurting you was never part of the plan."

"There was a plan?" She laughs, but it's a cruel, hostile thing. "That's real rich. You must've taken one look at poor, vulnerable me and thought, 'Now there's a gullible one.'"

"No, that's not—" I instinctively try to take a step forward, but something stops me: Officer Walton's firm hand on my arm. "I'm sorry."

I can't tell if that apology reaches Tessa's ears at all.

"You know what? Leave, Perla. And never come back. You shouldn't have been here in the first place."

Her last words are a thrown punch that hits its mark on a spot already bruised and bloodied. Then she turns and shoulders her way through the crowd that's gathered around us. I may have not had many friends growing up, but it's not hard to spot a broken heart when I see one. Especially when I'm the one who cracked it.

I want to explain and make her understand, to tell her that our friendship was the one true thing about this place. My words fail me. Instead, I watch her bright blue tresses fade in the distance, and I'm hit with a bitter vision of the late study nights we might have had, the silly Delmont traditions we'd dress up or down for, the tight hug at graduation.

I blink, and she's gone.

Officer Khan nudges me forward. "Let's go, Perla." Her words are softer now, a request rather than an order, and I'm thankful for the small mercy.

Officer Walton clears a path for us, and I spy some phones pointed at me. My face will be splayed across the top of their webpage in an hour, for everyone to see. I'm sure the *Daily Dragon* reporters will fill in the blanks of my story for me.

Four years ago, I made the front page of *Monte Verde Times* for being exceptional. Now I'm going to make the front page of the *Daily Dragon* for being a failure.

Some people will pretend they remember me. They'll say they saw me lurking around in class or that I was squatting in the dorm room down the hall from their friend. They'll say they always knew something was wrong with me, that I didn't quite fit in. And my truth—all the good and the bad parts of it—and I will be miles away from here, on the outside like I've always been, where maybe I should have stayed but didn't have the courage.

THIRTY-EIGHT

The quiet cuts far deeper than yelling would.

Since Dad shut the car door behind me a minute ago, we've been suffocating in silence.

I'm perfectly content to live in a world where we don't discuss this for a while. I came clean to Tessa, and the fallout, though deserved, was a stab in the chest. I don't know if I'm ready to talk to my parents about everything in the same way. Earlier, I'd made up my mind to try, but this will require strength and clear thinking I don't have at this moment. So I pull the hood of my Delmont sweater over my eyes and burrow down into the car seat for a nap.

I don't dare mistake their silence for acceptance though. Dad's knuckles are white on the steering wheel, and I get the feeling that he and Mom are simply letting the energy build up for an outburst the size of a hydrogen bomb.

Dad readjusts his seat belt and yawns.

"You can't drive another five hours straight," Mom says to him. "We should at least get a snack somewhere."

"Okay, but I don't want to spend too long. I just want to get back to Monte Verde."

The deep wounds from my run-in with Tessa still fresh, I know the fight is far from over. I drew heavily on the goodwill of those around me at Delmont. There's at least one other person I owe an apology to before we leave, even if this will slice me up too. I clear my throat with a cough. "I know a place with killer lattes and pineapple buns."

I use the bathroom as an excuse to sneak away from Mom, ordering at the register. I had a minute head start into the Bubble and Bean because Mom paused to fix her makeup before coming in. Even with everything crumbling around us, she puts on a flawless face.

Jackson's sister describes the snack box selections to Mom, which means Jackson is probably somewhere in the back room. He'd mentioned having a half day at school before Thanksgiving, and I'm hoping I get to talk to him, rather than his father, right now.

I step through the swinging door to the back room and let the café din die away. It's almost serene back here, and this small moment of peace offers me one insight: this is a mistake.

Texting in my resignation is just as good, right?

A "Hey, Perla! What's up?" stops me before I can turn and run.

Jackson pops out from behind a shelving unit. "Your shift's not for a couple hours."

"That's what I'm here to explain. I can't take my shift, I—"

"Didn't we have this whole conversation about you being reliable and—"

"I quit."

The phrase hangs in the air with the scent of freshly baked goods and cardboard packaging.

Jackson takes a step toward me. "What? Why?"

I inch back toward the door. "I'm leaving Delmont." There it is, but even that isn't entirely true, and the truth demands freedom after I kept it locked for so long. I bite my lip and try again. "I didn't actually get into the university. I faked it and got caught. I'm going home." My voice breaks with the last phrase, at that mention of home. "I'm so sorry for lying to you and your dad. I just really needed the money. I never wanted it to be like this."

I lower my gaze to the floor just in time for a tear to roll down my cheek. I didn't even realize I had any tears left.

Suddenly, Jackson's in front of me. I brace myself for a verbal onslaught, a scream, something thrown across the room: a reaction like Tessa's. But it's so much worse.

"Perla"—the gentleness in his voice is a blade—"are you okay?"

I meet his eyes then, and they shine back at me with concern. It's different than with Camilla: she knew all the damage I was doing to others and, worse, to myself, for a while now. But Jackson's concern is one that I, a person who lied and forged forms and wronged him and his family by being here, am certain I haven't earned.

This concern guts me in another way: it isn't anger. All this time, I'd expected everyone to be angry at me if or when my deception was discovered. Tessa showed me as much. Jackson's reaction completely catches me off guard. He hears what I've done. He sees me taking ownership of it and being truthful. He doesn't see Perfect Perlie Perez at all. He's never seen her, and he's still worried about me.

I don't realize I've hugged him until he squeezes me too. I lurch back, my face red, as if I have any room for being embarrassed about anything.

Jackson's eyebrows knit together. "Now I know something's up. You wouldn't even return my high five after I made that sick *Star Wars* reference, and I suddenly get a hug?"

Leave it to him to try to joke his way out of this. I would smile if I had the energy. "Thanks, Jackson."

"For what?"

"For not being angry with me."

"I mean, I am angry. But also, kind of impressed? I feel like I should applaud or something. Wait, am I on a reality show?" He smiles wide and poses then, as if there's some hidden camera and producers ready to jump out for a big reveal.

I shake my head. "No reality show, sorry. You get all of the mess, none of the fame." I hear Jackson's sister call out Mom's order, and I know I can't hide back here forever, joking around with one of the few people who gets me. Taking one last look at this place, I apologize again for everything and sprint toward the cash register before he can reply.

It's time for me to strike up the courage to face my parents.

It's time to leave Delmont.

THIRTY-NINE

The courage builds up, drip by drip, but not quickly enough for me to breach the silence in the car. I pretend to nap, but sleep doesn't come, even as drained as I am. I instead replay every moment from when Camilla smiled as she left her room, to the high fives after I pulled off a shocking *Super Smash Bros.* victory at Jimmy's, to the second Brand turned to me with the icy shock that he'd never known me at all. I replay the pity washed across Mr. Le's face. I replay Tessa and her newly blue hair, then Jackson posing as if on a hidden-camera show. The mental movie reel keeps me awake.

There's some murmuring against the low hum of public radio. I make the mistake of glancing in the rearview mirror and meeting Dad's eyes.

"Perlie, you know we need to talk about this."

I burrow farther into my seat. My courage tank still feels only half-full, and I'd rather wait until we're home, when there are stairs to stomp up and doors to slam. "I don't want to. Not now."

"Well, we're going to talk anyway." Mom's voice lacks all of Dad's softness.

Silence is my answer.

Mom lets out a sigh that makes me thankful we're all facing forward, not each other. I don't want to see their faces right now. I don't want to see the angry set of their lips, the shaking of their heads in denial, then disappointment, the looks they'll throw at each other that shout all the doubts about me that they don't want to say aloud.

"What in the world possessed you to do this, Perlie?" Mom says.

At the hint of disappointment in her voice, I'm instantly my ten-year-old self. I loathe myself for it. The courage I'd gathered up from my moment at the Bubble and Bean deteriorates. "I don't know . . . I—"

"You don't know? You must've known something if you managed to plot out this scheme to live in the dorm for three months, to trick us into believing you got in."

"I didn't mean for it to turn out like this."

"This whole stunt proves what you mean and what actually happens are two different things, doesn't it? And after this? Delmont was right not to accept you." The hardness in her voice has even Dad swiveling his head from the road to her.

Her words sting worse than I thought they would. I should've known that they, of all people, would choose anger rather than concern.

I finally see the pattern in it: at no other time in my life had they acted any other way. Not with my failed math quiz, our Saturday running sessions, or any of the times I've been so close to a breaking point that I reached to them for help and understanding. If I ever performed in a way that fell short of their standards, they responded with disappointment and immediate solution-finding.

Dad's hand strays from the steering wheel to rest on Mom's forearm. His lips purse, and he lets out a short breath through his nose before speaking. "Lina, I don't think this is helpful."

"Perlie lied to us, to the school, to everyone. This is going to be in the newspapers. It's probably all over the internet by now. Oh no, I should put our Facebook accounts on private. I don't want to see our vacation pictures on Channel Five."

Mom's anger is diverted, but it doesn't sting any less.

"Lina . . ."

Mom's head thumps back onto the headrest. "What are we going to tell people? Our coworkers? Our clients?"

"We'll worry about that later. We can hire someone to manage this. Right now, our priority is Perlie. That's what that Director Le said."

If he had stopped at "our priority is Perlie," I might have hoped that they were open to listening to me, for once. Yet the mere mention of Director Le means they're still not focusing on me.

The sound of my name stokes Mom's wrath. "She gets this from your side, Ernie. She thinks all this lying is okay because of your father."

My own anger bubbles over, blasting off the lid that stayed welded on for years but corroded and fractured in recent weeks.

I'm done letting them talk *about* me and what they think I should be doing and being. They should be talking to me, the actual one living this life, and if it means I have to kick and scream to get heard, I'm ready to do it now.

"Wow, so you don't even think I can make my own mistakes? That I inherited this from the grandfather who was essentially the poster boy for 'fake it till you make it,' except I didn't actually make it? That's what makes this a failure, then: not what I did, but that I got caught."

The attitude I'd thrown at them elicits just the Perla-targeted response I'm looking for. Mom turns her attention back to me. "You don't get to defend this! It's bad enough that you lied and didn't get into the school we worked so hard for since you were a kid, but what I don't understand is why you would embarrass us like this."

"Embarrass you? Are you serious?"

The hard armor I'd spent all morning reenforcing cracks at the audacity of her words. Any thoughts of waiting until we got home to hash this out dissolve. I'm fooling myself into thinking that there'll ever be a time when I'll be strong enough to handle this. Now is the time to lay everything bare because it's not about strength: it's having nothing left to lose.

I used to joke that living in Monte Verde is like living in a pressure cooker, but that isn't all that funny. I'm only beginning to unravel the ways in which this entire school complex—my family included—enforced these unrealistic expectations on each of us. Camilla saw it too, and even she hasn't been strong enough to break out of its grasp yet. We've just been struggling to find our own ways to work within the dysfunction.

I made myself accepted into a school that wasn't the place I'd dreamed up after all. And sitting here, in the back of my parents' car, returning home in shame, there's no way I can justify the pain of that pointless struggle anymore.

I rip my hood back. It's stifling. "The embarrassment is the part you want to focus on?"

"Perlie, we're not the ones who—"

"It's Perla."

Mom shakes her head. "I know we put a lot of pressure on you—"

The understatement of the century.

"—but pressure isn't an excuse for what you did. We've done so much to help you succeed. We want the best for you."

I shake my head. I've heard this all before, even from myself, and I can barely wrap my head around the damage that this kind of excuse has wrought. How many times have we excused people's anger, their disregard, their coldness because of this? It isn't a justification; it's a poison, and we've let it ruin us.

"No, no you don't. You want the best, period. You want the best of everything so you could show it off to the world like a new luxury car or a designer purse. I'm just another accessory that needs to fit with this image of perfection that lives in your head."

A tear drops onto the sleeve of my Delmont hoodie. The freedom that my Delmont destruction brought starts to shape the feelings I've grappled with all these years. At long last, they materialize into real, sharp words.

"But you know what I've realized?" I continue. "You collect all these things you think make you the best. But you're not lifting yourself to some higher level: you're building yourself a stronger cage. And you tried to lock me in with you."

"That's not true," Dad cuts in. The microsecond of a look he shares with Mom tells me they've had this conversation before. They'd wondered why I couldn't just be the obedient, faultless daughter who didn't throw wrinkles into their already-busy, already-successful professional lives.

A silent second beats by, my parents both stunningly speechless, and in that second, bile rises in my throat. "Pull over."

"At the next exit, we'll—"

"Pull over. Now!" I yell. In this closed, coffee-scented space, the words bounce off the windows and channel into Dad's arms. He flicks on the emergency lights.

I barrel out of the car once it stops beside a grove of endless almond tree rows and make it a good twenty feet away before my lunch spills onto the red brown dust. We're halfway to Monte Verde, and farmland and freeway stretch as far as I can see. A mud-caked white truck surrounded by a handful farmworkers sits at the far edge of the field. The air reeks of manure, which seems more than appropriate for how I'm feeling.

My body racks under the stress. The horror of what I've said and done flows out of me as chunks of the Bubble and Bean pineapple buns and stomach juice. I plant my hands on my thighs, and I heave again. My throat burns raw.

Steps thump against the dirt beside me, and a hand lands lightly on my back.

I shrug it off and lunge away. Distance may have been what I always needed.

"Perlie—Perla, we never said you had to be perfect," Mom says, her voice low.

I give a hoarse laugh, a wry, disbelieving sound. "You didn't always have to say it for me to feel it. I didn't get the highest GPA or take the most AP classes. I wasn't Camilla."

"You never needed to be," she says, in a slow way, as if she's testing out the foreign taste of that idea.

It makes me wonder whether her verbalizing it is the first time she's seeing its truth. It's possible she and Dad sincerely didn't realize that they didn't have to keep one-upping themselves and everyone else.

In a way, I'm thankful I realized this now and am owning up to these mistaken beliefs. I'm sixteen. I'll have time to fully shed the emotional weight of obligation while shaping my life how I want it. I don't want to wake up twenty years from now realizing that everything I've ever done was in pursuit of some useless prestige, some pointless high opinion of people I don't care about. I've already seen how that turns out.

I wipe the clamminess on my palms onto my jeans. "Then why did you say so? You made me feel like everything I said or did on my own was inferior somehow. You and Dad challenge my every decision, my every preference. It made me doubt myself so much that it just become easier to do what you wanted. Except it wasn't easier at all, not for me."

I'm hit with memories of so many late nights, lies, held-back tears. Crushing, deeply internalized guilt continued their hard work while they got their beauty rest.

The crease in Mom's smooth forehead deepens for once.

"It was supposed to encourage you. Drive you to do better, the way my parents did with me and your auntie Trish."

A shout in the distance from someone at the white truck cuts her off. Her lips purse slightly, like the words are warring within her. Her eyes drift to the heart pendant on my necklace, the one she gave me before Monte Verde graduation. I wonder if she regrets that gift now that she knows the truth. Her voice hardens. "But this? This is unacceptable, Perlie. I don't know how you can expect us to forgive you for this."

She takes a step back, then another, and I can practically feel herself dissociating from this conversation, from me. My disappointment grows with her every inch away. It was naive of me to think that my parents would easily see the error of their ways. They don't even think anything's wrong with how they view the world, and Mom's clearly refusing to listen.

I let Mom retreat. I can't help but feel a pang of sadness, but I don't beg her to come back or promise I'll change my ways if only she'll smile and throw an encouraging word at me again. If she can't handle the first time I've truly expressed myself, that's on her.

I glance over my shoulder at my dad, standing there, watching my mom open her car door and slide silently inside. When he looks at me then, something about his slumped shoulders and tired eyes whispers of regrets and broken hearts. Part of me doesn't care that he's upset. I'm still hurt. Him feeling bad about it doesn't absolve him of the damage, but it might mean he's willing to hear me.

I straighten and face him, the burden on my shoulders lighter now. I don't need to blame him or Mom anymore because I don't feel as pressing of a need to be who they want me to be.

"Look, I'll be the first to admit that what I did means I'm going to need some serious help building myself back up into some functional, non-constantly-law-breaking member of society. I can see that. But you two?" I point over at Mom, in the car, not even looking in my direction. "You're both going to need to grow up too. It doesn't matter what your law partners think, what your Botox client crew thinks, what Channel Five thinks. In fact, I don't think it even really matters what you think of me anymore. This"—I wipe the acid from my lip with the back of my hand—"is me, and I'm not perfect. I don't need to be."

The words leave me empty but healing. I thought getting admitted into Delmont would wipe my soul clean, but I know now that wouldn't match the impact of letting years' worth of my truth out. There's a space in my chest that I can only fill with honesty and goodness, and I promise myself that's what I'll do.

Dad closes the distance between us and pulls me into a tight hug, and even with my cheeks sticky with drying vomit, he brushes a tear off my face. I can't remember the last time he hugged me like this—not at graduation, not at Delmont move-in. But he was hugging a whole different Perla then. After the surprise wears off, the familiar smell of our home fabric softener begins to calm the roiling waves in my heart.

"All we wanted was what was best for you. I hope you know that," he says. "But I think I'm starting to see how we let so much trivial stuff get in the way. Work is work, grades are grades, but you're my Perla. I'm sorry I forgot that. We never really listened to you on what that was or what path you wanted to take to get there."

He offers me a wad of paper towels, balled up in his clenched hands, and a half-empty bottle of water. I take it, and after I rinse out my mouth and mop up my face as best I can, I peer over at Mom. She hasn't moved from her place in the passenger seat. In fact, she's put on her sunglasses, one more physical barrier between her and me. Months ago, this would've torn me up, made me grasp for ways to clear the air between us and win her approval. Now I see her for who she is: a work in progress in her own right, with her own unseen pressures and wordless expectations to live up to. This iciness? It's always been her way. Admitting you're wrong takes practice: I know this from experience.

I look up at Dad, and over his shoulder, I spot a small, wild tree growing through a boulder at the edge of the almond grove, the rock split in half to let the sapling through.

Dad brushes a hair off my hoodie, the way he used to do when I was kid. "I'm sorry we made you feel anything less than perfect. When I look at you, I sometimes still see the toddler who learned how to unlock my smartphone and take selfies, did you know that? You were always so smart; it was astounding."

He shakes his head and drops his gaze to the ground. "I don't know how our dreams for you warped into keeping you from becoming your own person. I guess we need to work on that."

I think of what Mr. Le suggested. "Maybe a therapist. But you can't put this all on me again. I'm not going to let you."

Dad nods. Fixing one leg of a rotting stool doesn't make the whole thing sound. "Then maybe a therapist not just for you, maybe for all of us, okay? I'll talk to your mom about it."

We both glance over at Mom, and to my surprise, she's staring at Dad and me now. Her fingers worry the seat belt strap across her chest, but she doesn't make a move to rise and join us. She and Dad aren't perfect either—I understand that better than anyone—and this feels like a slow, messy beginning toward something new.

I take one more deep breath and head toward the car. Each step back from the dusty roadside is easier. It's how I felt leaving Perfect Perlie back in Monte Verde in September, except now I'm leaving Delmont Perla here, in this patch of dirt between the freeway and an almond grove. None of those personas suited me truly. They can both stay buried. The person I'm supposed to be will come to me, eventually.

Dad tosses me the paper towel roll as I buckle in and closes my door. Mom slouches farther into her seat. There's no way she wouldn't have witnessed everything that transpired between Dad and me, but she must not have anything further to say.

"Guess we'll have to hit up a McDonald's or something, then," Dad says, "considering your lunch is on the side of the road now."

I snicker, the vice around my heart loosening. "Guess so. No Happy Meal though."

Dad nods once, seriously. "Got it, Perla."

Perla (to Tessa)

Can we talk?

Sent 12:11 pm

Perla

Please?

Sent 12:22 pm

Perla

I'm sorry

Sent 12:29 pm

Perla (to Camilla)

Heading back to MV now w/parents.

Sorry again I got you involved.

Sent 12:33 pm

Camilla

Take care of yourself, sis. Good luck with your parents.

Read 12:34 pm

Camilla

Also, we should both delete these last few texts.

Read 12:34 pm

Delete Messages.

Deactivate PicLine Account: Yes or no?

Yes.

FORTY

Dear Ms. Perez,
We regret to inform you that we are unable to offer a place
in our spring class.

I'd waffled on opening this envelope. It isn't hard to guess what the thin paper inside said. Even if I was qualified, there's no way anyone at Delmont wouldn't have recognized the name Perla Perez, not after what I'd done.

I want to frame this new rejection letter from Delmont and replace the Einstein quote above my desk, but Dad worries that'd be a bit deranged. I've only been home and in treatment for three weeks, and he wants to check with our therapists first. He and I burn it in the fireplace instead, then go out for ice cream. Mom stays home, saying she has a lot of paperwork to catch up on.

I take down the Albert Einstein quote. I can't believe I ever considered Einstein a reachable role model. I'd attempted the absurd, and it hadn't gotten me any closer to being an admitted Delmont student. In fact, it probably resulted in me and any descendants being banned from there permanently.

We still can't watch the local news. They keep finding new angles on my time at Delmont. This week they're interviewing a panel of my elementary school teachers to figure out if there were any psychological hints back then as to what I would do years later. As if my third-grade PE teacher was so involved in the inner workings of my brain and home life.

Dad's firm is in active negotiation with Delmont over the quietest way to address my living at large on their campus for such an embarrassing-for-them period of time. They're trying to convince the school not to press charges and to use their considerable influence to get the district attorney to do the same.

It doesn't escape my notice that someone without a highly paid lawyer dad and his highly paid lawyer friends wouldn't be waiting out possible punishment at home like I am. What an oddly beneficial twist to my family's brutally relentless drive to financial and social success.

While they're working on that, my job is to prove I'm an otherwise-upstanding member of society. This includes paying off the credit card debt I accrued, then maybe putting the rest of any earnings or savings into escrow in case Delmont demands payment for "hosting" me. My therapist agreed that it'd be fine for me to get out into the working world for a while, in a place where my worth isn't dependent on a pop quiz or term paper, if that's what I wanted. Dad inquired as to whether I could fill in for his firm's receptionist while he's out on parental leave, but the other partners claimed some conflict of interest. Mom didn't offer anything. She doesn't say it, but I can tell she doesn't want me dragging down her reputable practice with my scandalous presence.

So I've started busing tables at the local Bartleby's. Of all people, Camilla's boyfriend, Rich, came through with the hiring connection when no one else wanted to have the infamous Perlie Perez in-house. Despite trying to lie low, I've unfortunately become somewhat of a local celebrity, and the Monte Verde Bartleby's has seen an increased flow of business in the week I've been working there. I consider it a sort of cosmic penance for how much I lied to everyone when I have to clear the mess of a gawking group of Monte Verde High graduates, whispering and snickering under their breath.

Through it all, Dad and his associates still sound hopeful when they give me updates about their negotiations with Delmont. They say I might not face time in prison. Fines, therapy, and community service may be enough to assure Delmont I've thoroughly learned my lesson. They pat me on the back and tell me I don't have to worry about it one bit, but I've become an expert at spotting liars.

I drape my blue Bartleby's apron over my pink computer chair and rummage around my dresser for some comfy joggers to change into: a reward for eight hours of a job well done. The only reward, considering all my earnings are spoken for.

Mom's heart pendant necklace is tucked into that top drawer of the dresser. I don't wear it anymore, not because I didn't earn it, but because sometimes, it feels more of a yoke than a gift. I'll wear it again one day, maybe when my mom and I are in a better place relationship-wise, when her love isn't something she can give and take away at will based on her perception of my actions. In the meantime, I'll hold on to it, because it means something to me that she didn't ask for it back like I half expected her to.

I plop onto my bed next to Bip and Bop, the only stuffed animals I refused to donate. Goodwill received a generous donation of the rest of my childhood toys, my free First Cal-Am Bank shirt from Delmont, and the pink bedspread and daisy rug gathering dust in my room. My room is slowly going from pink to cream, which isn't ideal either but is a start.

From under my pillow I pull out the journal my therapist's been asking me to keep. She assigns me prompts each week in between our sessions, and it's up to me if I want to share my writing with her. My journal cover is red, like the Perlie's Academic Plan binder that Dad and I chucked in the recycling bin when I got home. But this journal doesn't feel like some restrictive, straight-line plan. Instead, it's page after page of me ruminating about the life I've lived and want to live: no set destination, no grades, no points for getting something "right" by someone else's standard.

Today's prompt is broad, asking about ways I can draw strength from my loved ones.

I copy the prompt onto a fresh page in my journal. Sneaky of Dr. Wan to slip this prompt in here after we spent the whole last session talking about whether I feel supported by—her words—"loved ones."

I'd done one of those sad laughs in response. "Loved ones. Do I even have any of those?" My answer at the time was that I don't feel supported all the time, especially these days. But I understand why, after what I did. No one asks me about whether I'm going to return to school, nor does anyone other than Dr. Wan ask me about everyone I'd left behind at Delmont. Not a peep from Brand, and Tessa didn't respond to any of my initial texts, so I deleted their numbers from my phone two days after I moved home, out of respect. My actions hurt them, and I don't get to keep hurting them just to make myself feel better. They know where to find me.

Camilla texted me happy birthday and we traded a few texts when I was securing this Bartleby's job, but we didn't make plans to hang out over winter break. Based on my tissue-box-destroying last session, Dr. Wan thinks I have some more work to do before opening that in-person connection again.

Jackson let me know his dad didn't get in trouble for hiring me, and he even asked about whether there are any empty bubble-tea-shop-ready storefronts around Rancho Community College. He said there was no way I'd ever be able to work there, though they'd of course welcome my business, and I totally understand that.

I set down my pencil. Through it all, I guess I do still have loved ones: family and friends who are still willing to reach out when I'm at my worst. Auntie Trish even took me to the art fair last weekend as more of her self-care evangelizing and a partial apology for contributing to the pressure that led me to Delmont.

In addition to two scoops of gelato and a new game, Auntie Trish bought me my choice of a new art piece to replace my Einstein quote. I glance up at it on my wall.

It's a helluva start, being able to recognize what makes you happy.
—*Lucille Ball*

I close my journal. I'll answer the prompt later, but I suddenly feel inspired to do something else. I open up my laptop and navigate to the Rancho course catalog. It'll be a miracle if Dad and his associates could help me clear this all up without me working day and night to repay my debt or being incarcerated. But I've spent so long planning the worst-case scenarios on someone else's behalf that I only want to plan the best of it now, for me.

I cast away all the uncertainty, all the fear about things out of my control, all thoughts of anyone else's opinion, and I click open a new, blank spreadsheet.

Warmth spreads in my chest from something I haven't felt in years: excitement about what lies ahead, on a path I'm going to forge myself.

ACKNOWLEDGMENTS

Now to the part that actually is a personal statement.

I owe my thanks to my agent, Natalie Lakosil, for believing in me and my work, being such a wonderful advocate, and answering my questions, big and small. My thanks also to Em Dickson: your enthusiasm for my work was contagious and so welcome as we shaped this story and sent it out into the world.

To my editor, Jen Ung—you pushed me to take this story into deeper waters, always trusting that I could swim, and for this, I'll always be grateful. It helped to have the occasional life preserver in the form of corgi pictures, as well.

Thank you to the phenomenal Quill Tree Books team and all those who lent their talents to help bring this book to life, particularly Rosemary Brosnan, Celina Sun, Erin Fitzsimmons, Alex Cabal, Mikayla Lawrence, Jacqueline Hornberger, Sean Cavanagh, Suzanne Murphy, Jean McGinley, Sabrina Abballe, Patty Rosati, Tara Feehan, Laura Raps, Andrea Pappenheimer, and the Harper sales team. I consider myself the luckiest for getting to work with people as brilliant and attentive as you.

To Alechia Dow, Sam Farkas, and Jessica James—thank you for your early notes. You helped me find the heart of the story, kept me focused, and offered the gentlest suggestions on when I mistitled classic books or described a baked good or drink poorly. And to Rae Castor, Alyssa Colman, Kat Enright, Jenn Gruenke, Kalyn Josephson, Ashley Northrup, and Brittney Singleton: your encouragement and friendship mean the world to me, and I can't thank you enough for being just a click away whenever I need to commiserate or celebrate.

My thanks as well to Shaan Akbar for your gaming industry expertise and Roanne DeGuia-Samuels for your invaluable insight into Filipino and Filipino American minds and hearts.

To Traci Adair, Jennifer Franz, Brittani Miller, and Rossini Yen: your friendship, texts, and toasts are always bright moments. A special thanks to Traci, for supplying such lovely names for characters in this book.

Thank you to the wonderful folks at Better Books Marin, the retreat at which I was hit by the spark for this story. Being around such amazing storytellers was a truly remarkable experience, and I value every lesson and moment from our time together.

To my FALSD, NFALA, and Pinay Powerhouse families—you continue to awe and inspire me with your strength and dedication to our community and the way you work to evolve and expand what it means to be Filipino American.

My family, as always, has been key in everything I do. Thank you to my parents for being so supportive (and not like Perla's parents) in all things professional and personal, to my brother for inspiring and challenging me to keep learning and growing every day, and to my wide, wonderful extended family for always cheering me on.

To my children: if I ever put as much crushing pressure on you as Perla's parents, please feel free to refer me back to my own book. I already know you're wonderful. You don't have to prove it to me.

And to my husband, Rahul Reddy, thank you for your never-ending support and all the times you've jumped at the opportunity to tell anyone and everyone about my writing. Whether it's talking through plot points over some craft brews or picking up takeout so we can spend our precious free time together as a family instead at the stove or sink, you make our version of perfect possible.